THE SINGING ROCK

THE SINGING ROCK

& OTHER BRAND-NEW FAIRY TALES

Written by
Nathaniel Lachenmeyer

Artwork by
Simini Blocker

:01

First Second
New York

For Arlo, who long ago asked
for a story about frogs.

—Nathaniel

For my family—I'm glad to have you.

—Simini

HOP HOP WISH

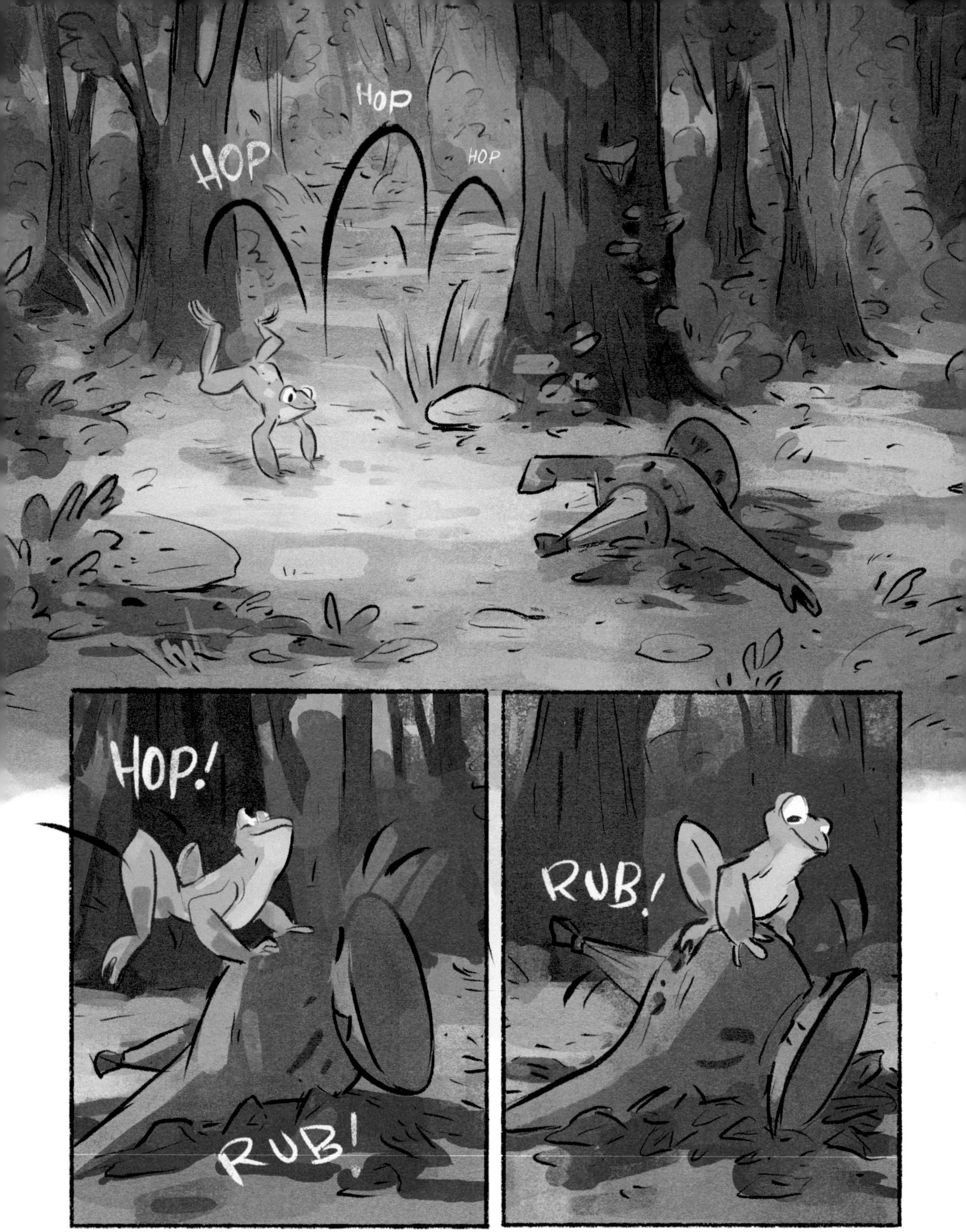
HOP
HOP
HOP
HOP!
RUB!
RUB!

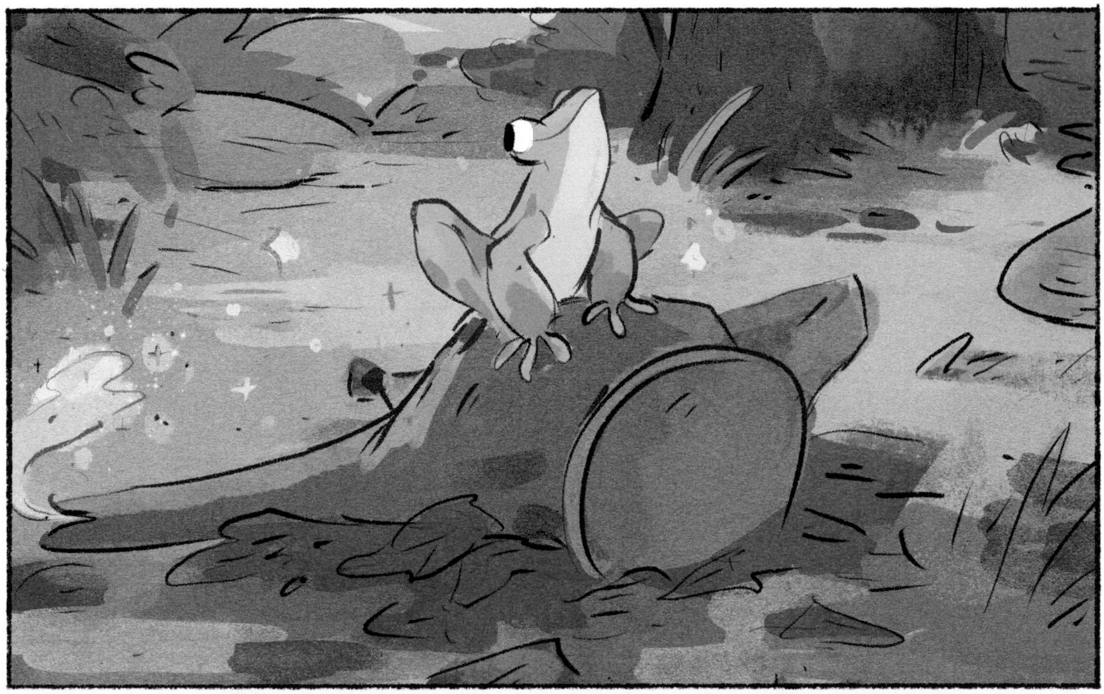

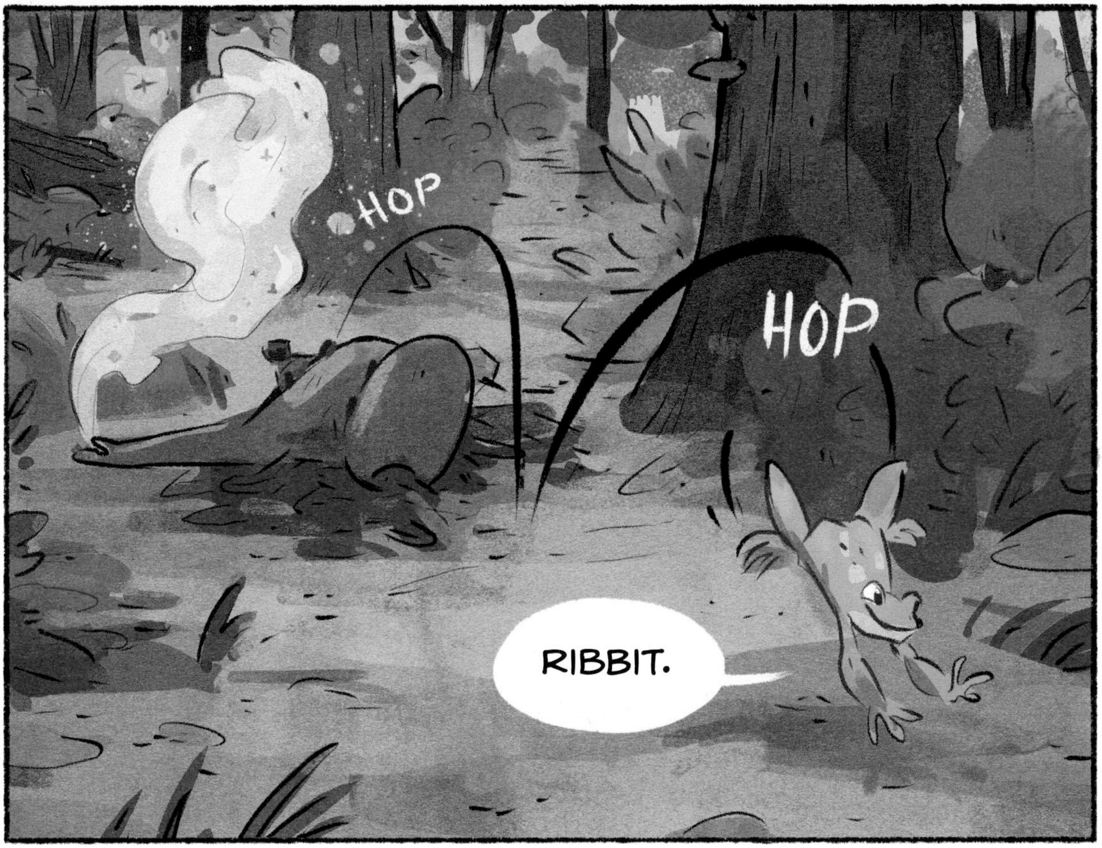
HOP
HOP
RIBBIT.

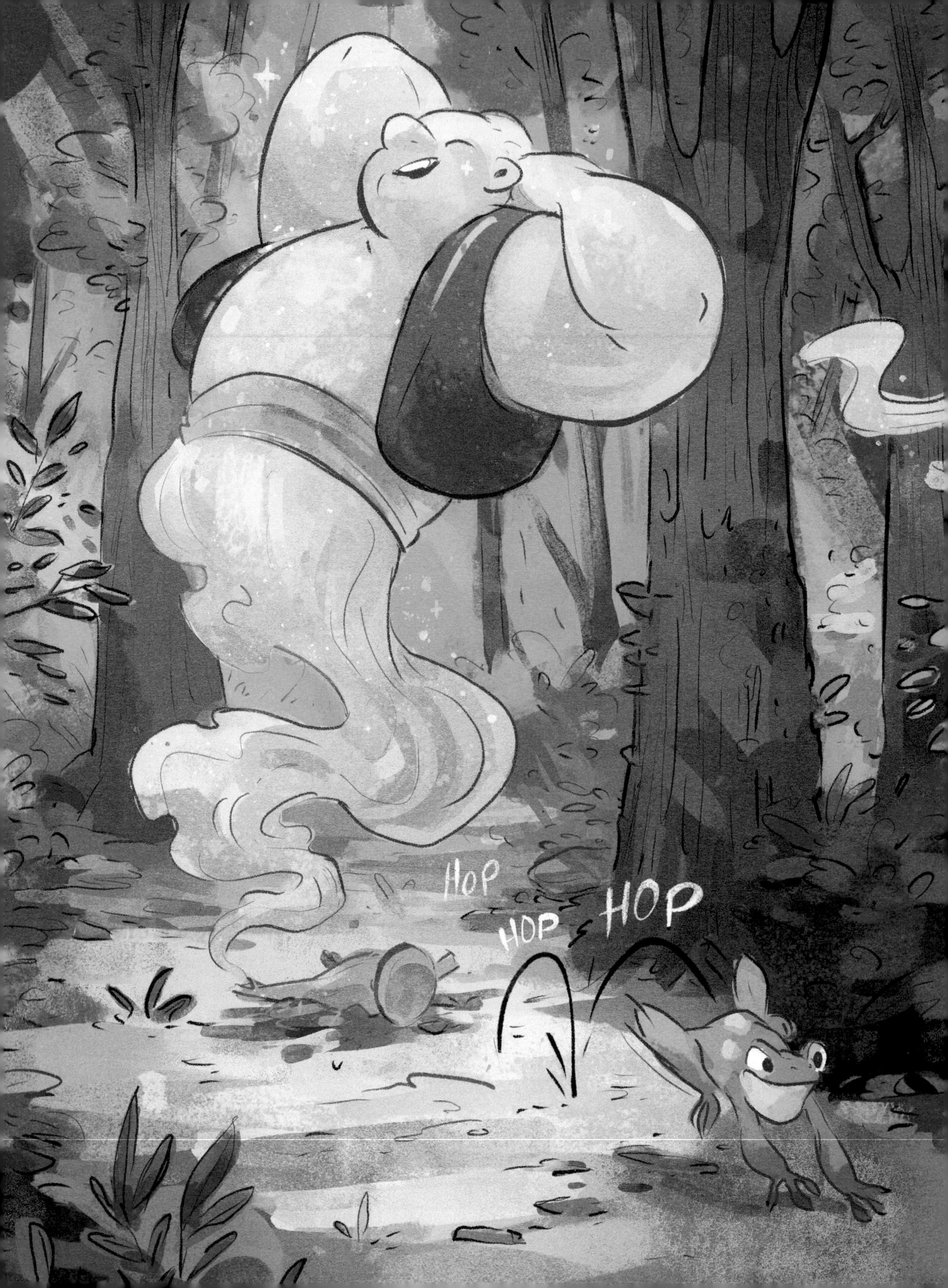
HOP
HOP
HOP

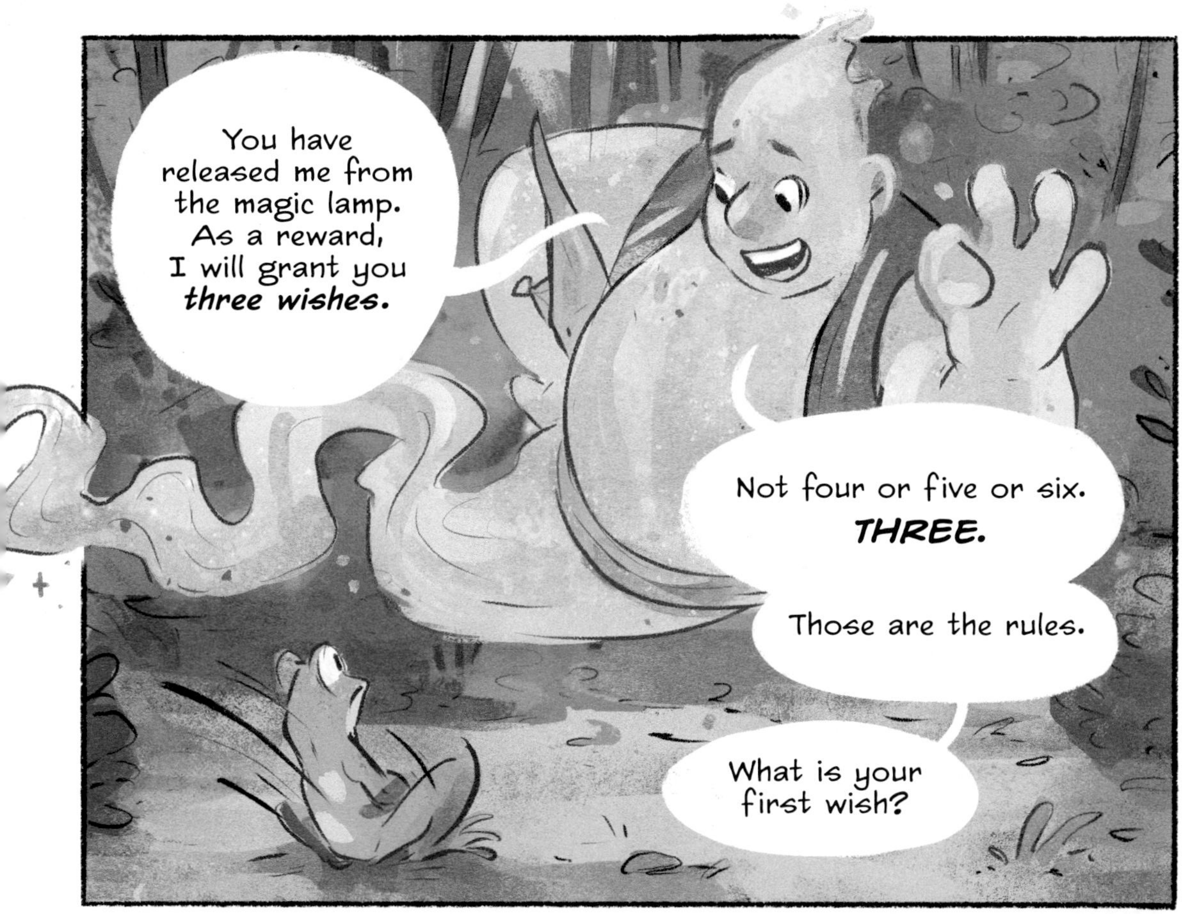

You have released me from the magic lamp. As a reward, I will grant you *three wishes.*
Not four or five or six. ***THREE.***
Those are the rules.
What is your first wish?

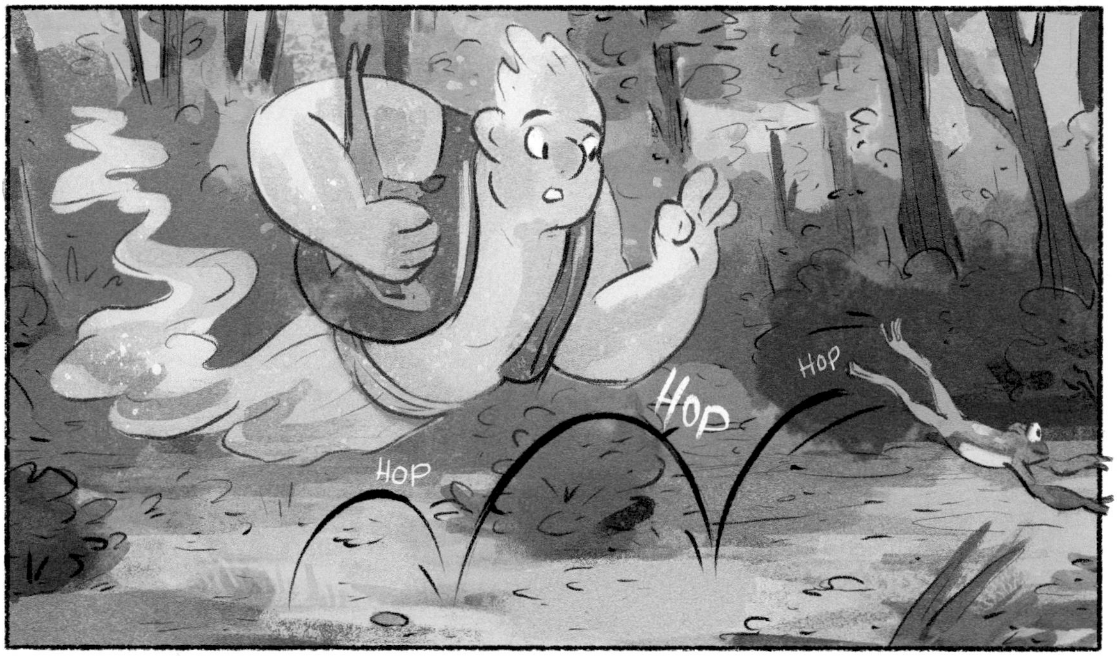

HOP
HOP
HOP

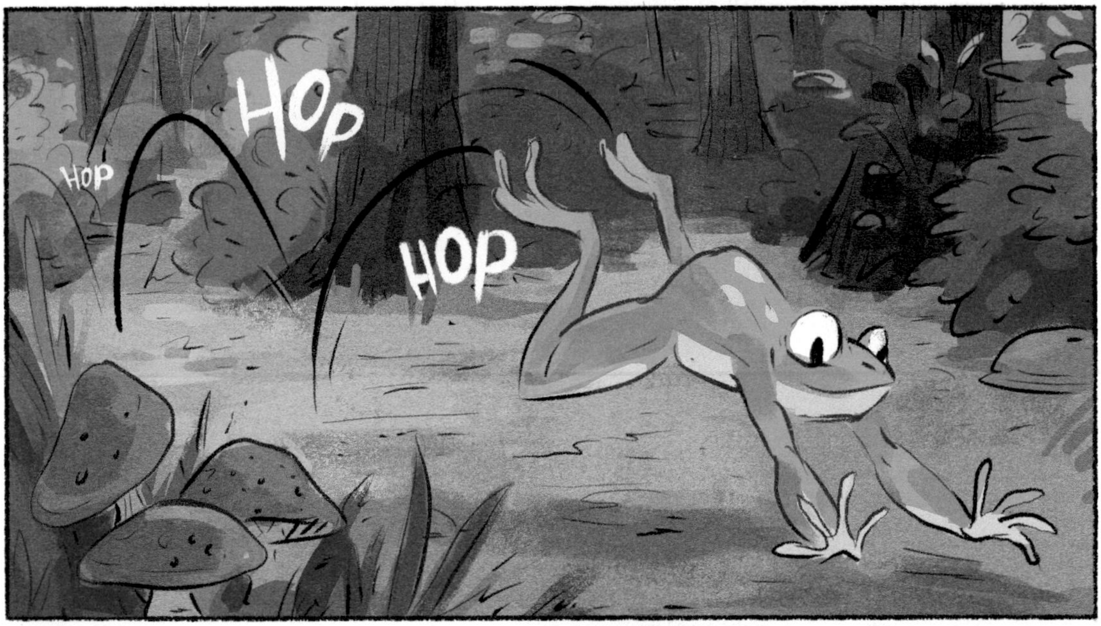
HOP
HOP
HOP

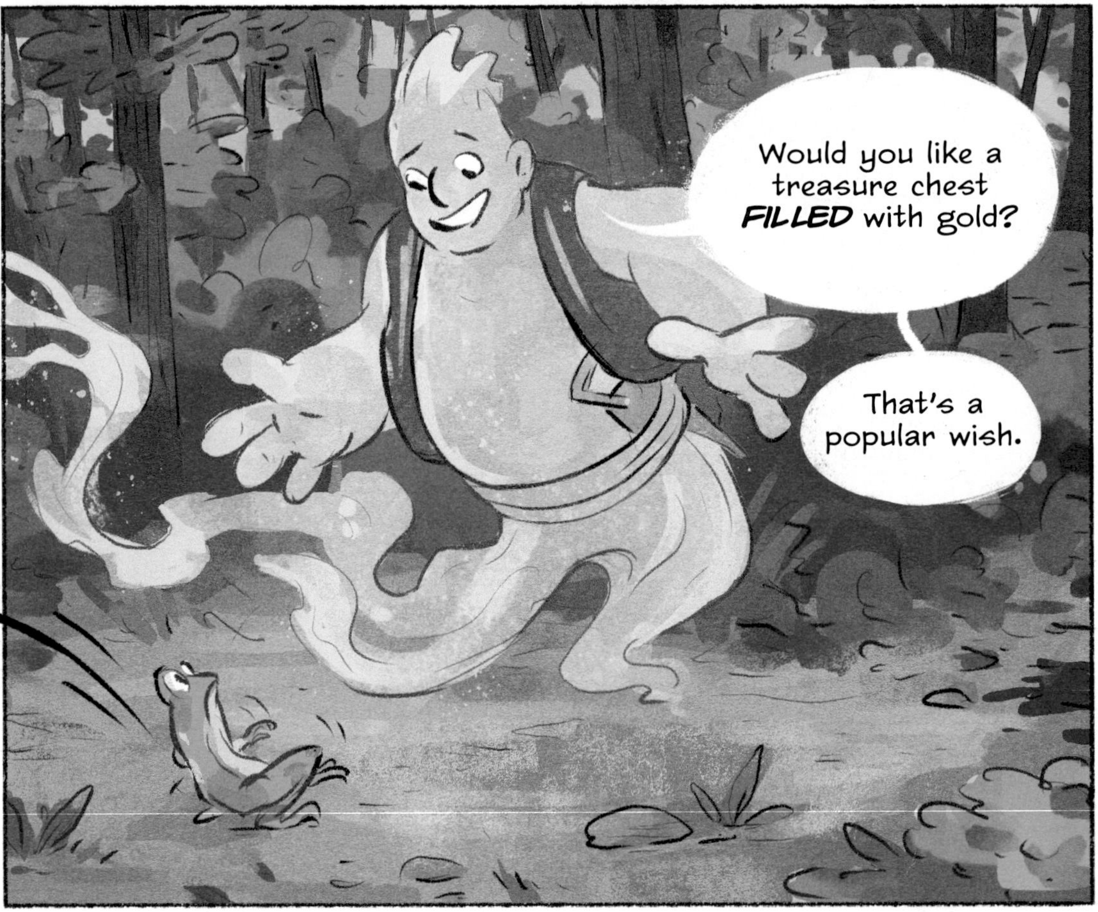
Would you like a treasure chest **FILLED** with gold?
That's a popular wish.

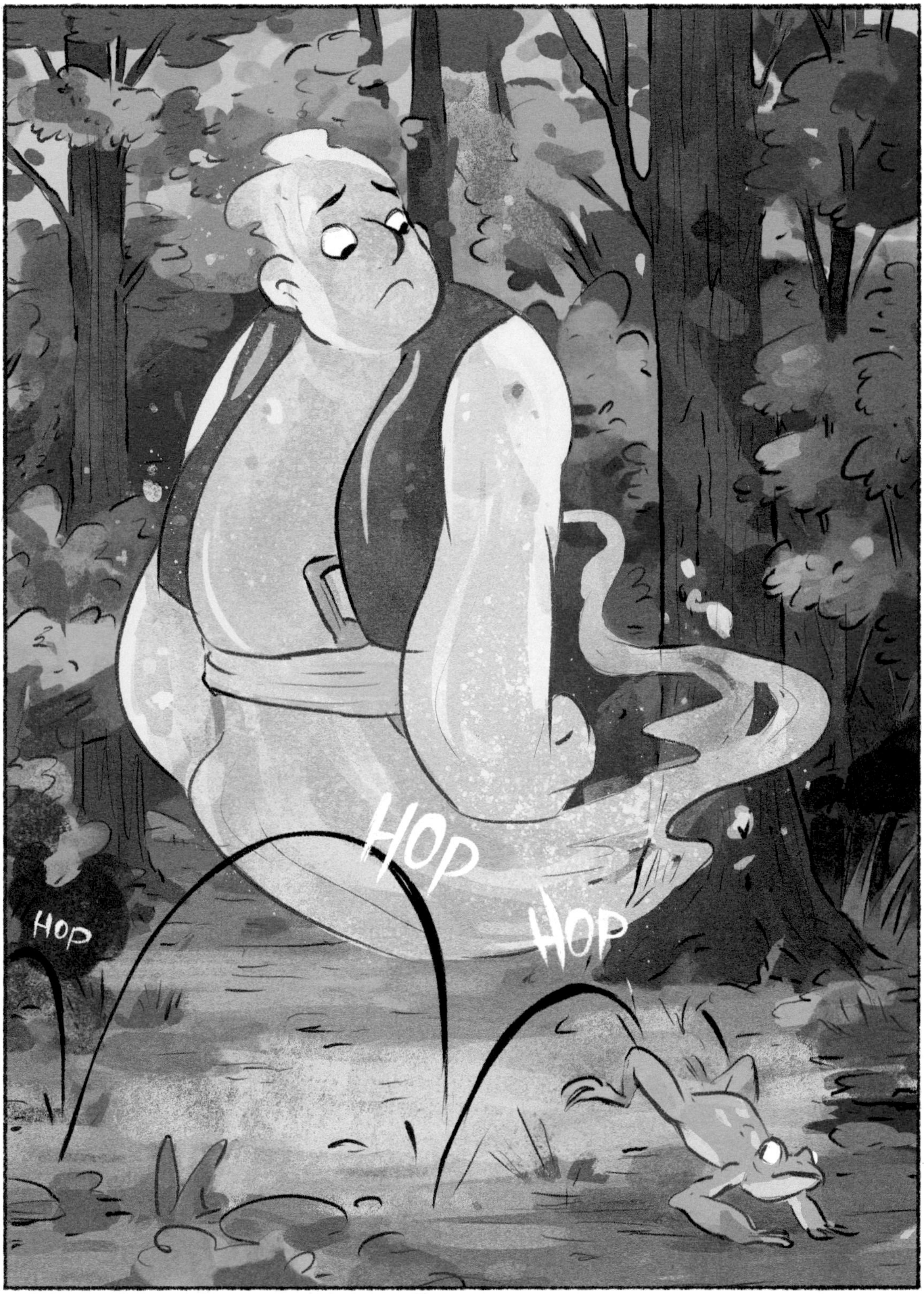
HOP
HOP
HOP

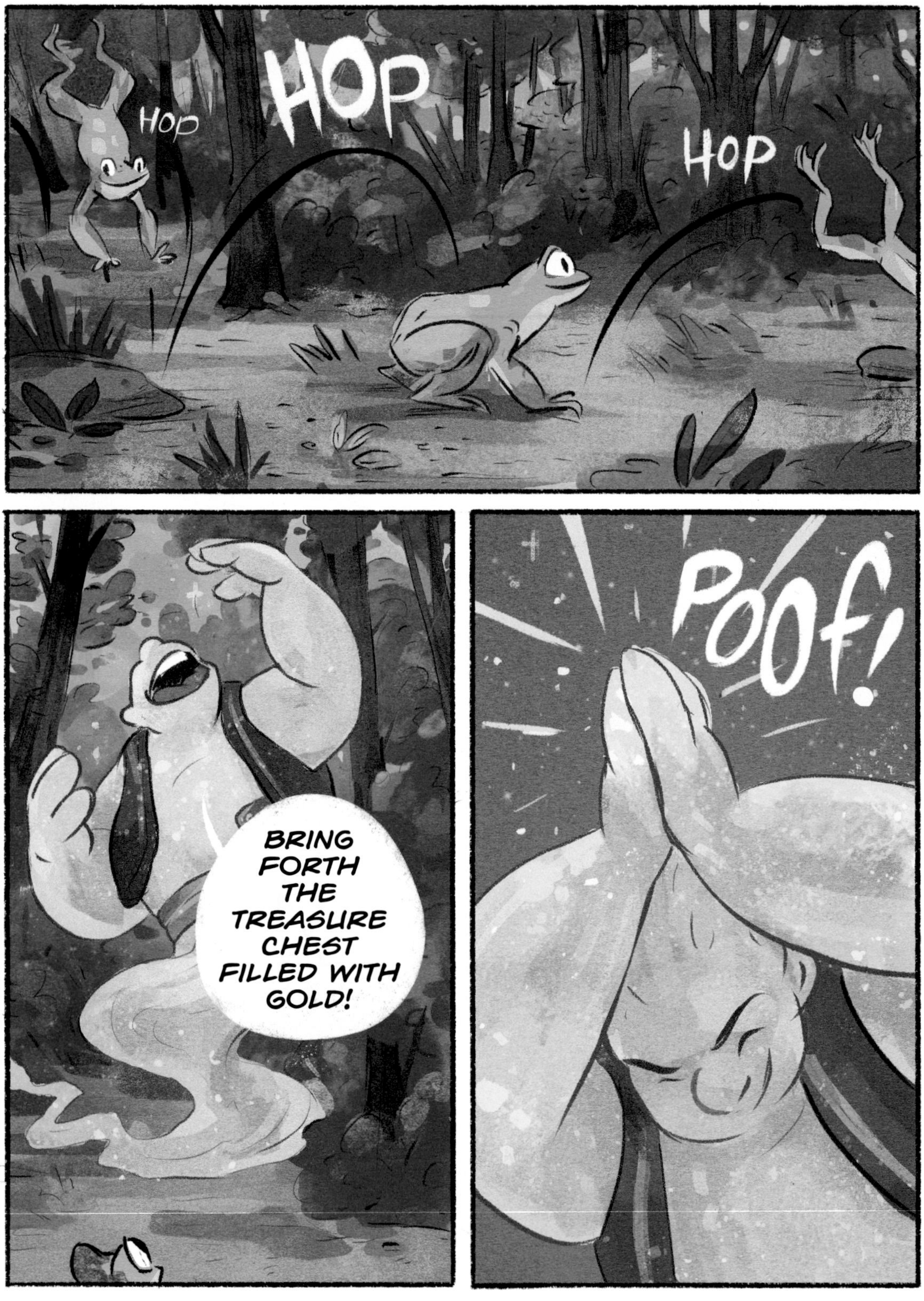
HOP
HOP
HOP
BRING FORTH THE TREASURE CHEST FILLED WITH GOLD!
POOF!

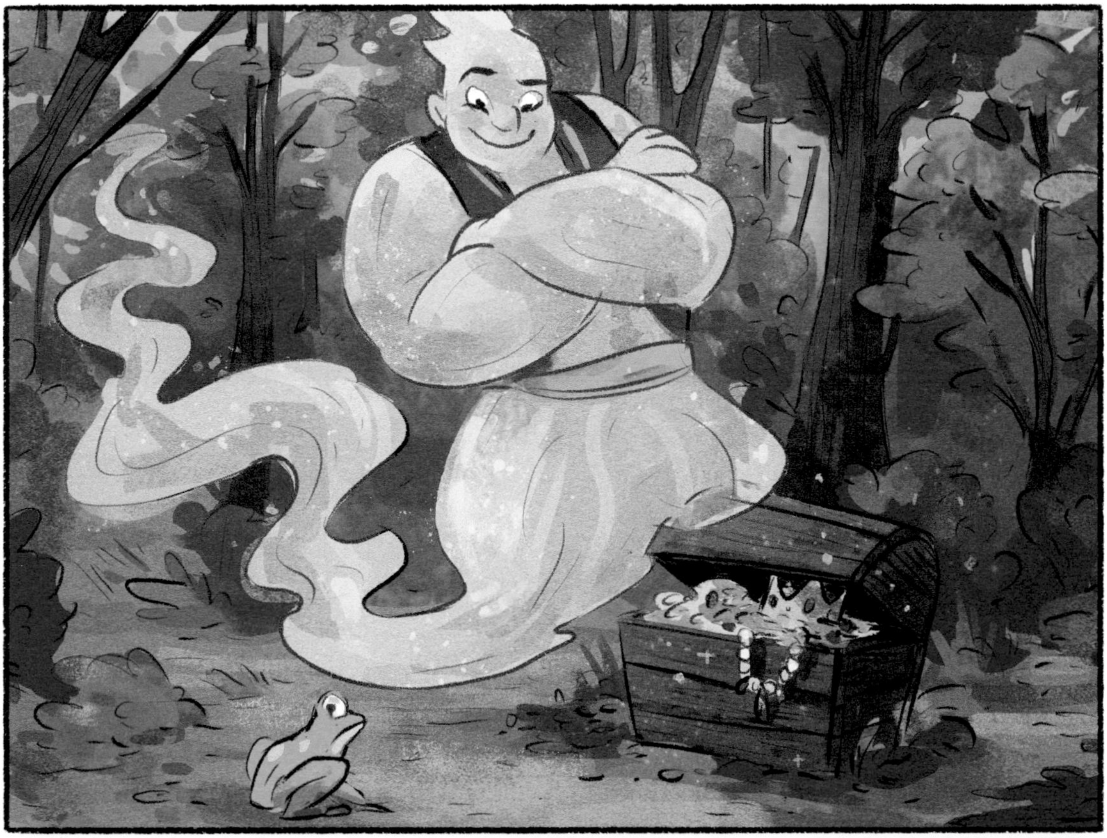

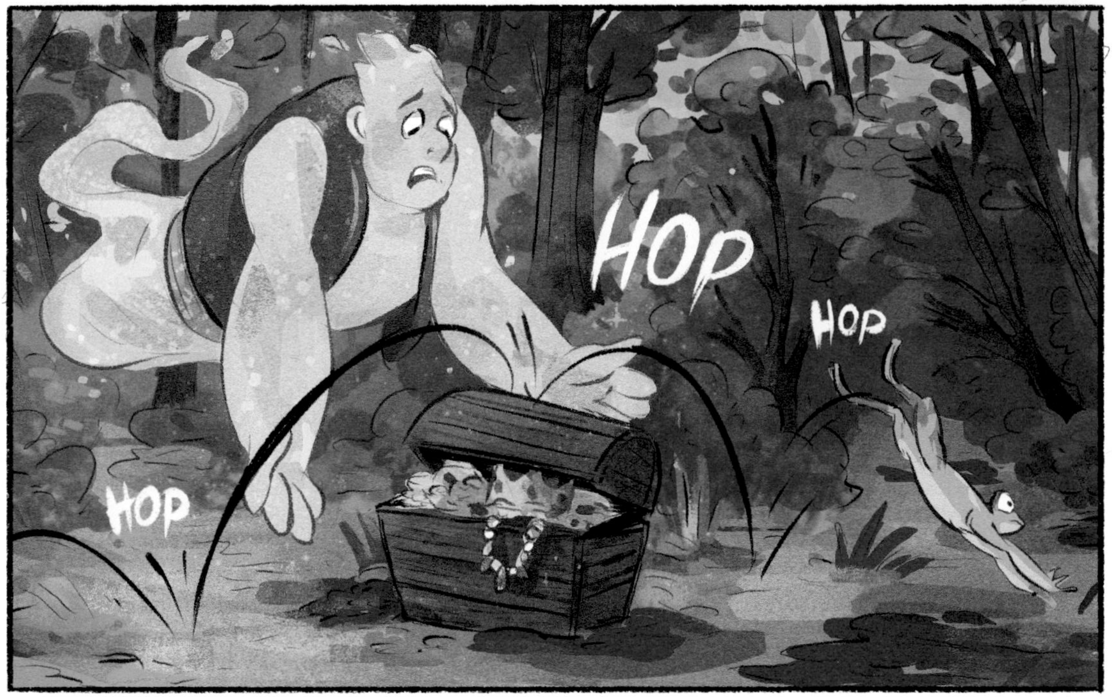
HOP
HOP
HOP

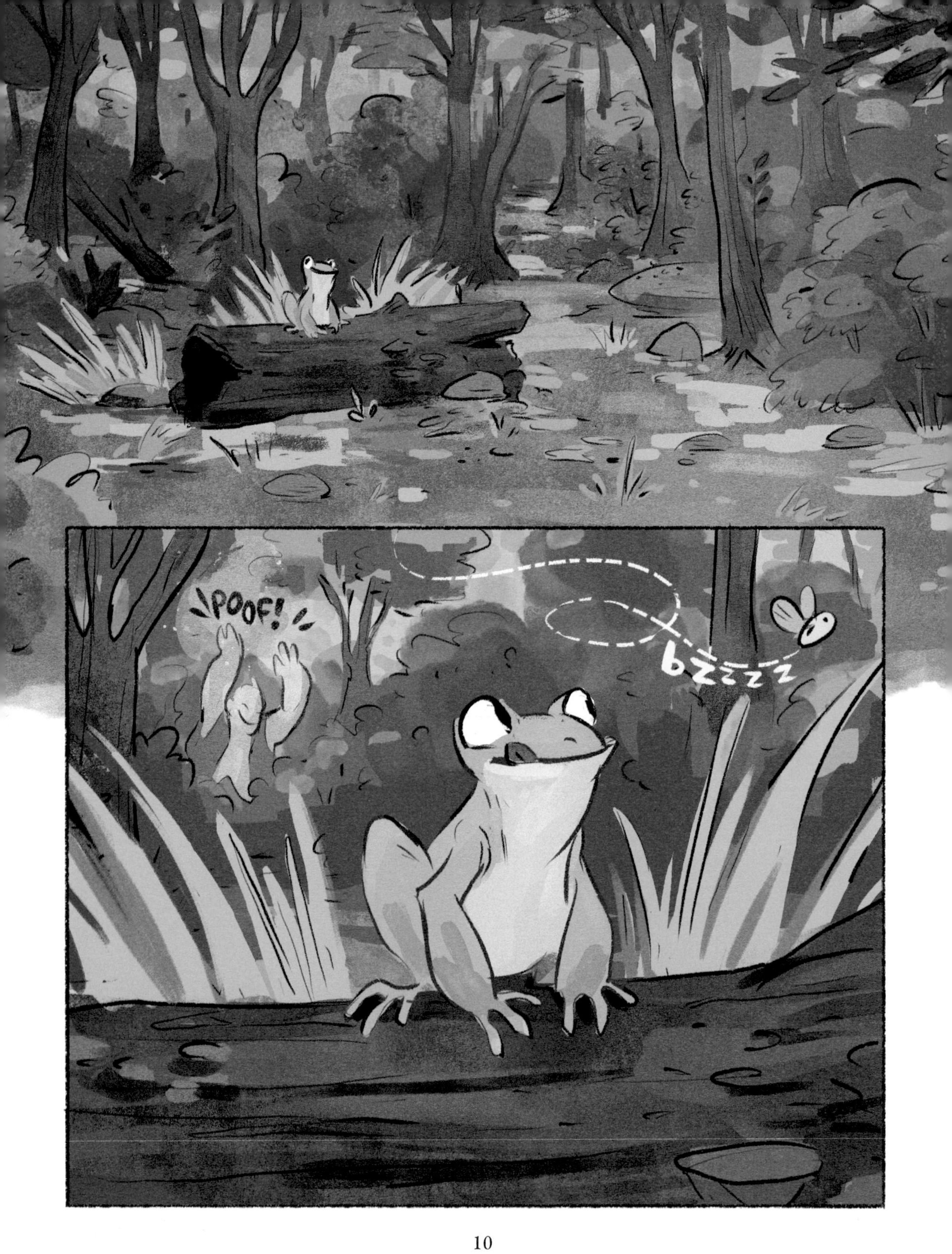
POOF!
bzzzzz

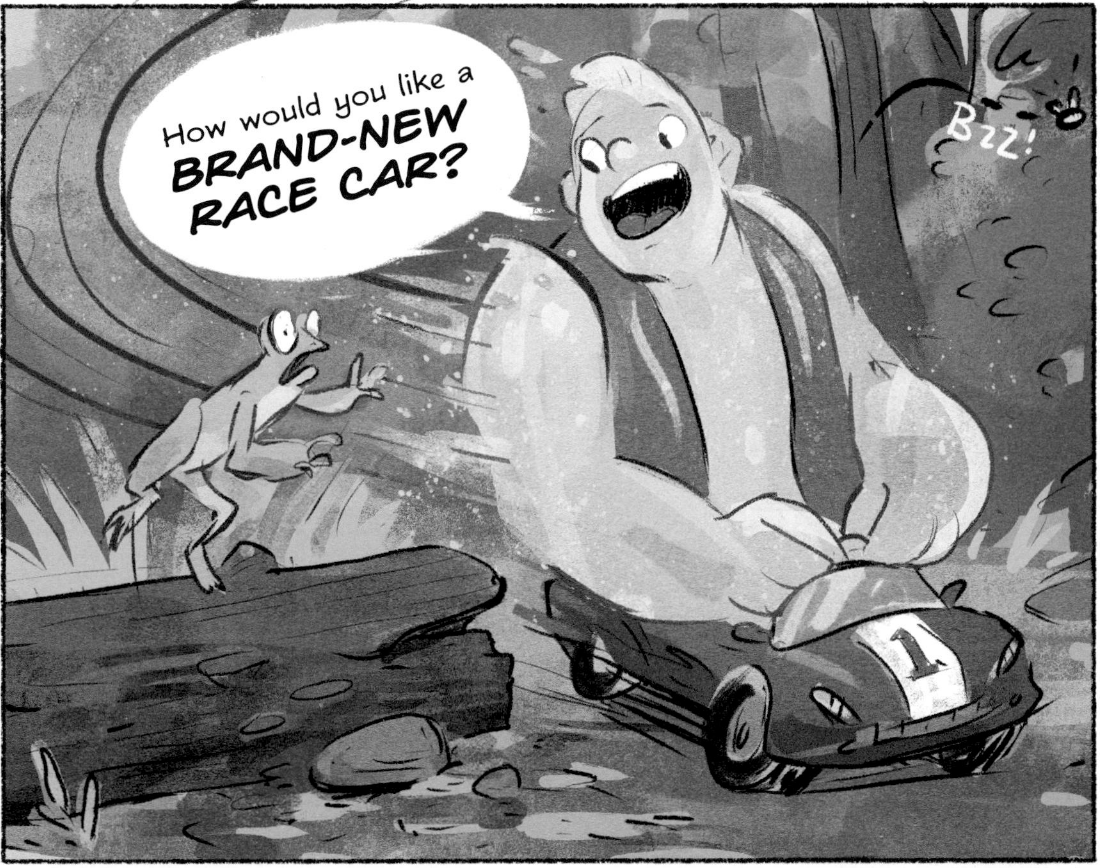
How would you like a BRAND-NEW RACE CAR?
Bzz!

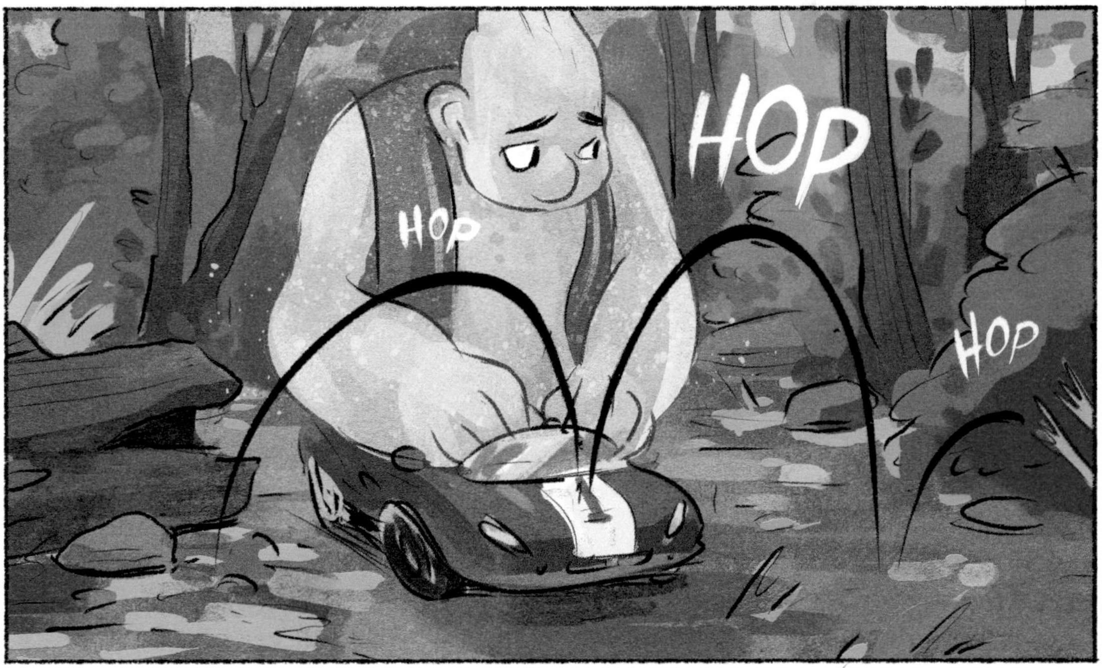
HOP
HOP
HOP

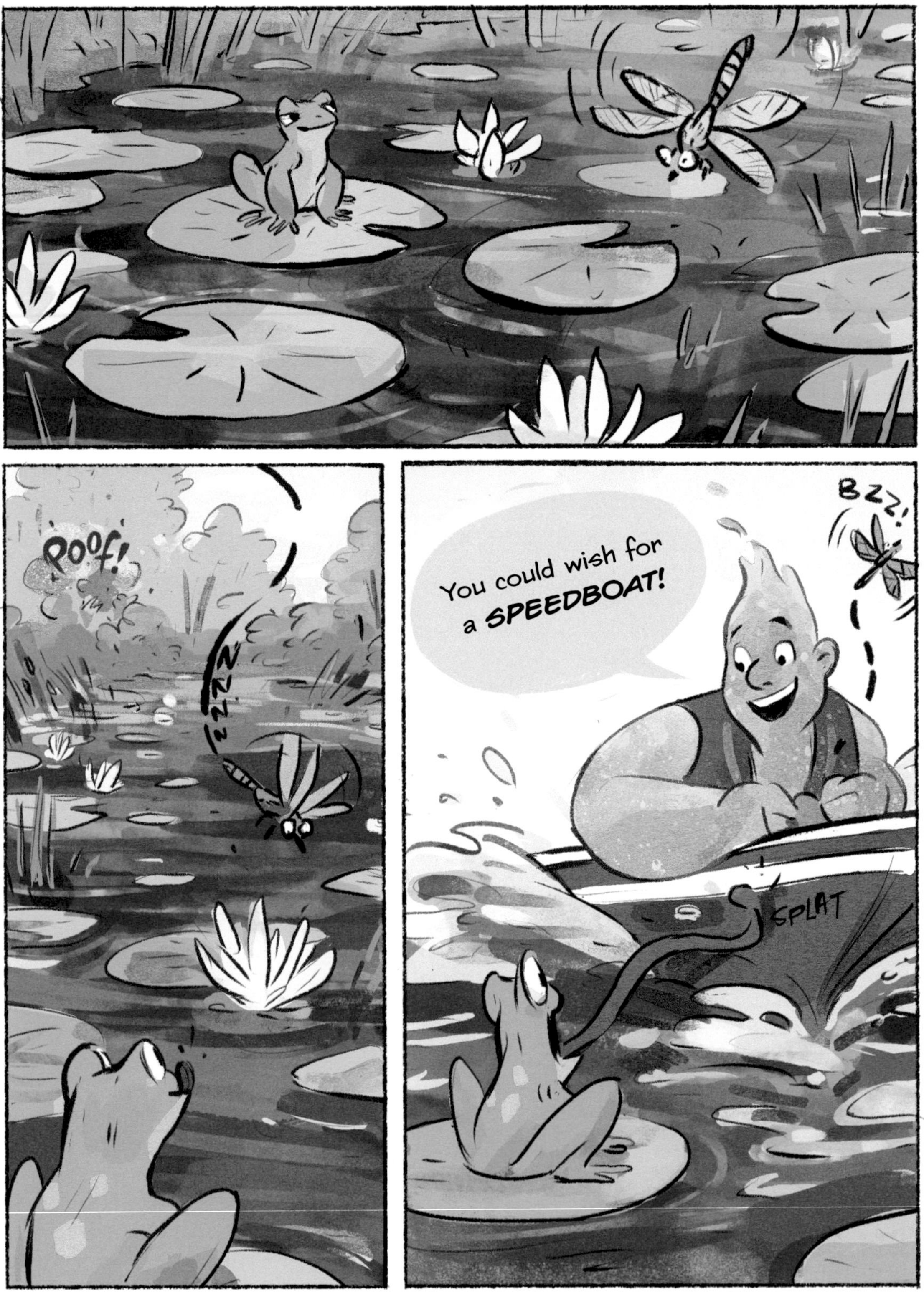
POOF!
ZZZZ
BZZ!
You could wish for a SPEEDBOAT!
SPLAT

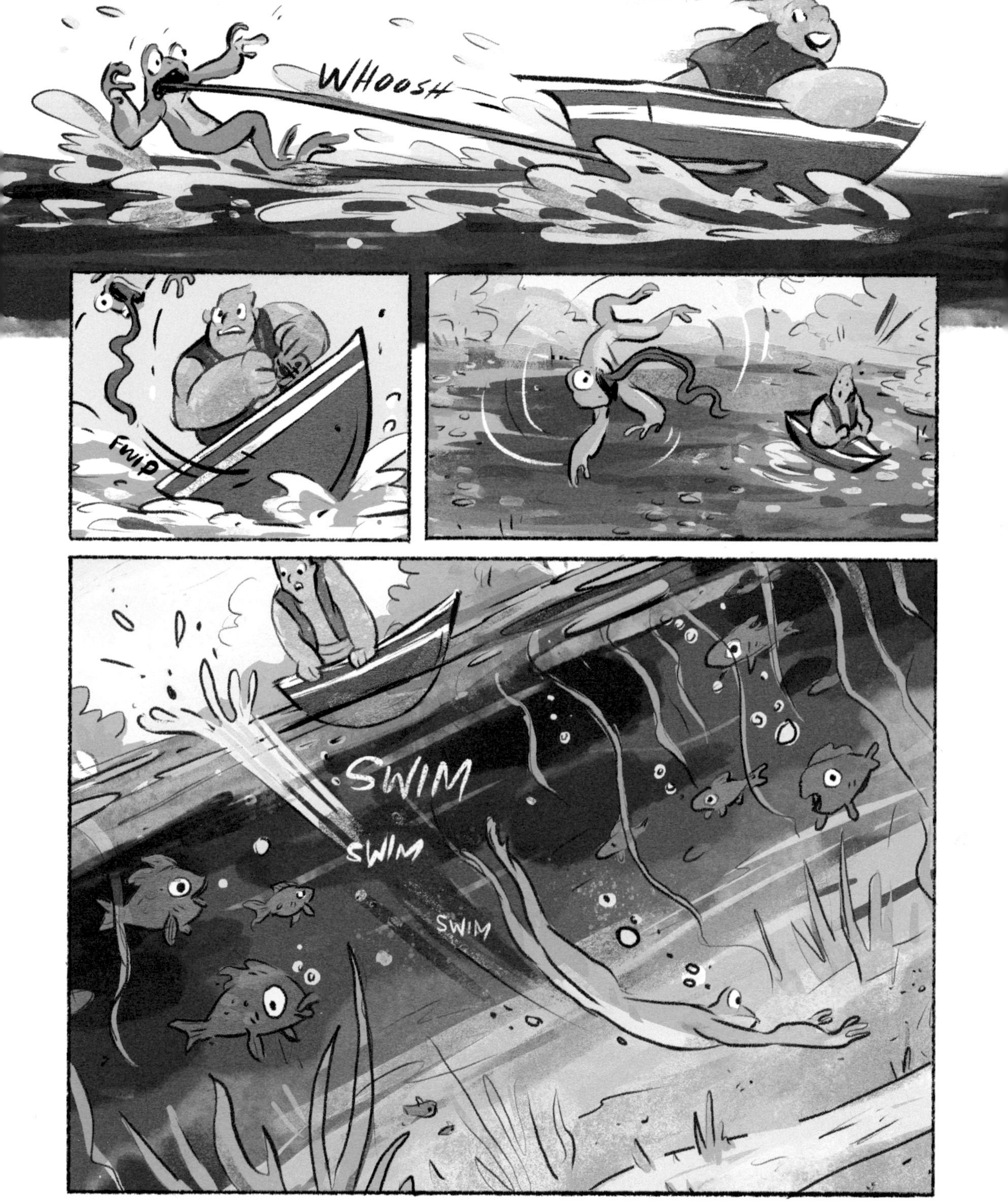
WHOOSH
FWIP
SWIM
SWIM
SWIM

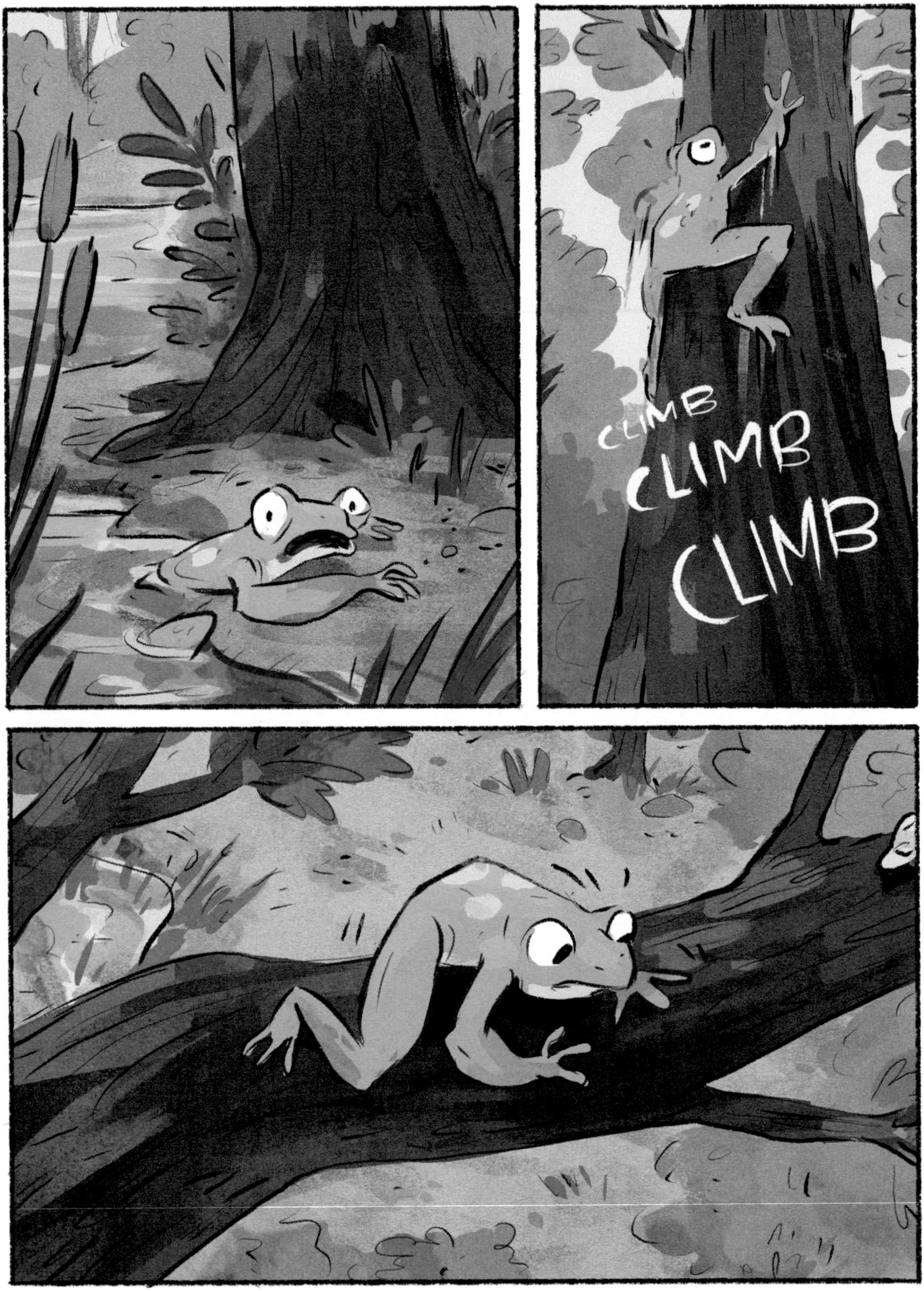
CLIMB
CLIMB
CLIMB

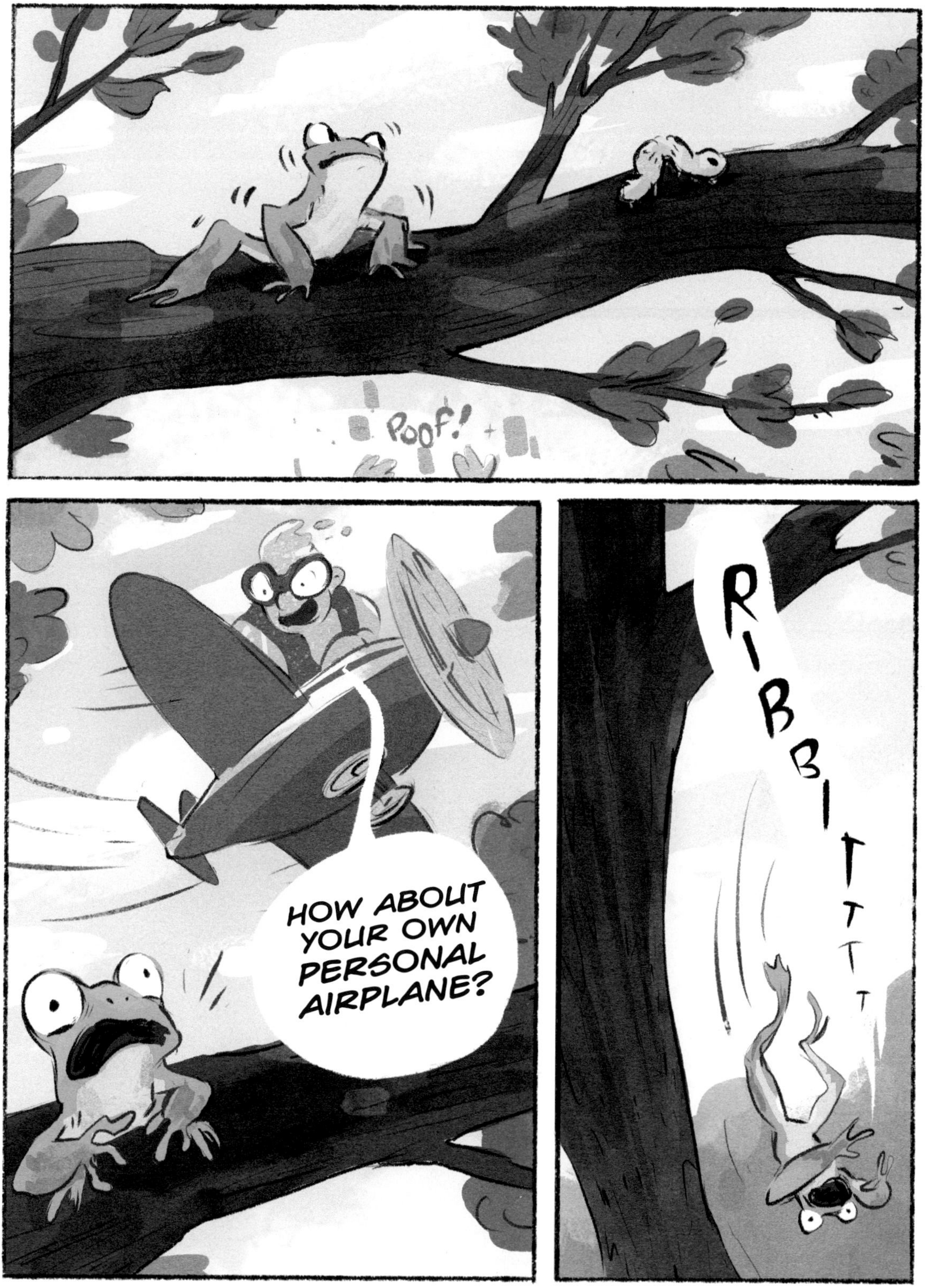
POOF!
HOW ABOUT YOUR OWN PERSONAL AIRPLANE?
RIBBITTTTT

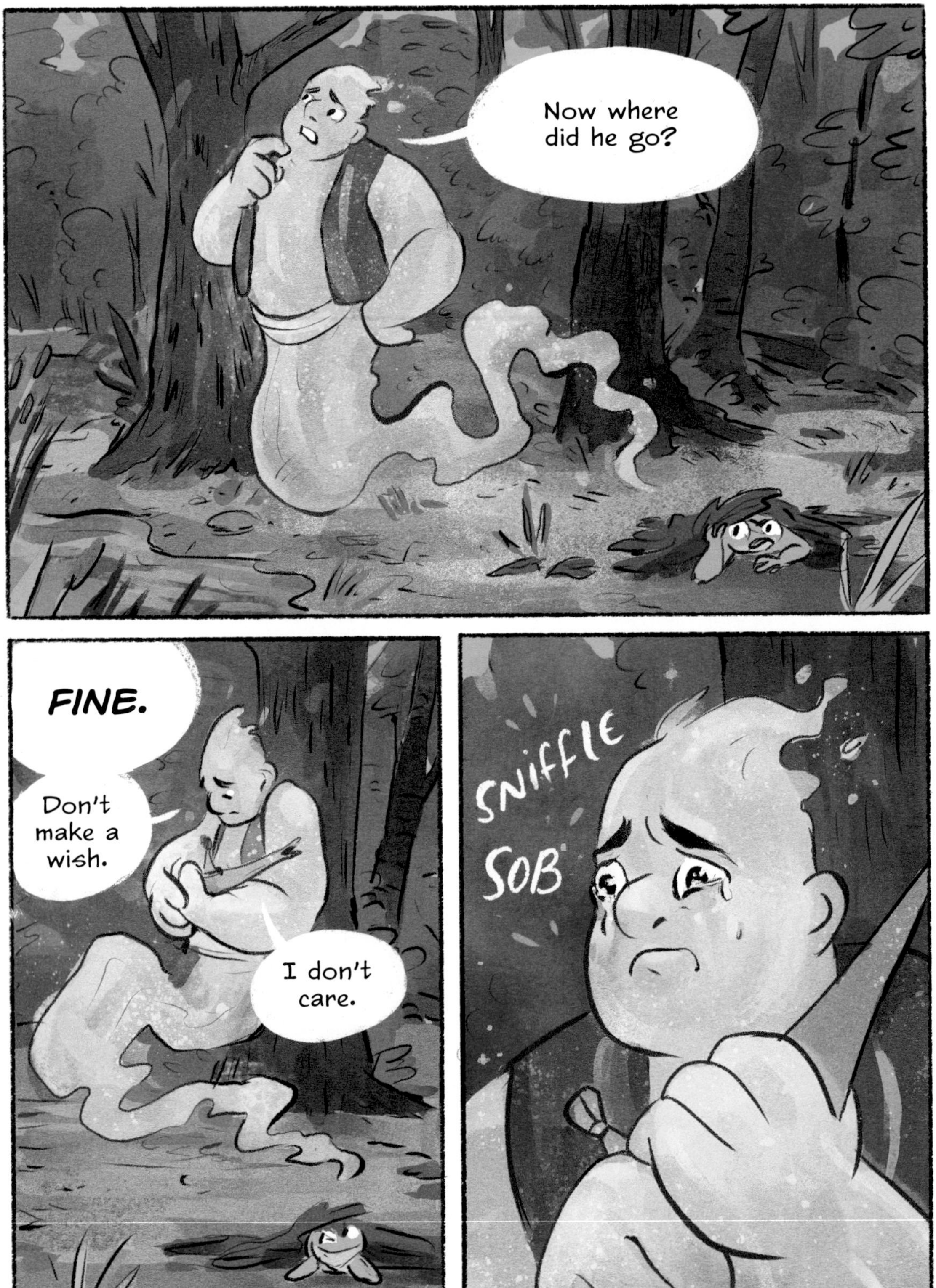
Now where did he go?
FINE.
Don't make a wish.
I don't care.
SNIFFLE
SOB

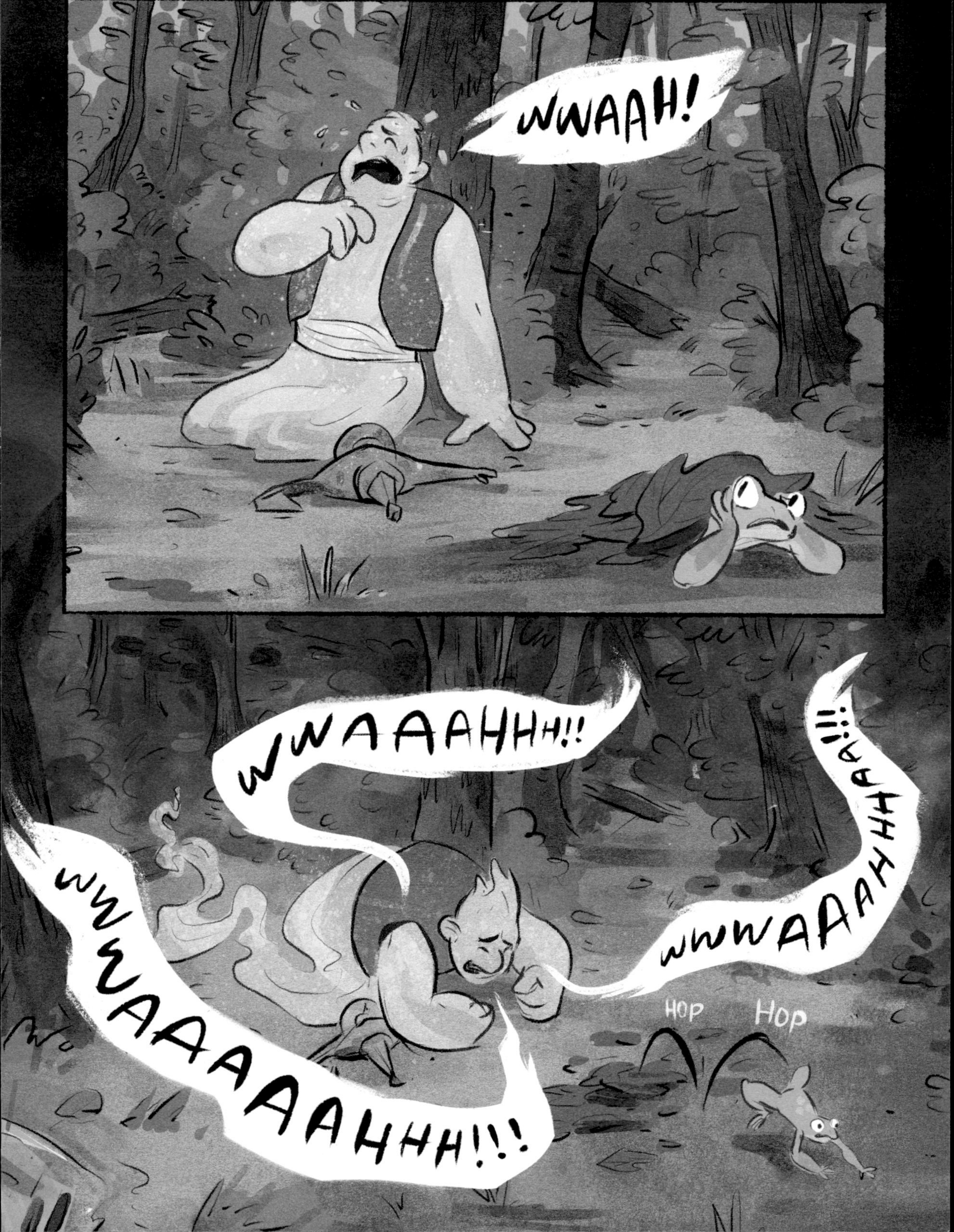
WWAAH!
WWAAAHHH!!
WWWAAAAAAAHHH!!!
WWWAAAAHHHAA!!!
HOP
HOP

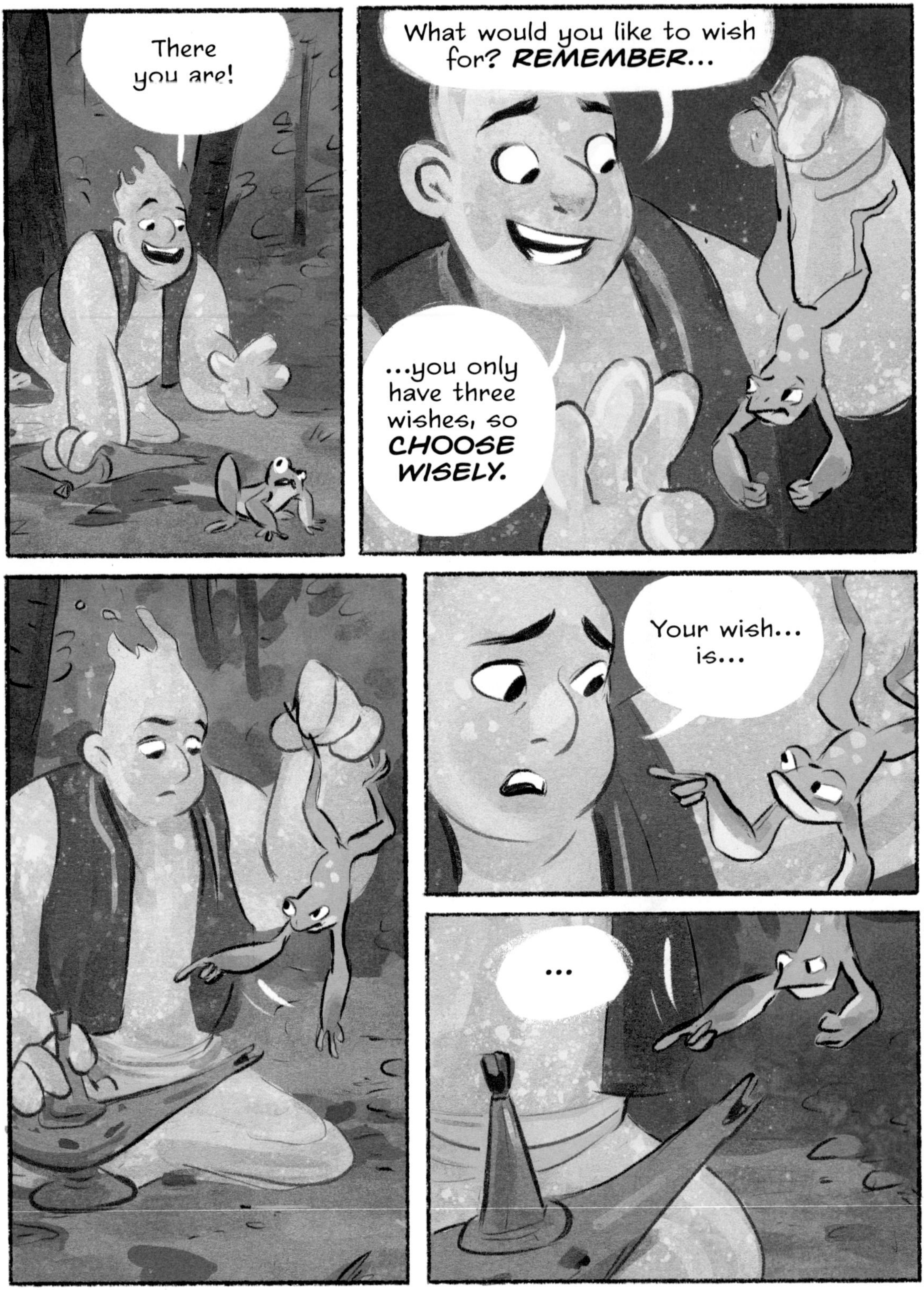
There you are!
What would you like to wish for? REMEMBER...
...you only have three wishes, so CHOOSE WISELY.
Your wish... is...
...

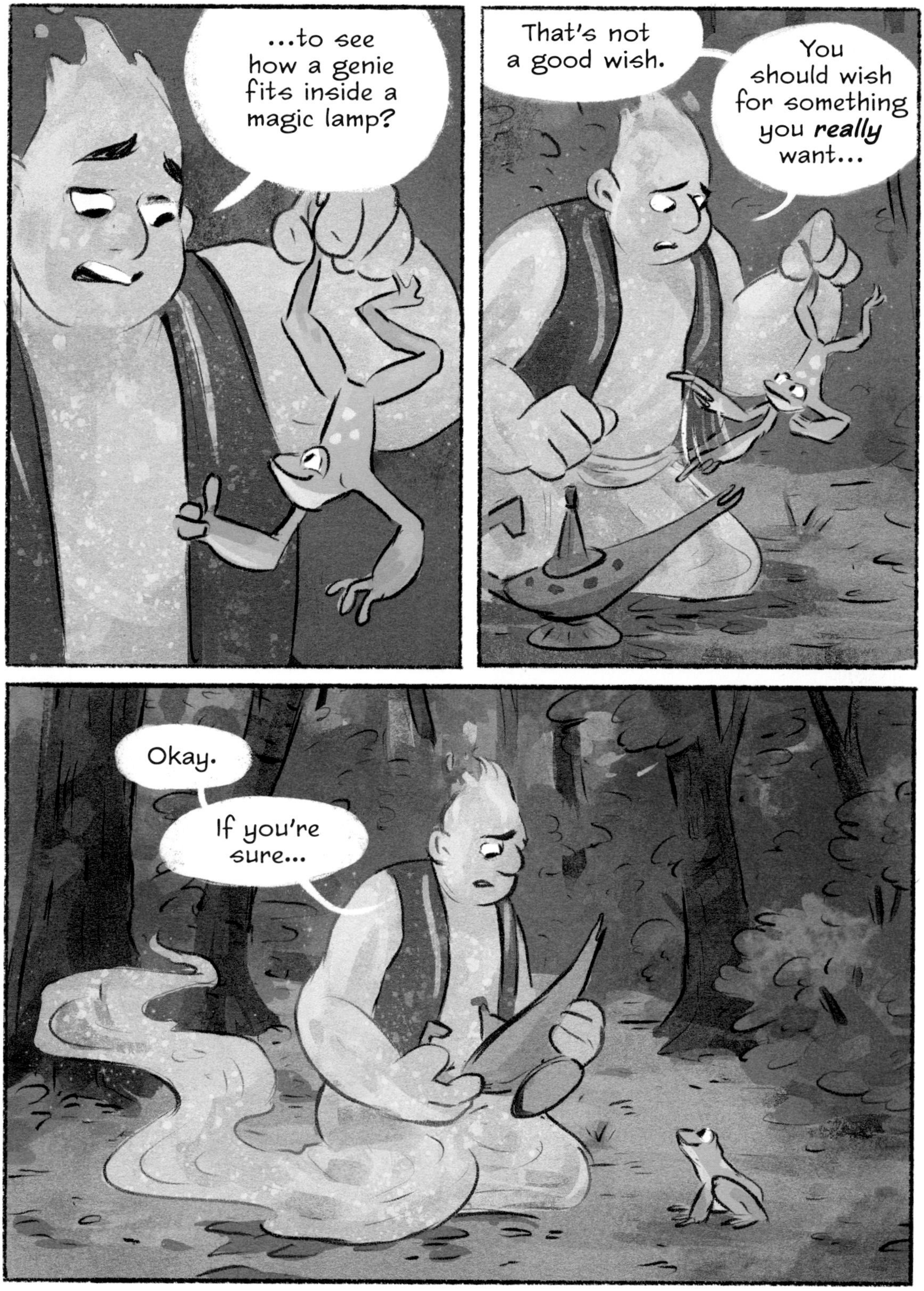
...to see how a genie fits inside a magic lamp?
That's not a good wish.
You should wish for something you *really* want...
Okay.
If you're sure...

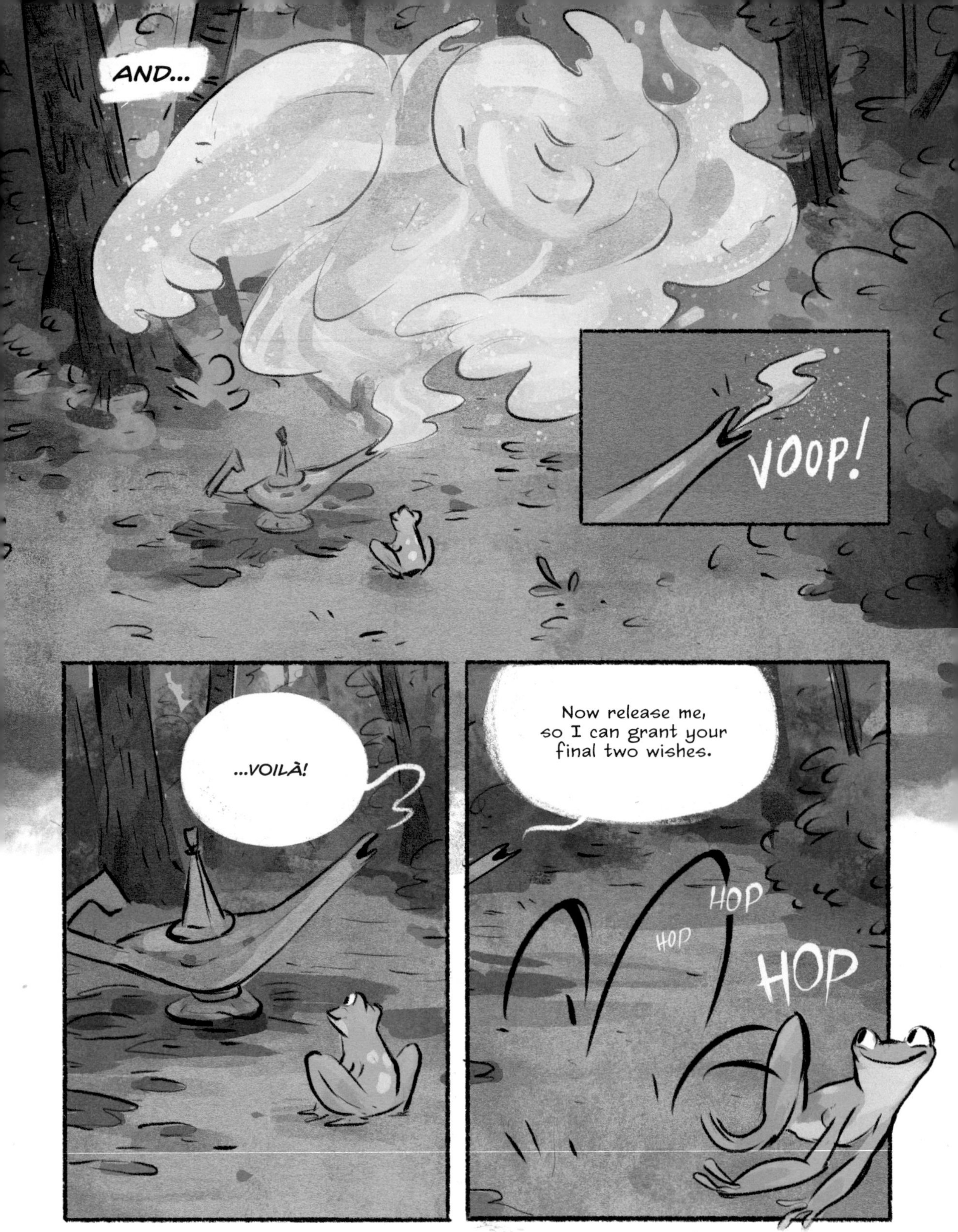
AND...
VOOP!
...VOILÀ!
Now release me, so I can grant your final two wishes.
HOP
HOP
HOP

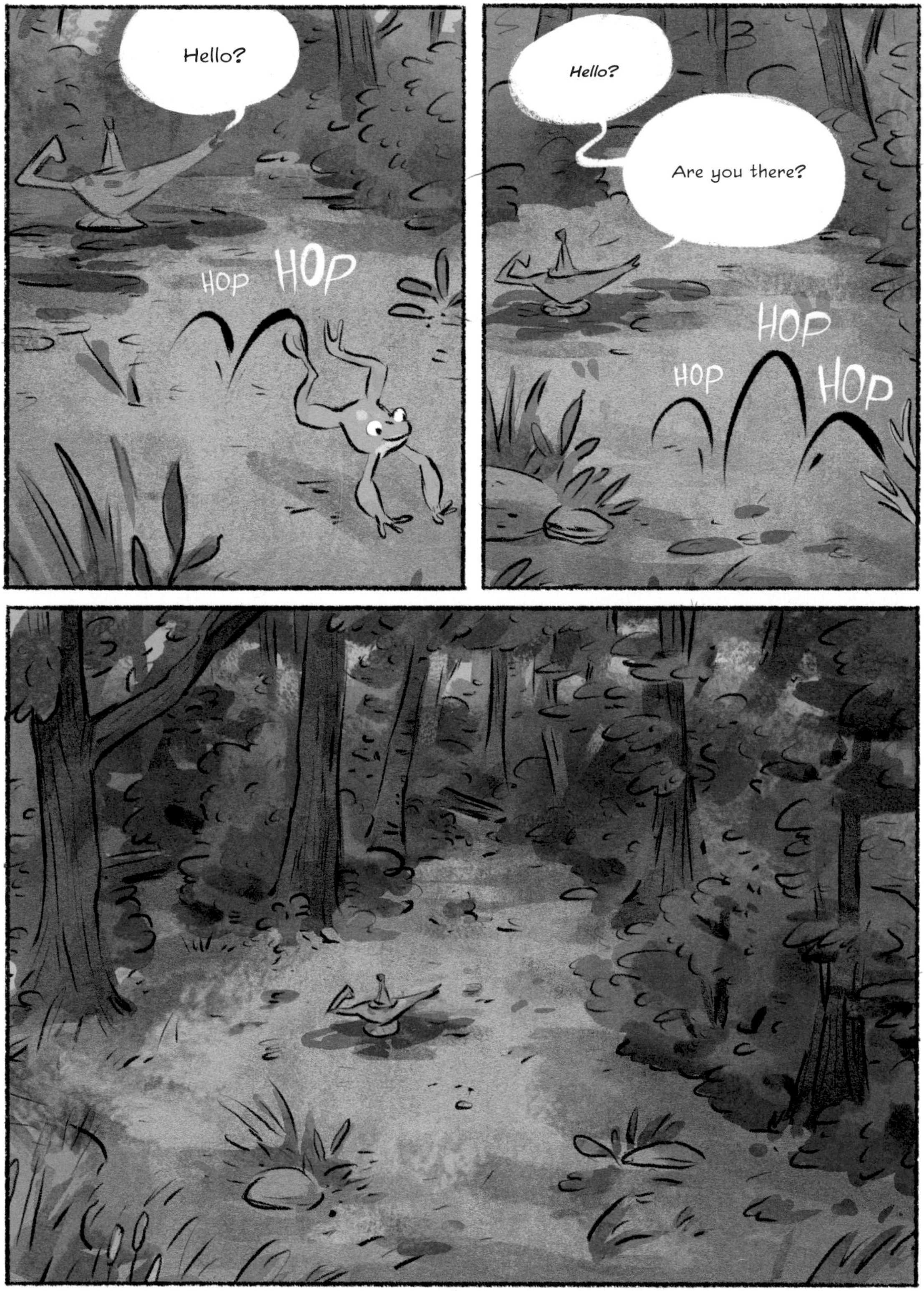
Hello?
HOP HOP
Hello?
Are you there?
HOP HOP HOP

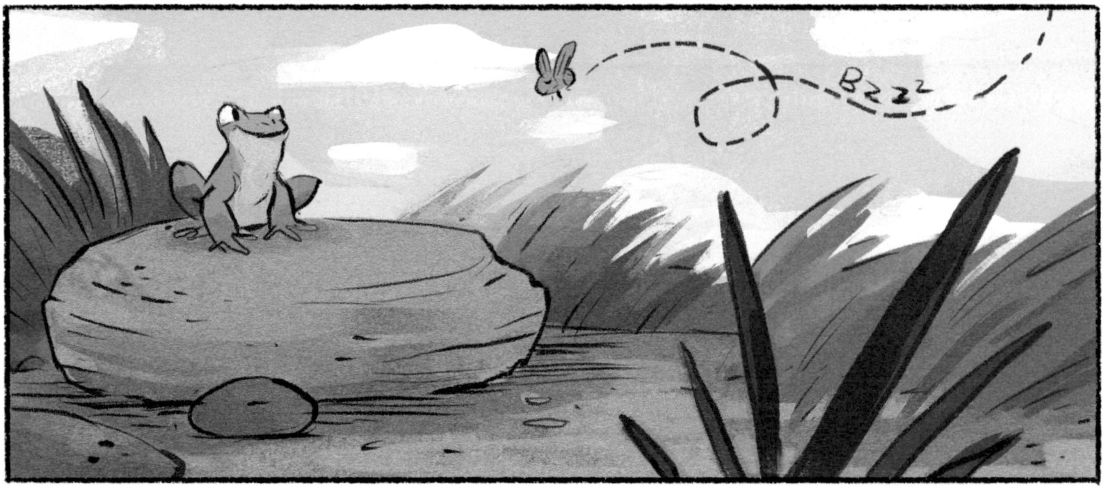
Bzzz
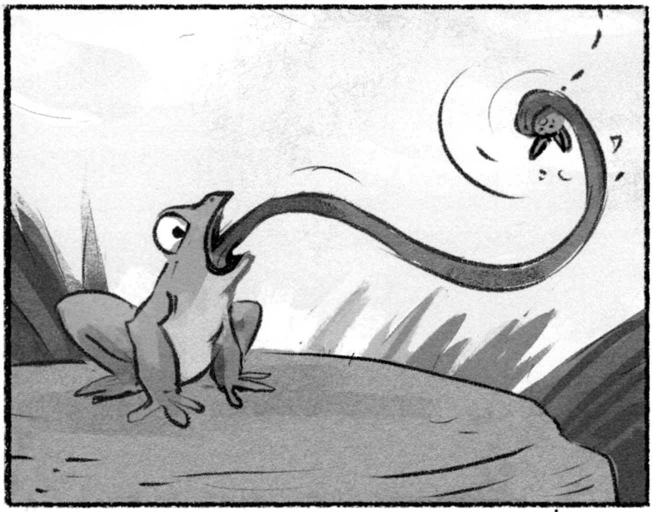
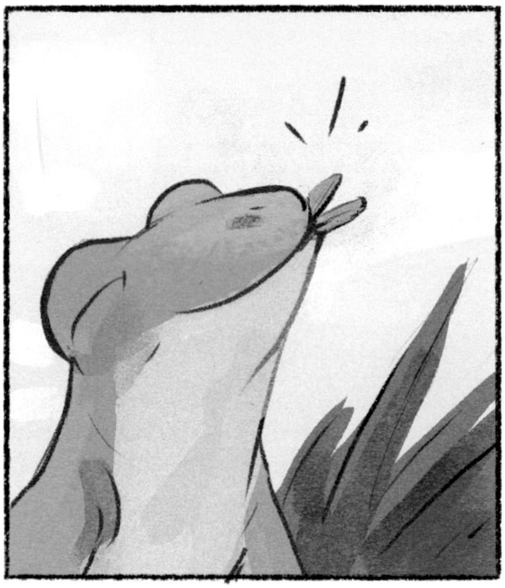
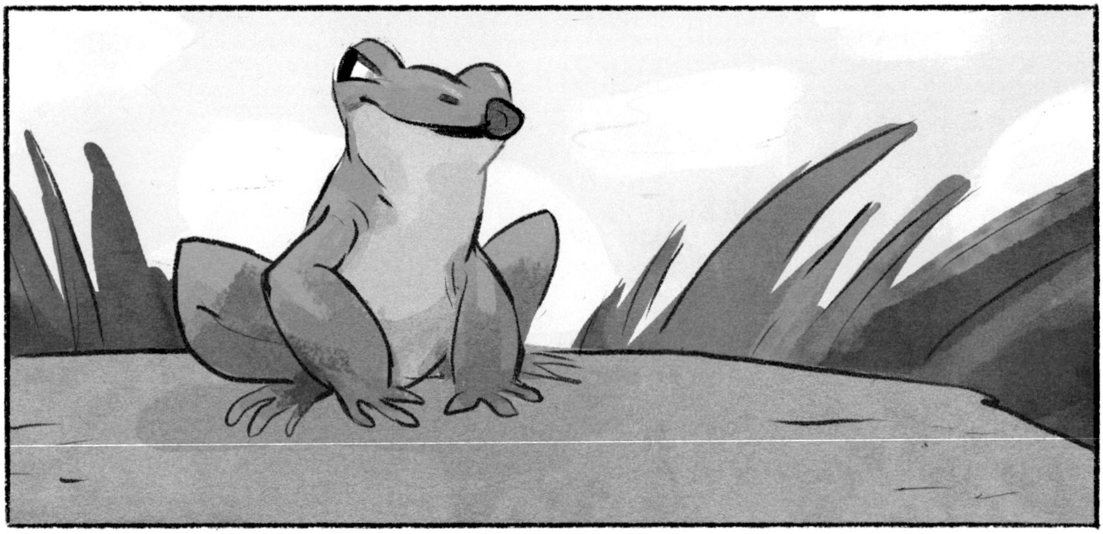

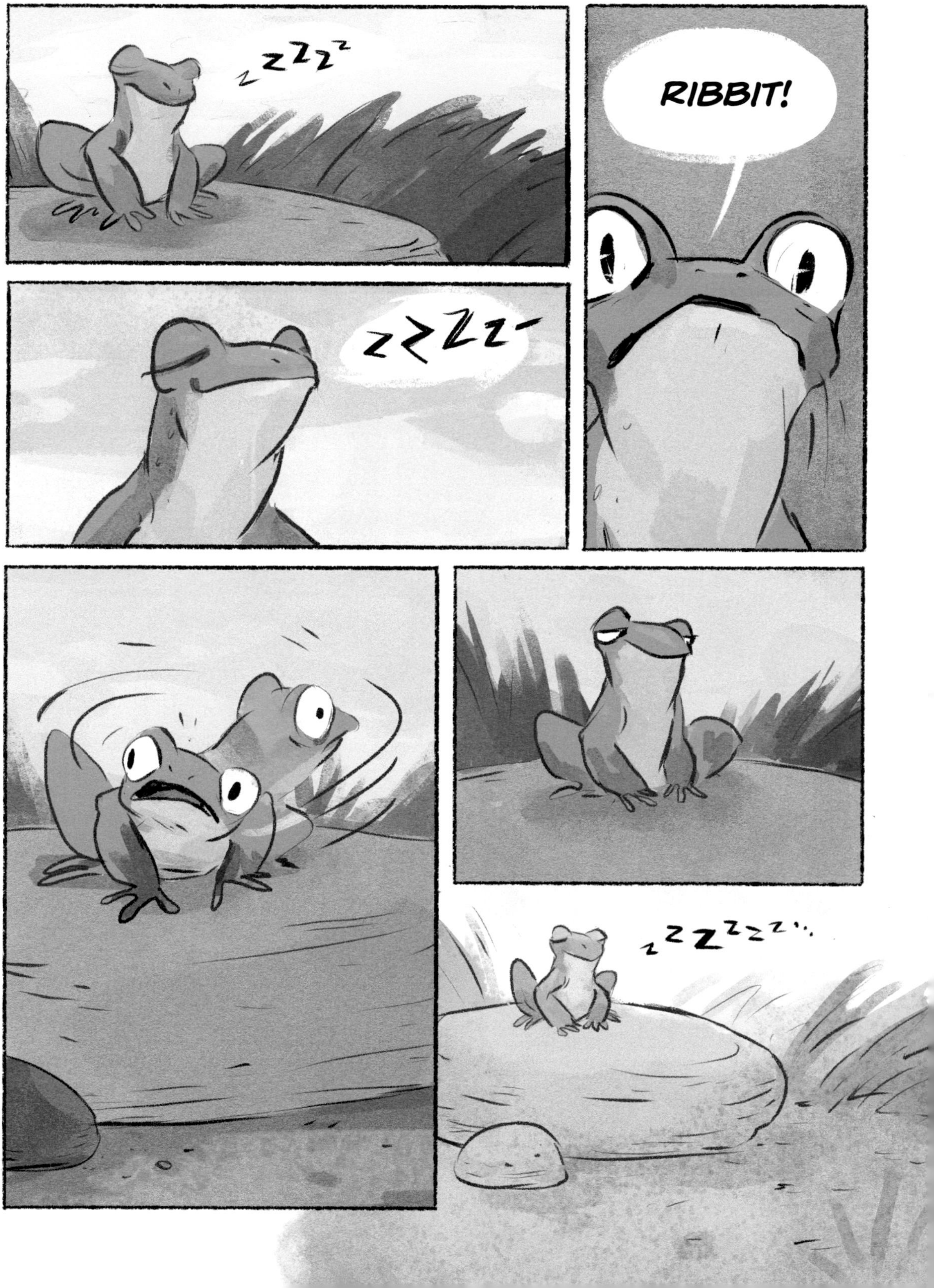
zzzz
RIBBIT!
zzzz-
zzzzzzz...

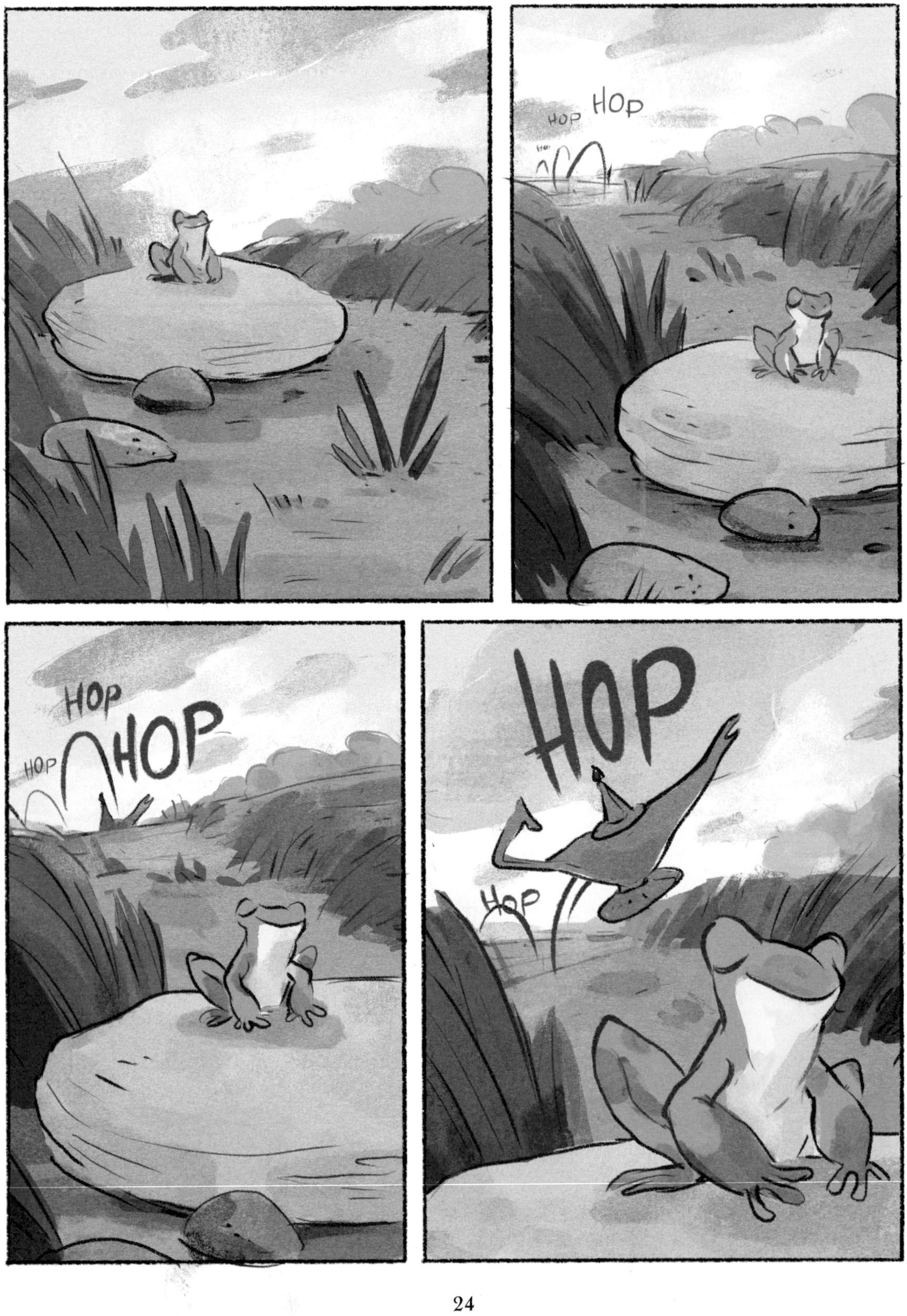
HOP
HOP
HOP
HOP
HOP
HOP
HOP

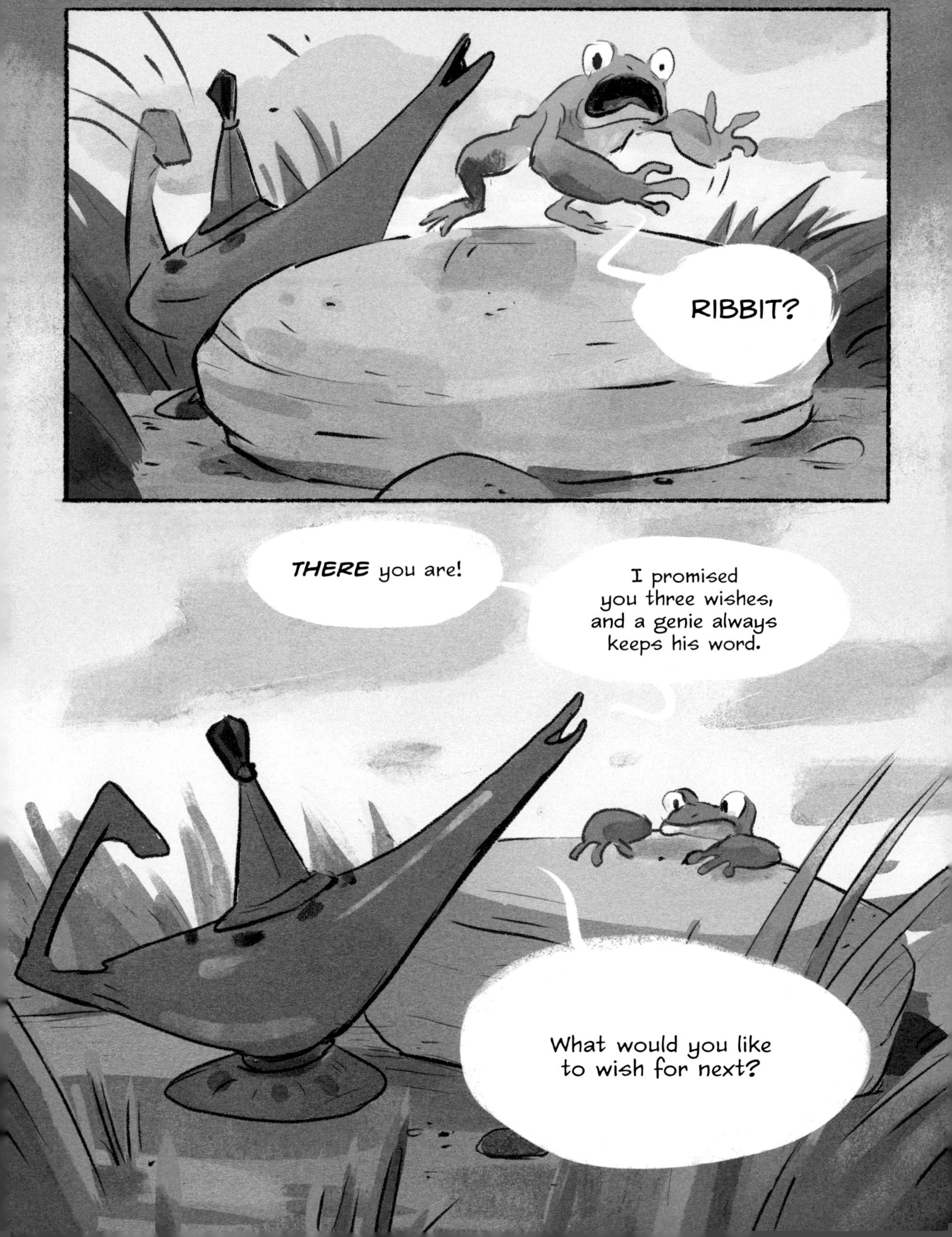
RIBBIT?
THERE you are!
I promised you three wishes, and a genie always keeps his word.
What would you like to wish for next?

THE SINGING ROCK

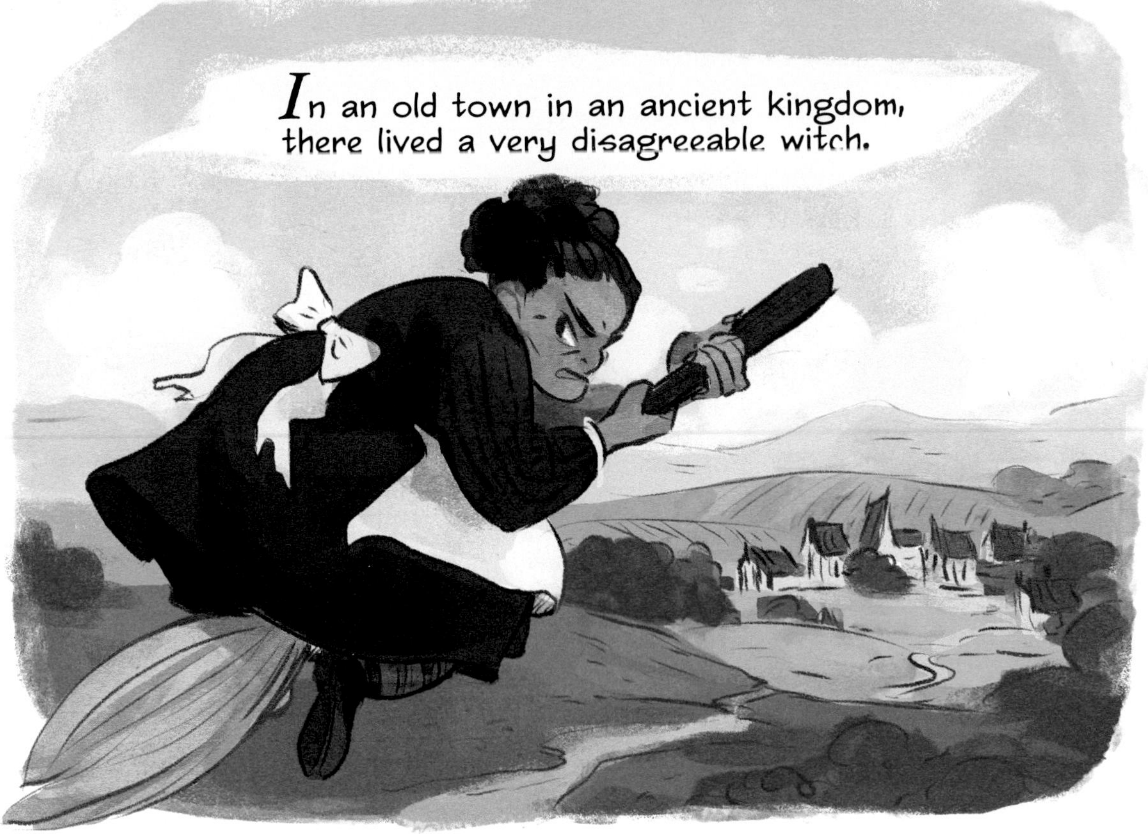
In an old town in an ancient kingdom,
there lived a very disagreeable witch.

The witch hated many things...

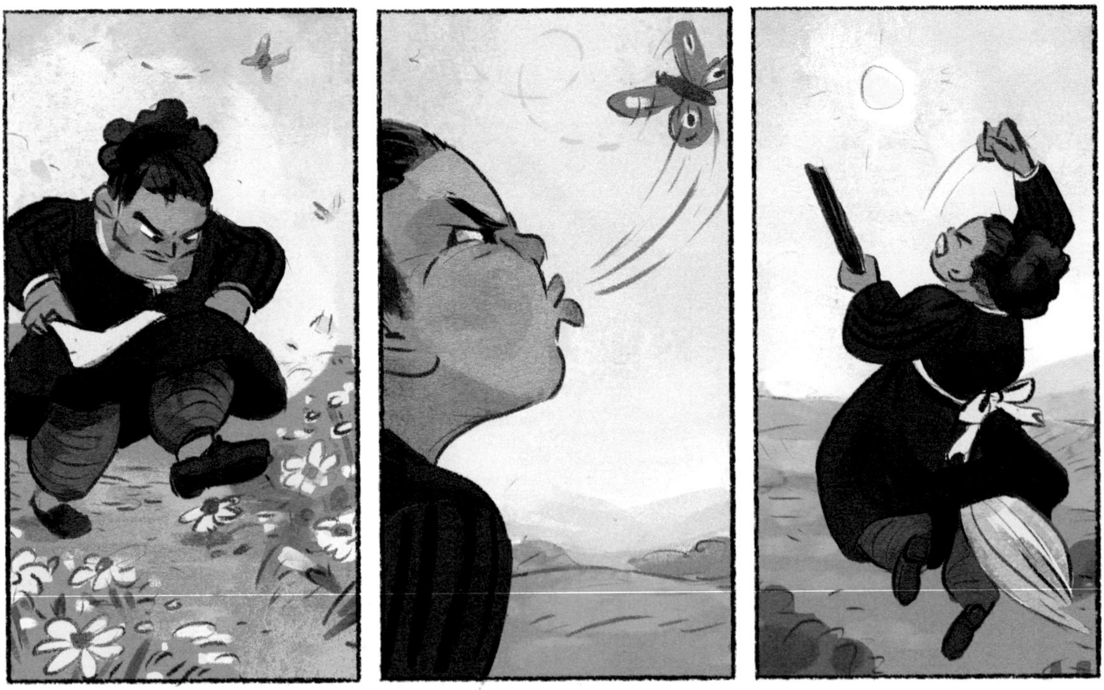

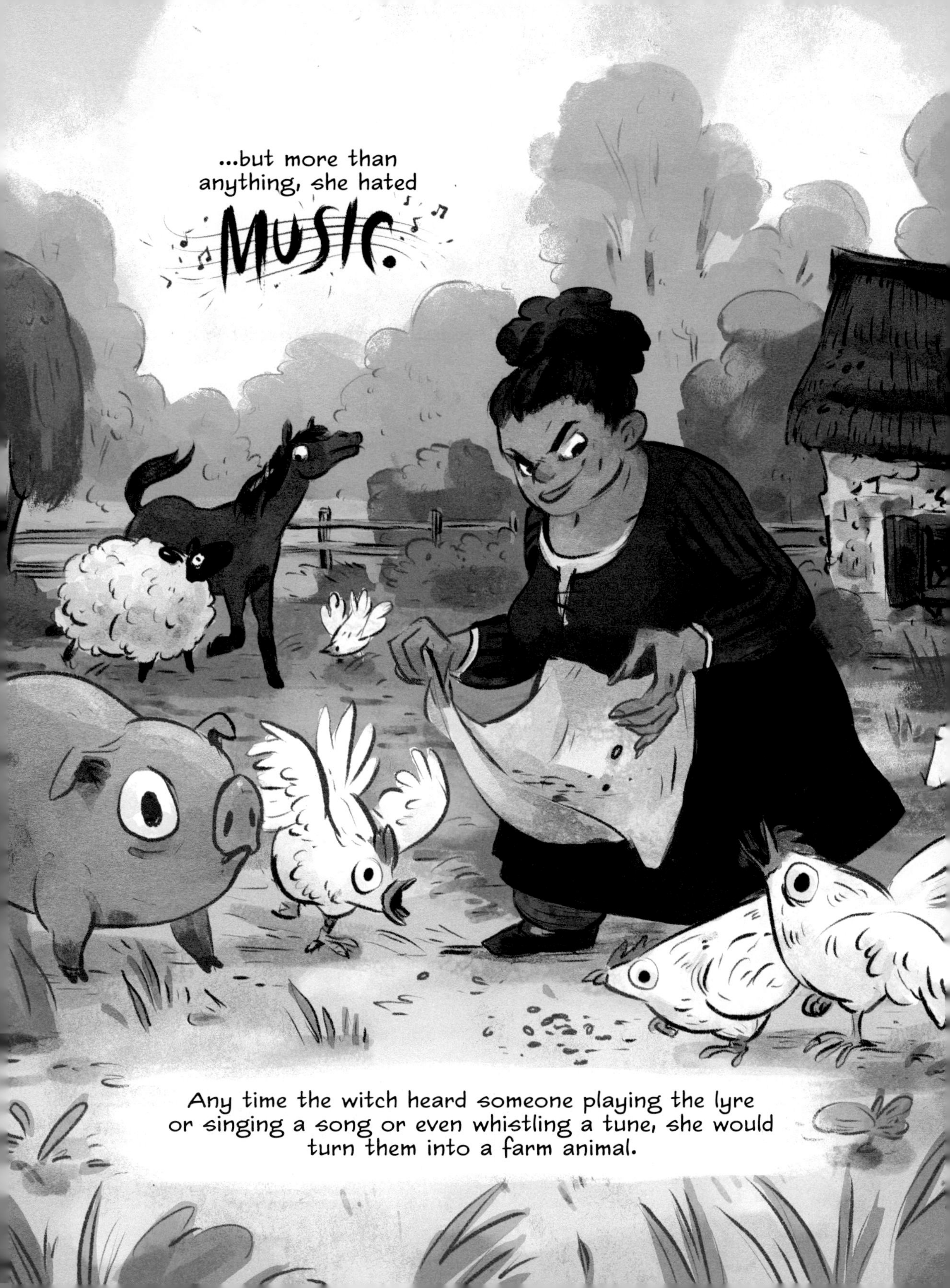

...but more than anything, she hated
MUSIC
Any time the witch heard someone playing the lyre or singing a song or even whistling a tune, she would turn them into a farm animal.

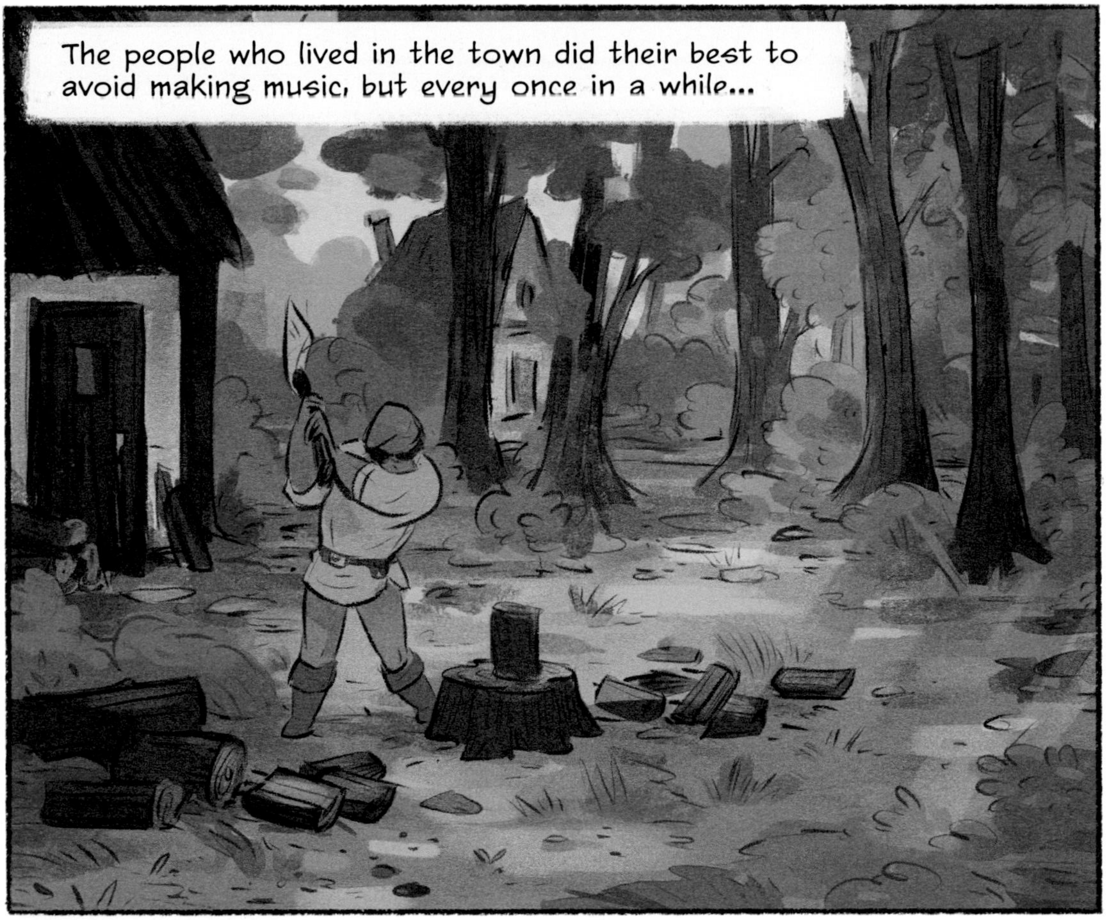
The people who lived in the town did their best to avoid making music, but every once in a while...

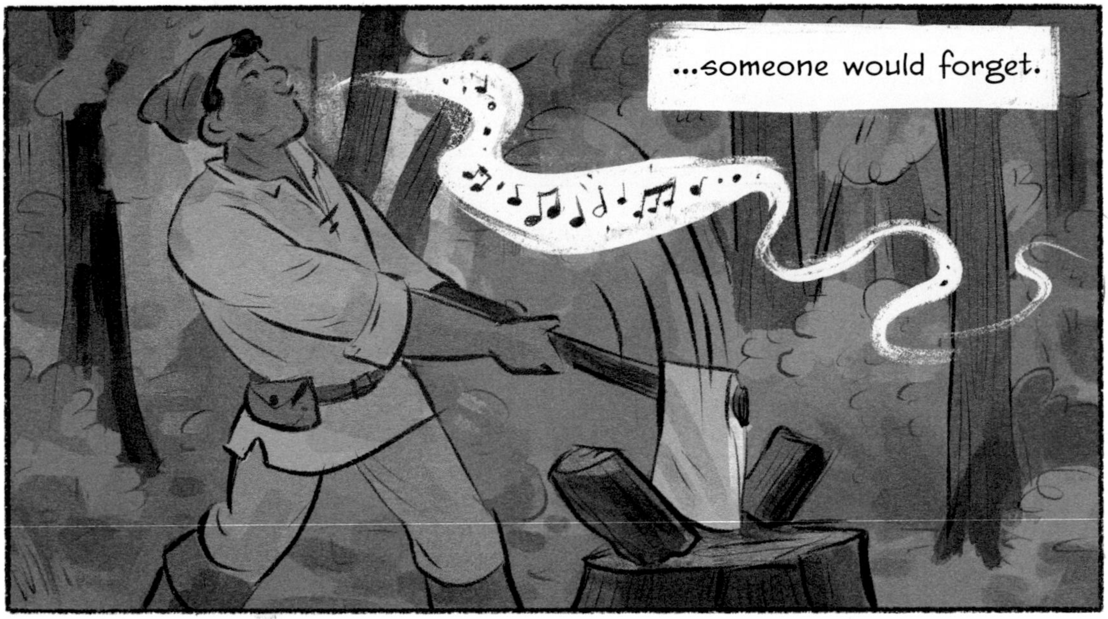
...someone would forget.

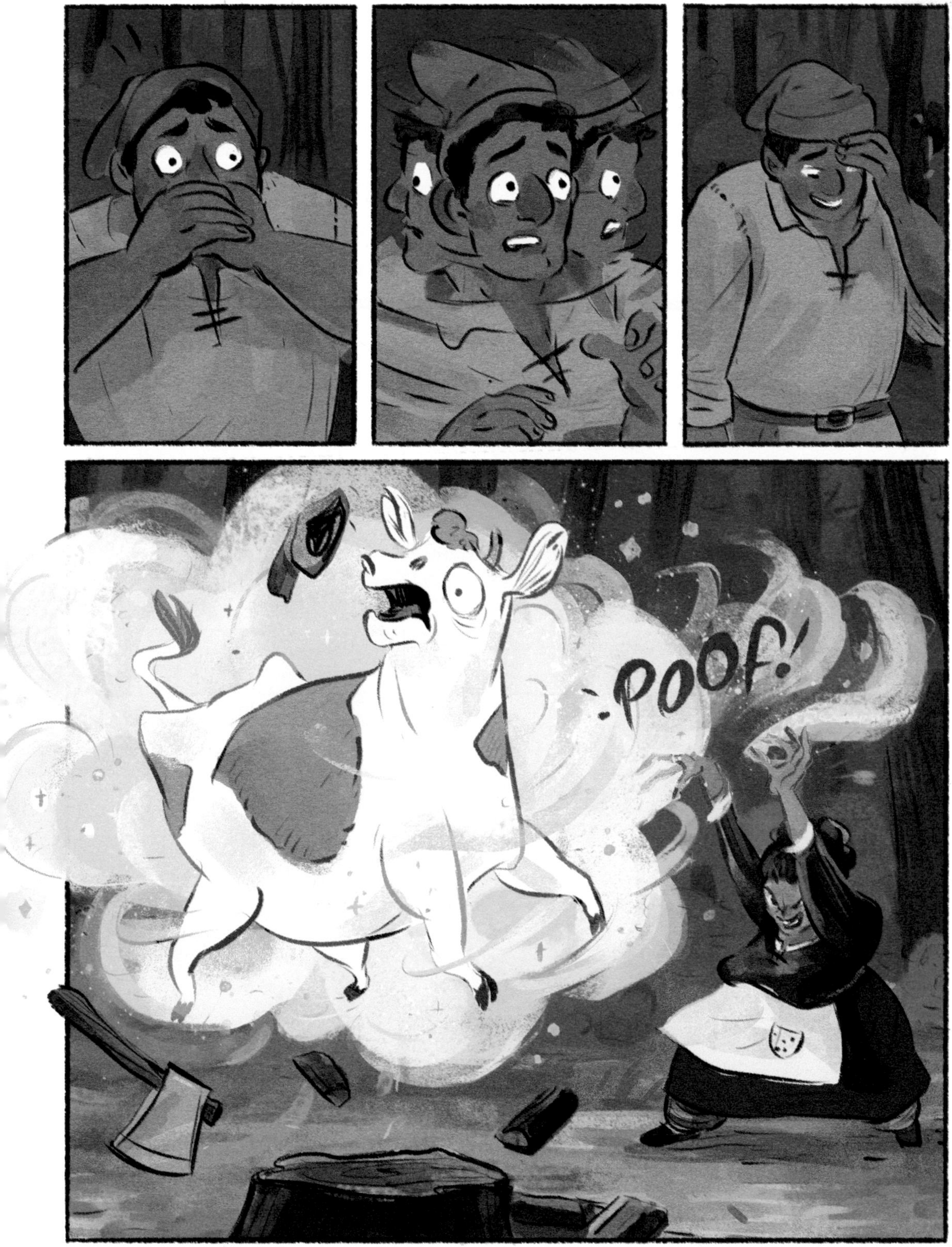
POOF!

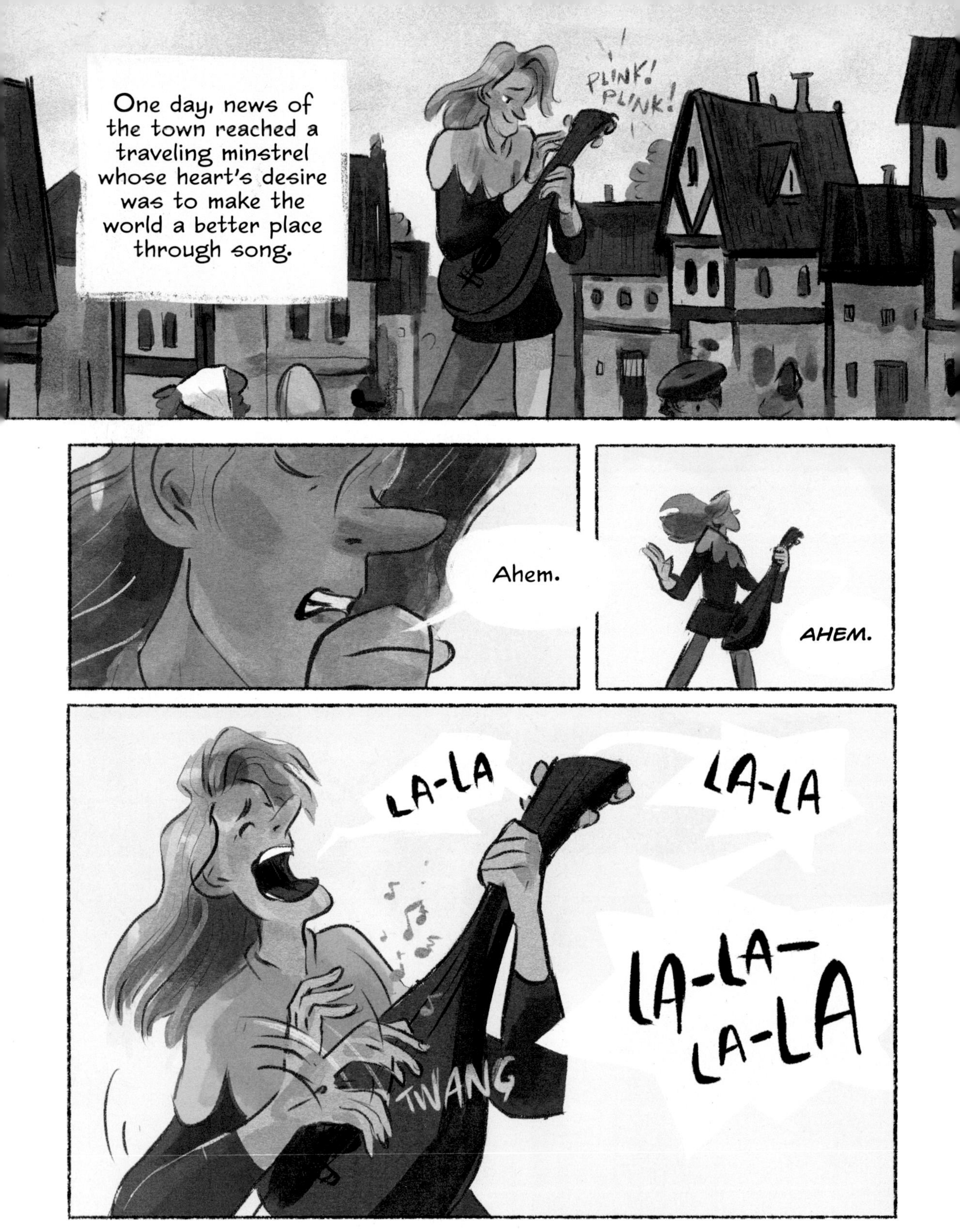

One day, news of the town reached a traveling minstrel whose heart's desire was to make the world a better place through song.
PLINK! PLINK!
Ahem.
AHEM.
LA-LA
LA-LA
LA-LA-LA-LA
TWANG

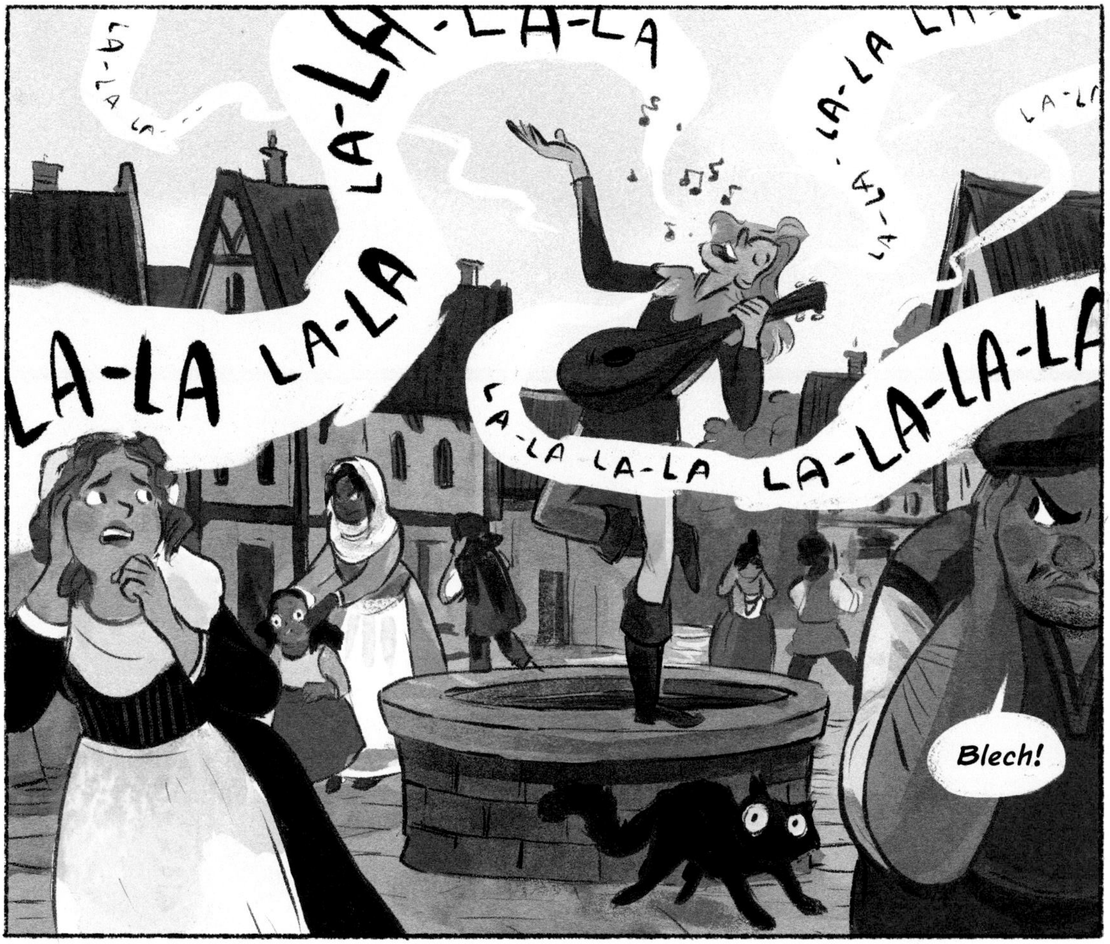
LA-LA LA-LA-LA-LA
LA-LA LA-LA LA-LA
LA-LA LA-LA LA-LA LA-LA-LA-LA-LA
Blech!

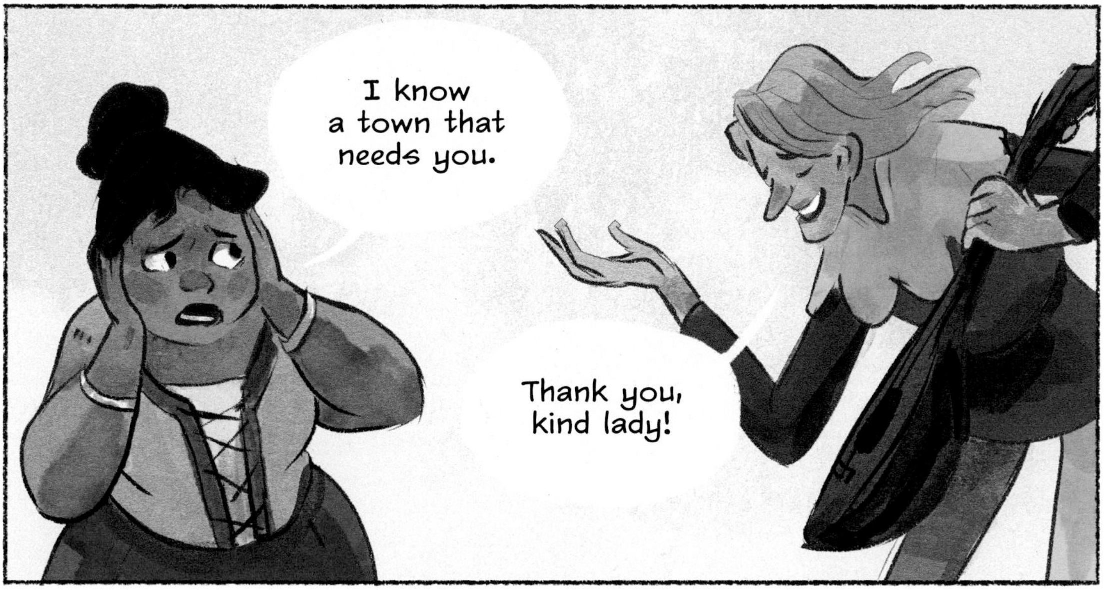
I know a town that needs you.
Thank you, kind lady!

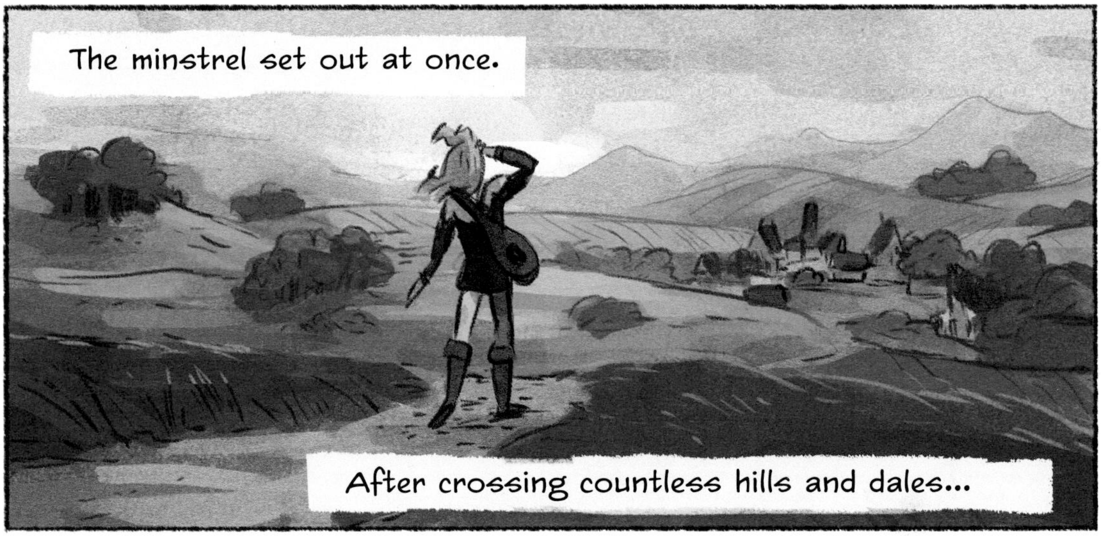
The minstrel set out at once.
After crossing countless hills and dales...

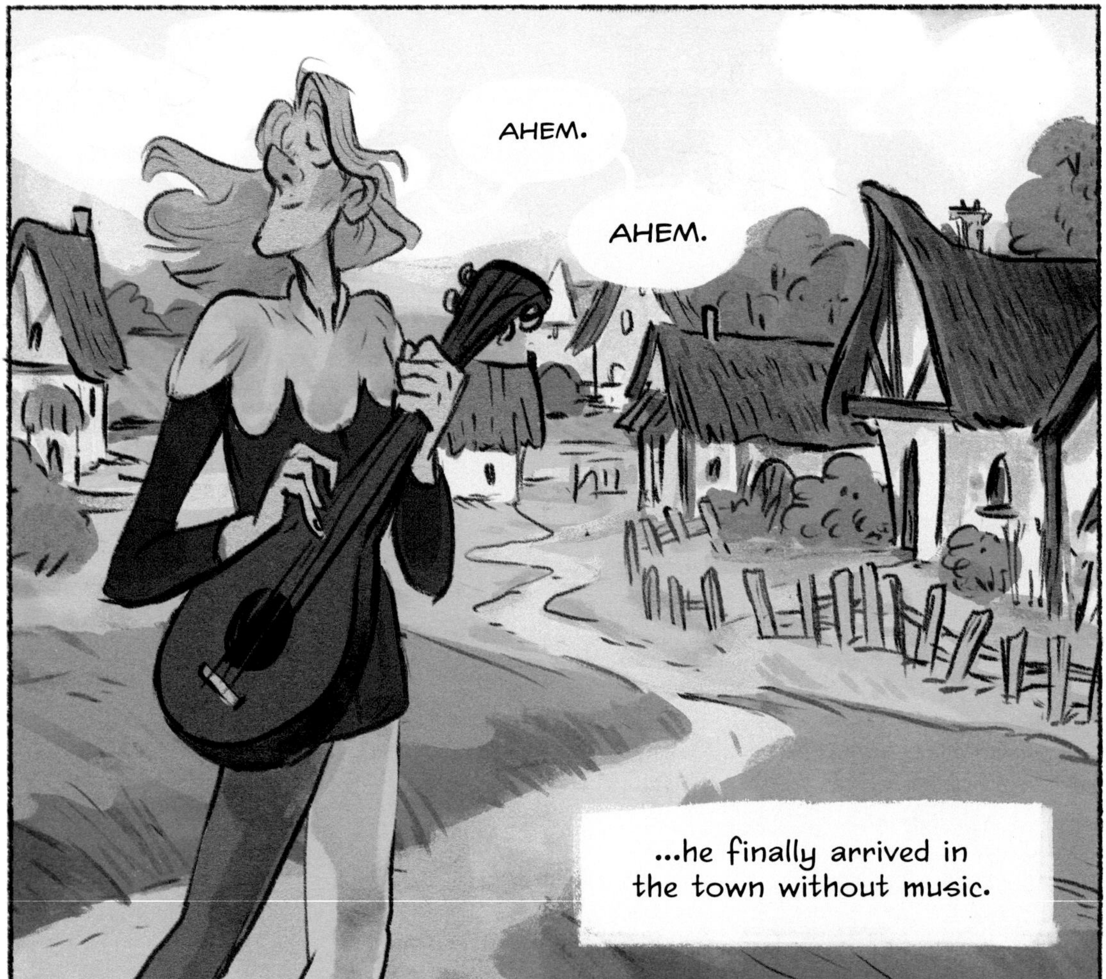
AHEM.
AHEM.
...he finally arrived in the town without music.

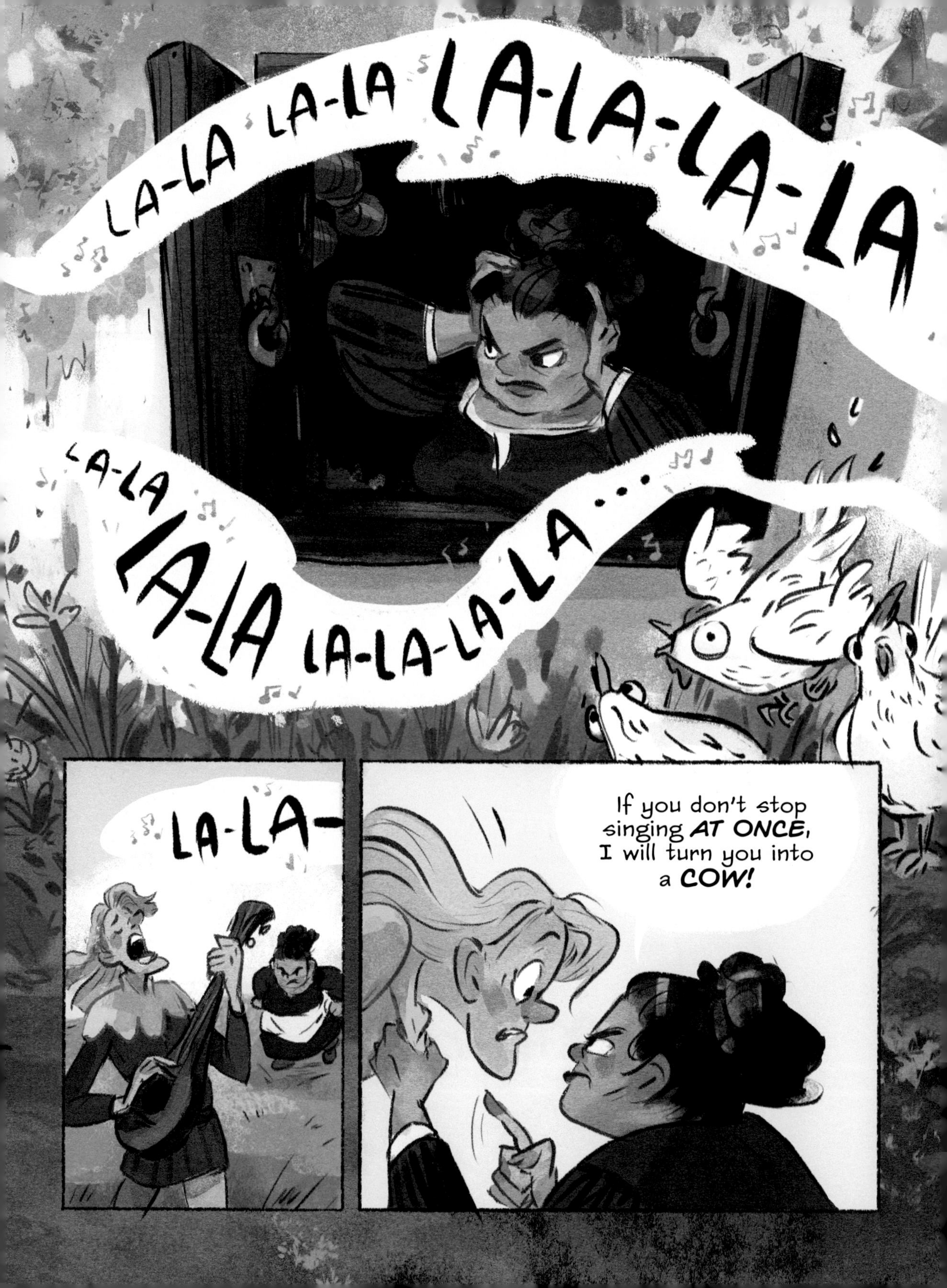
LA-LA LA-LA LA-LA-LA-LA-LA
LA-LA LA-LA LA-LA-LA-LA...
LA-LA-
If you don't stop singing AT ONCE, I will turn you into a COW!

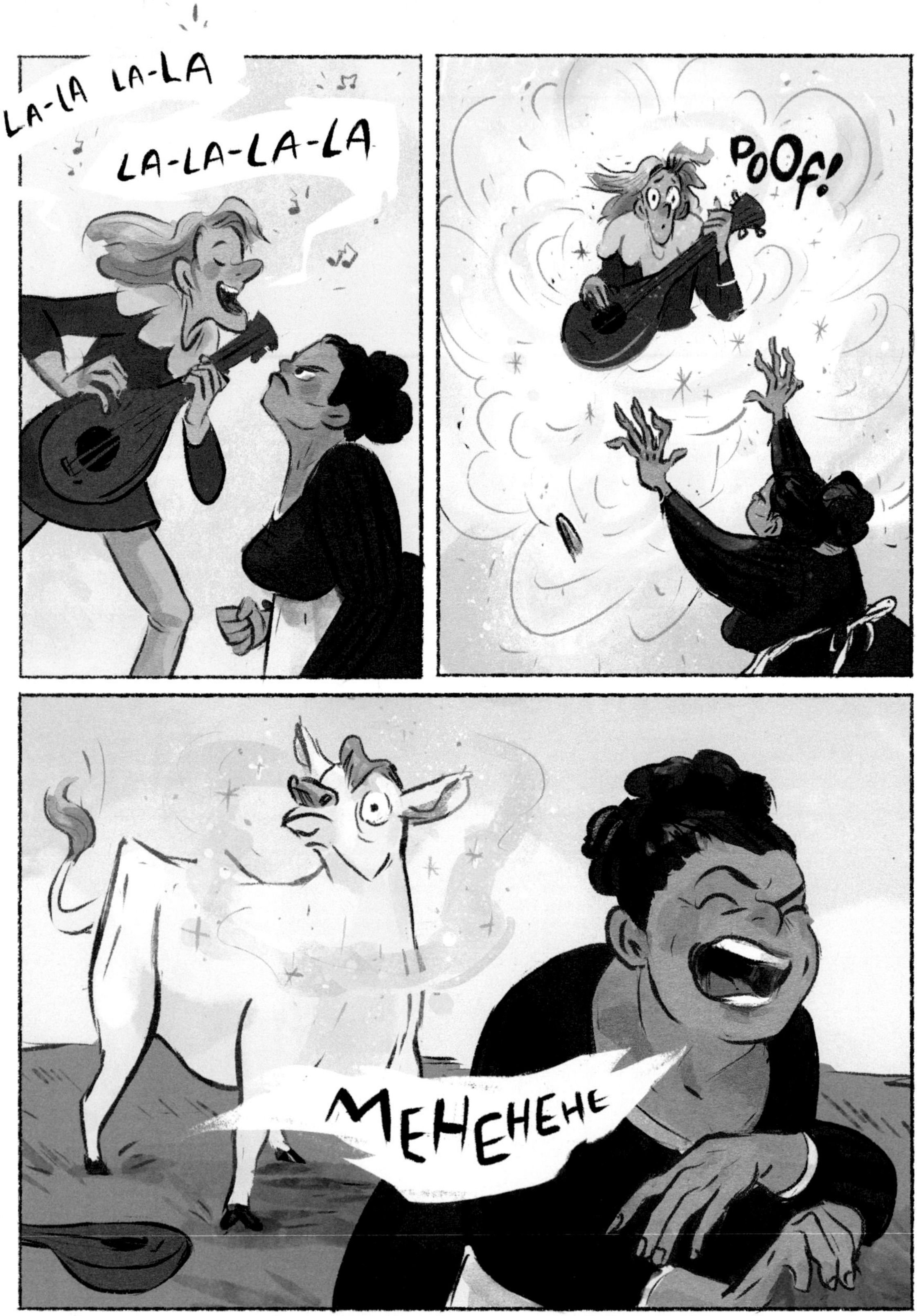
LA-LA LA-LA
LA-LA-LA-LA
POOF!
MEHEHEHE

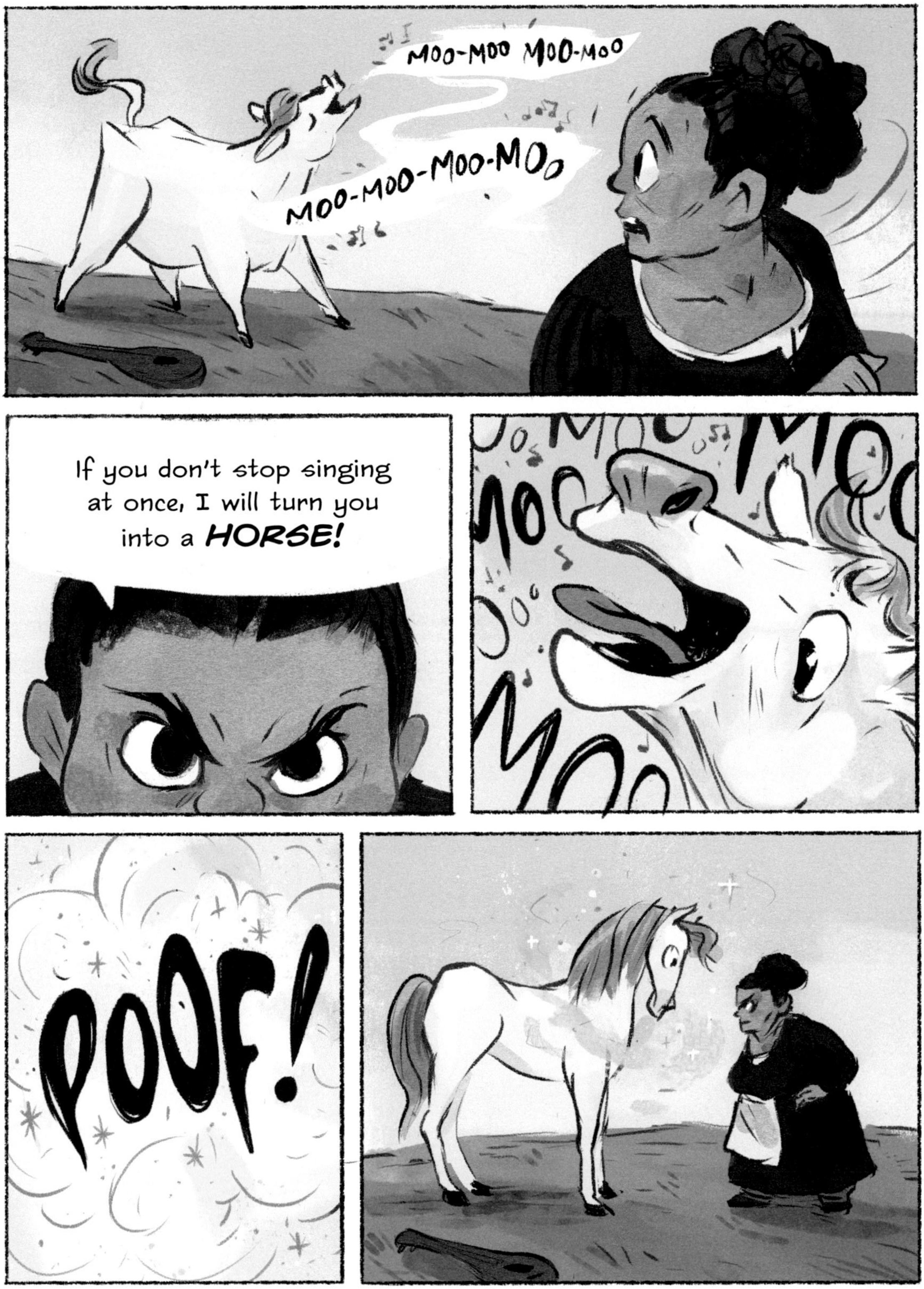
MOO-MOO MOO-MOO
MOO-MOO-MOO-MOO
If you don't stop singing at once, I will turn you into a ***HORSE!***
POOF!

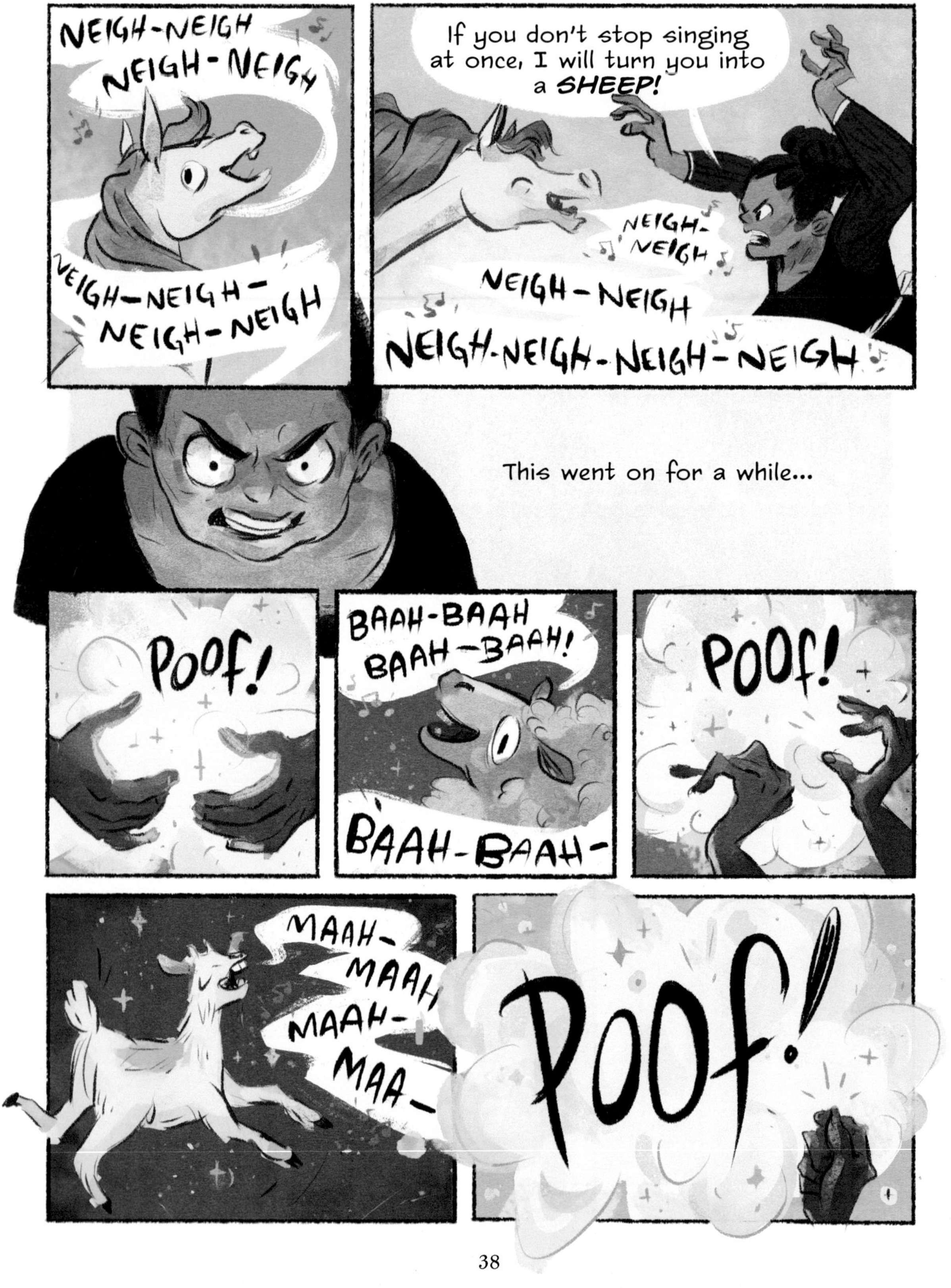
NEIGH-NEIGH
NEIGH-NEIGH
NEIGH-NEIGH-
NEIGH-NEIGH
If you don't stop singing at once, I will turn you into a SHEEP!
NEIGH-NEIGH
NEIGH-NEIGH
NEIGH-NEIGH-NEIGH-NEIGH
This went on for a while...
POOF!
BAAH-BAAH
BAAH-BAAH!
BAAH-BAAH-
POOF!
MAAH-
MAAH
MAAH-
MAA-
POOF!

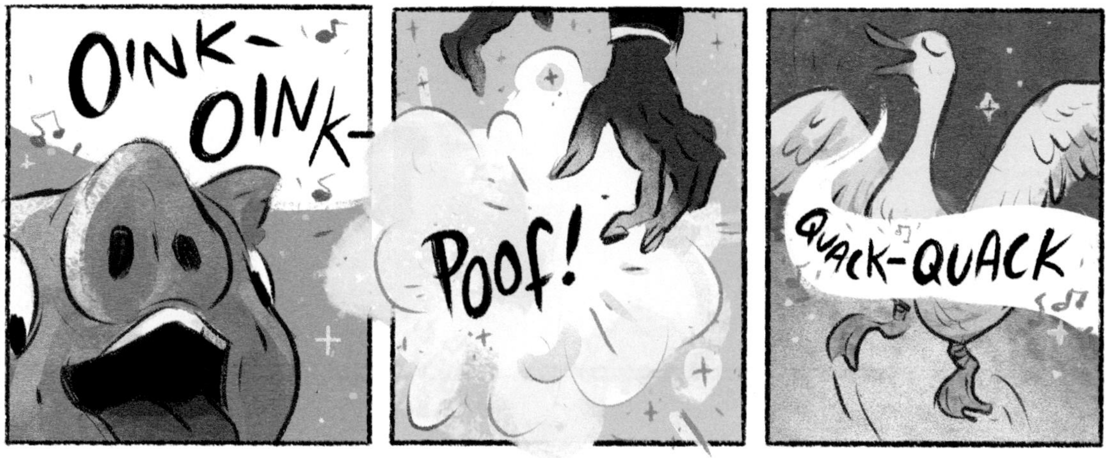
OINK-
OINK-
POOF!
QUACK-QUACK

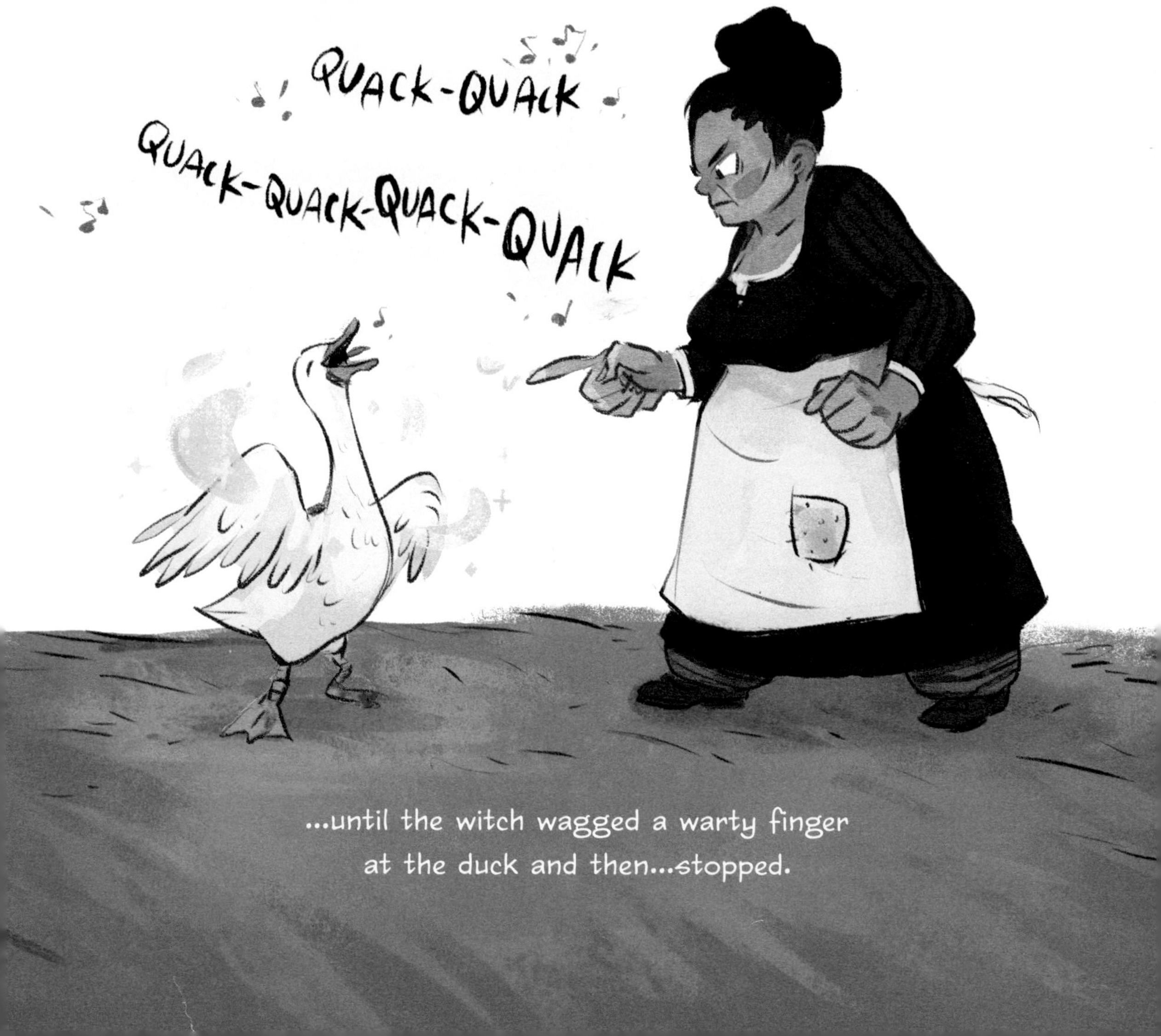
QUACK-QUACK
QUACK-QUACK-QUACK-QUACK

...until the witch wagged a warty finger
at the duck and then...stopped.

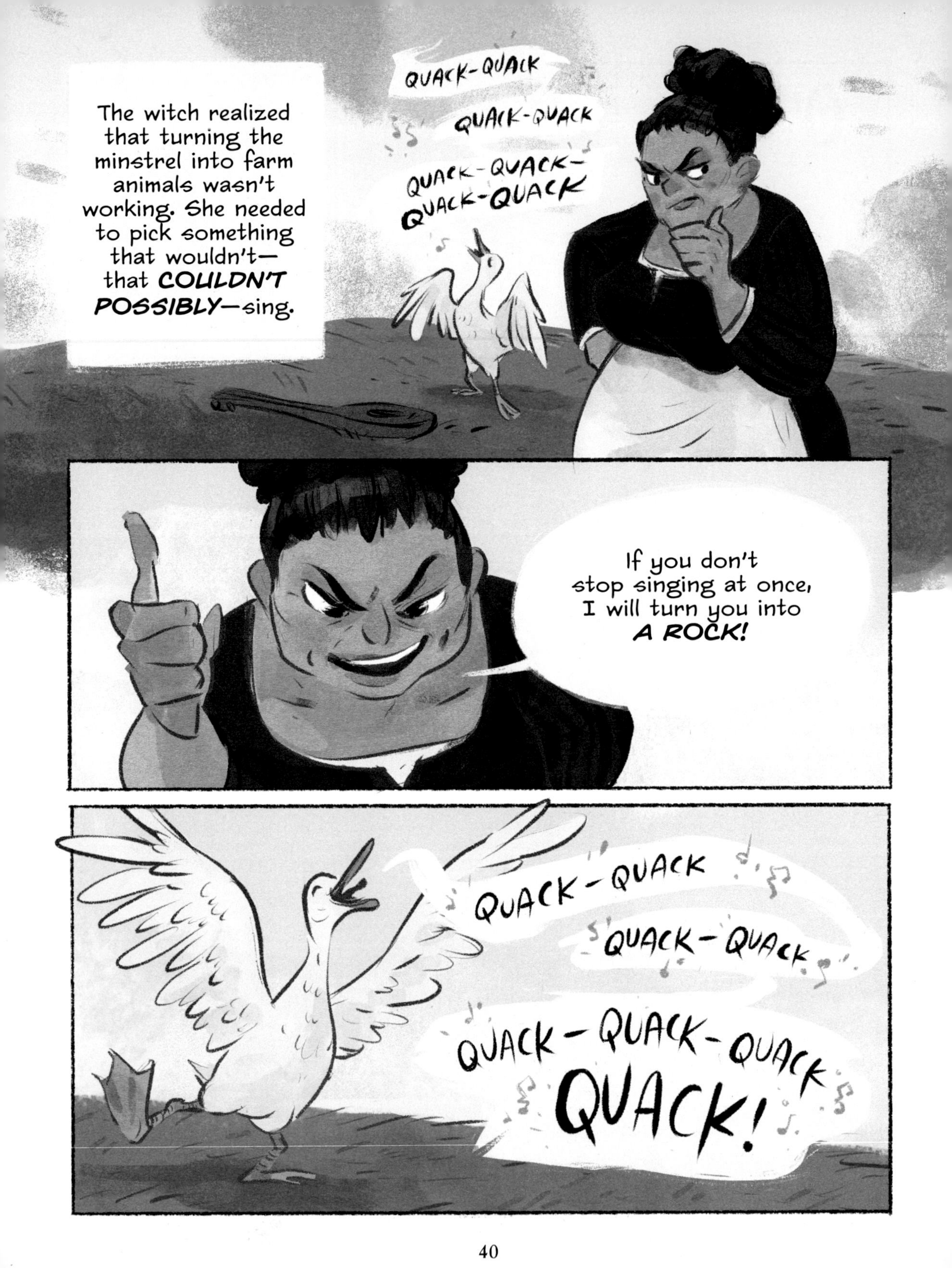

The witch realized that turning the minstrel into farm animals wasn't working. She needed to pick something that wouldn't—that **COULDN'T POSSIBLY**—sing.
QUACK-QUACK
QUACK-QUACK
QUACK-QUACK-QUACK-QUACK
If you don't stop singing at once, I will turn you into **A ROCK!**
QUACK-QUACK
QUACK-QUACK
QUACK-QUACK-QUACK
QUACK!

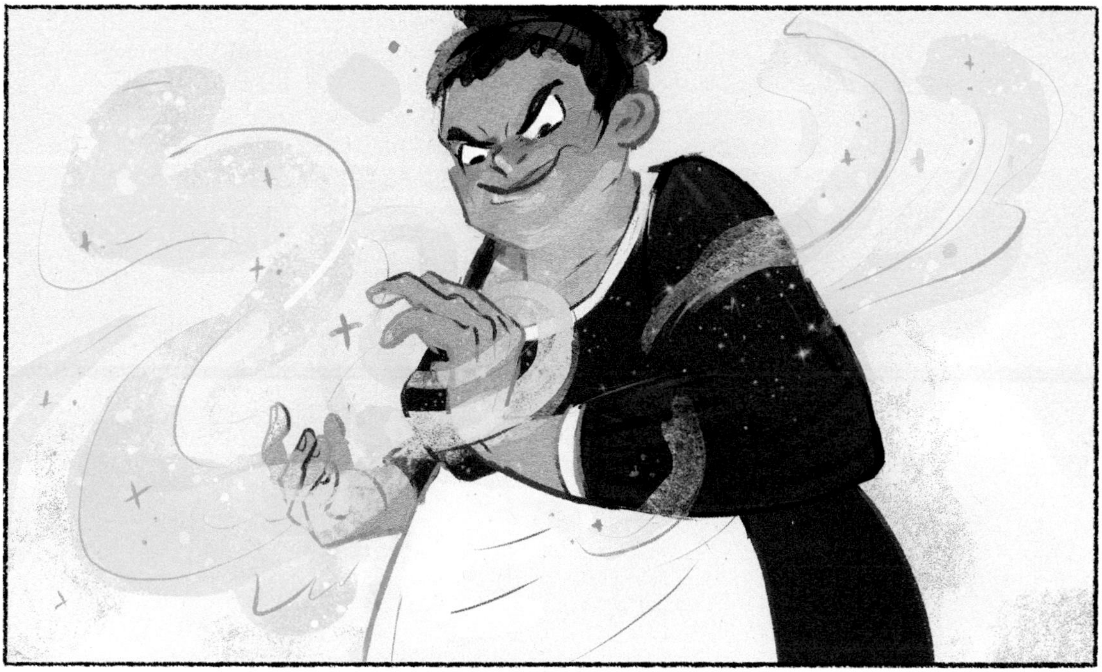

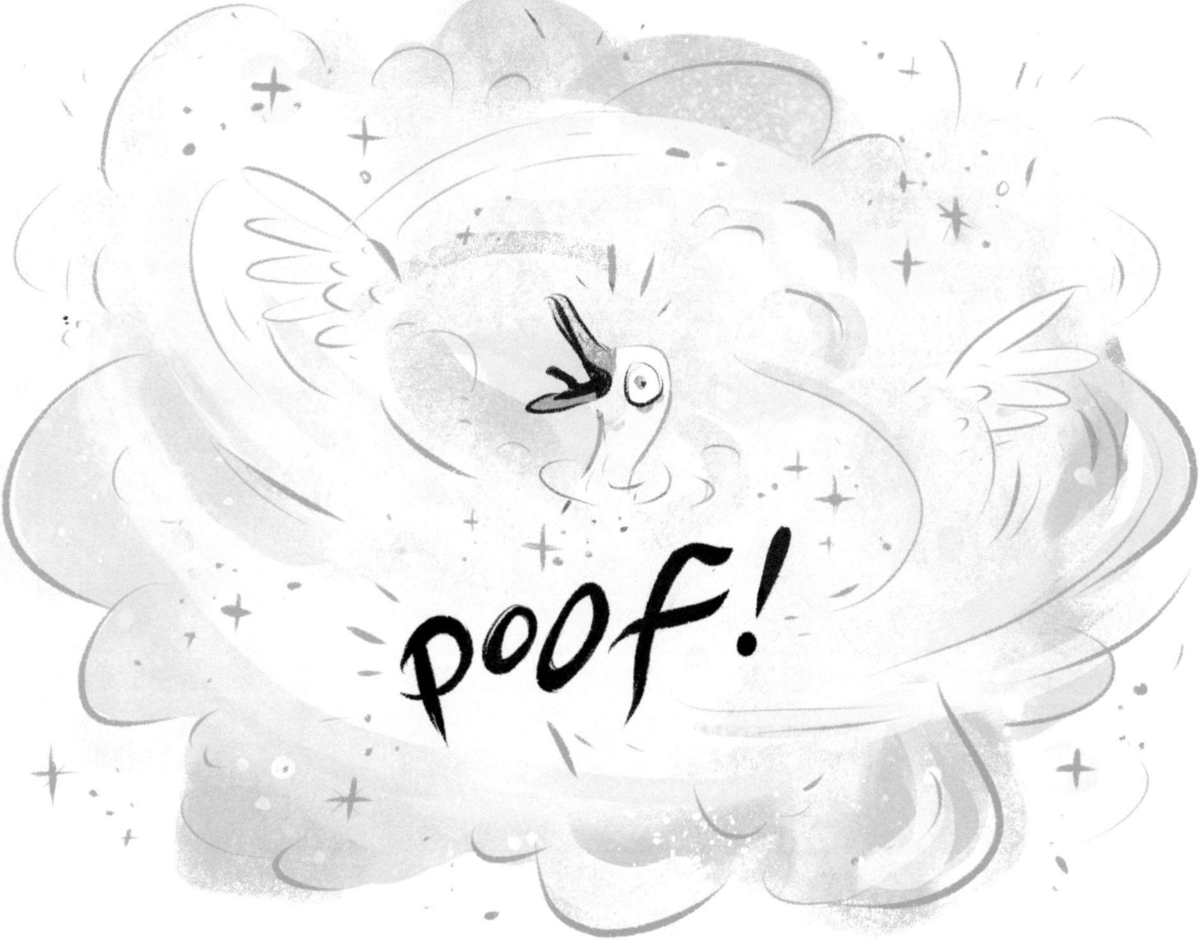
POOF!

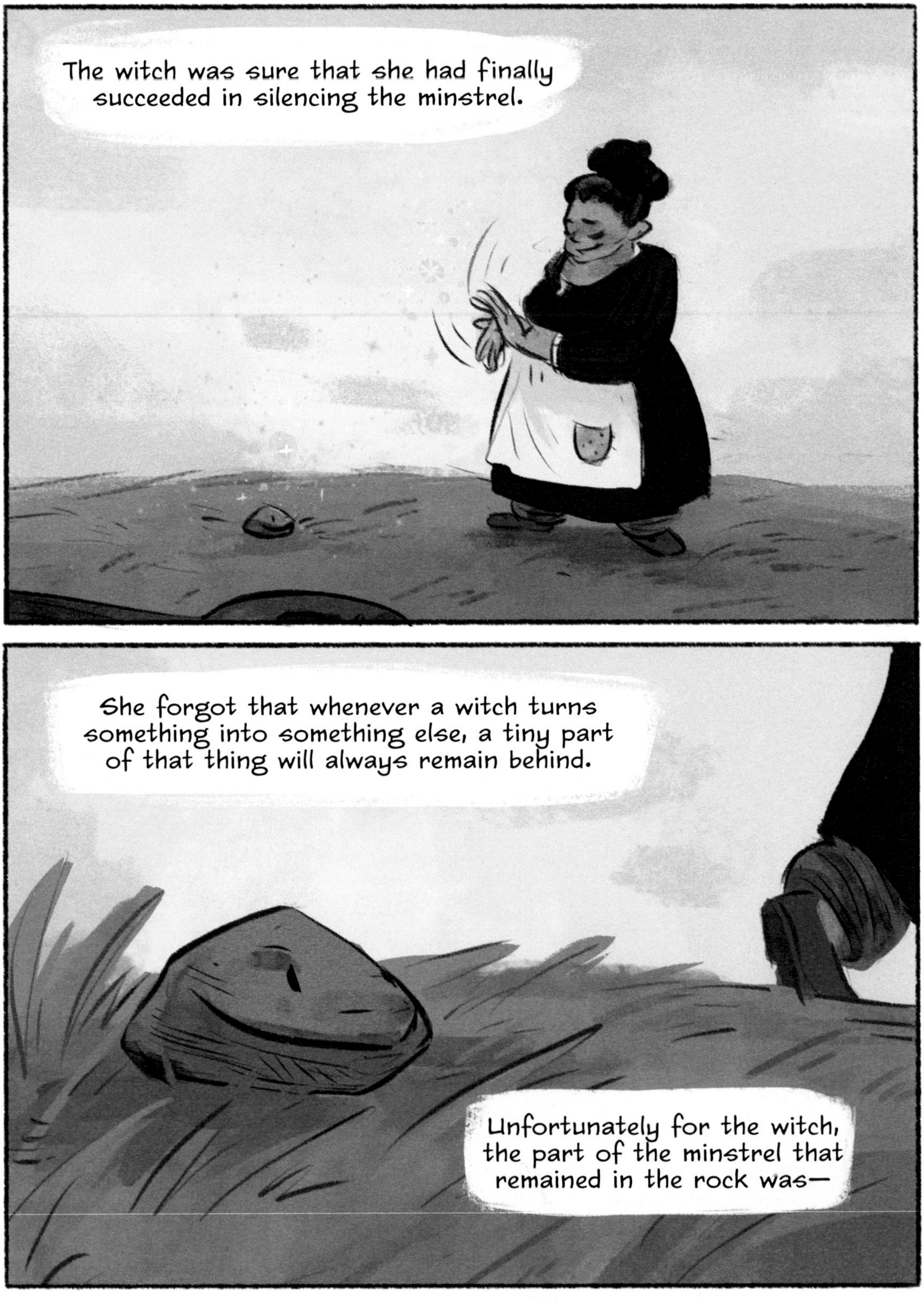
The witch was sure that she had finally succeeded in silencing the minstrel.
She forgot that whenever a witch turns something into something else, a tiny part of that thing will always remain behind.
Unfortunately for the witch, the part of the minstrel that remained in the rock was—

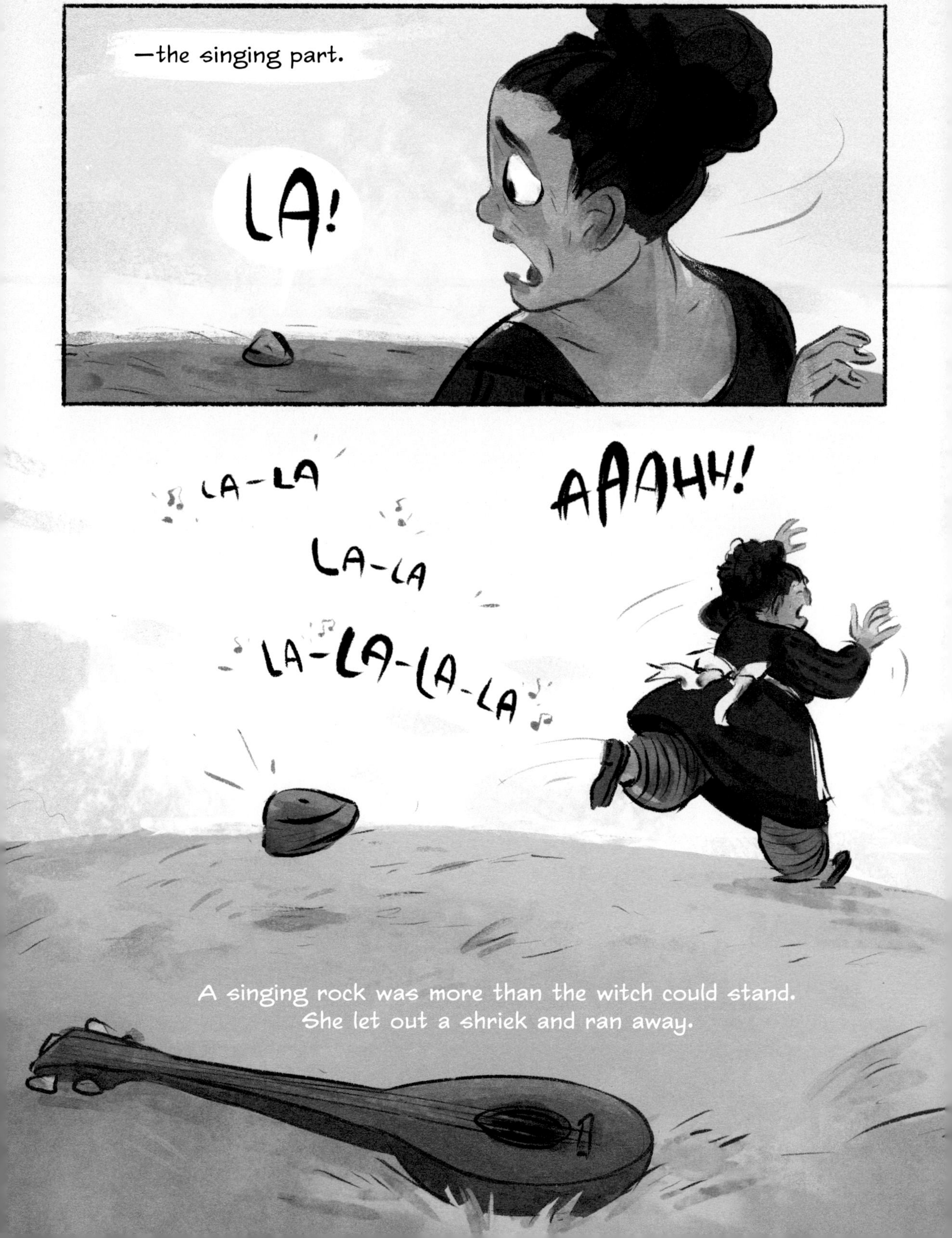
—the singing part.
LA!
LA-LA
LA-LA
LA-LA-LA-LA
AAAHH!
A singing rock was more than the witch could stand.
She let out a shriek and ran away.

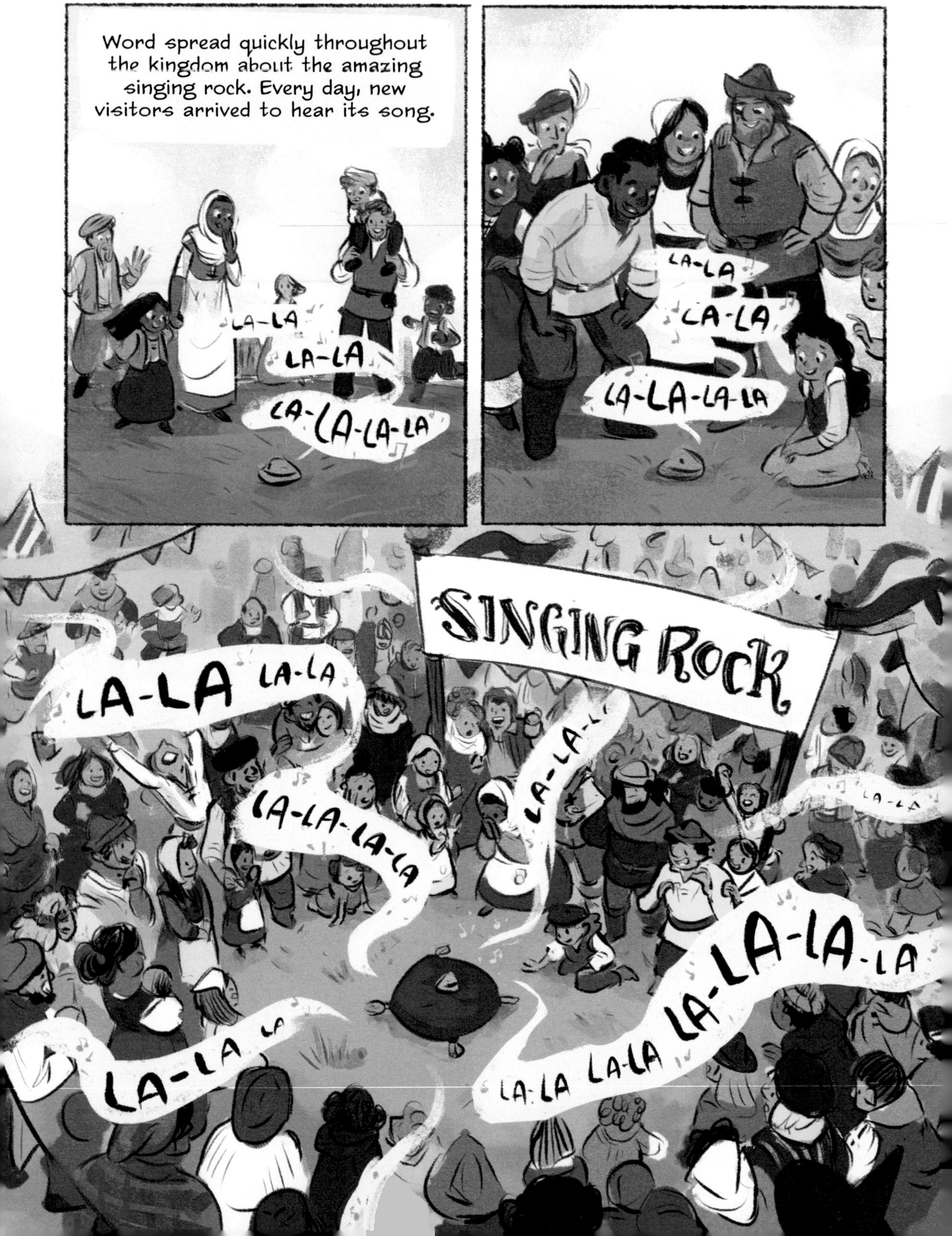
Word spread quickly throughout the kingdom about the amazing singing rock. Every day, new visitors arrived to hear its song.
LA-LA
LA-LA
LA-LA-LA-LA
LA-LA
LA-LA
LA-LA-LA-LA
SINGING ROCK
LA-LA LA-LA
LA-LA-LA-LA
LA-LA-LA
LA-LA
LA-LA LA
LA-LA LA-LA LA-LA-LA-LA

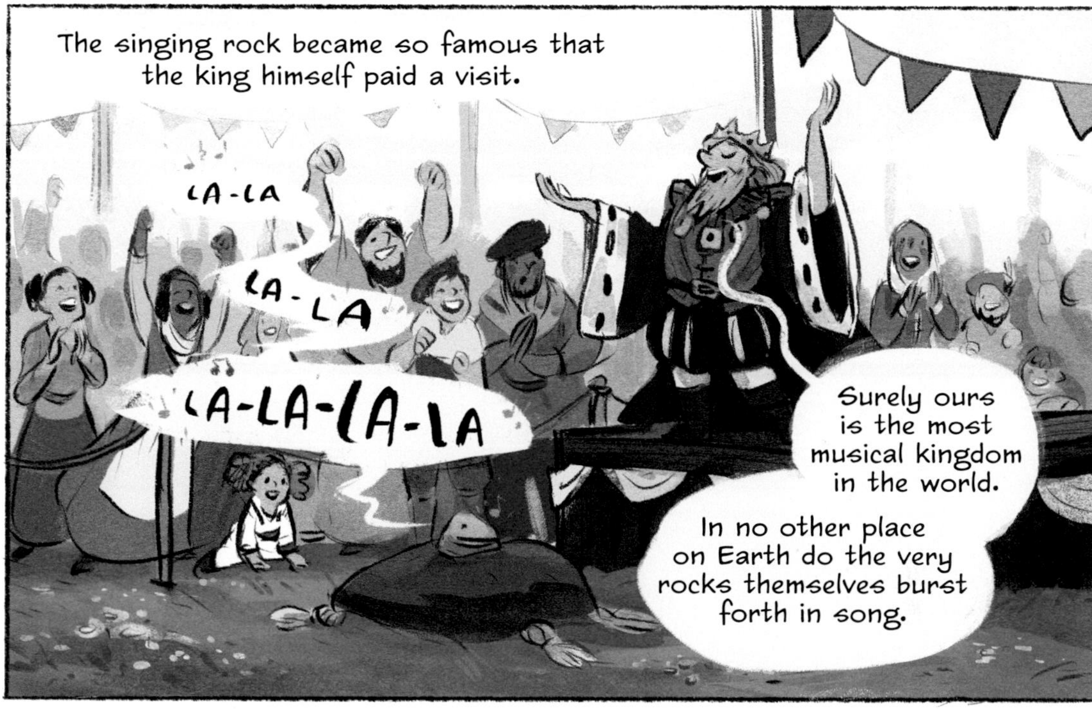
The singing rock became so famous that the king himself paid a visit.
LA-LA
LA-LA
LA-LA-LA-LA
Surely ours is the most musical kingdom in the world.
In no other place on Earth do the very rocks themselves burst forth in song.

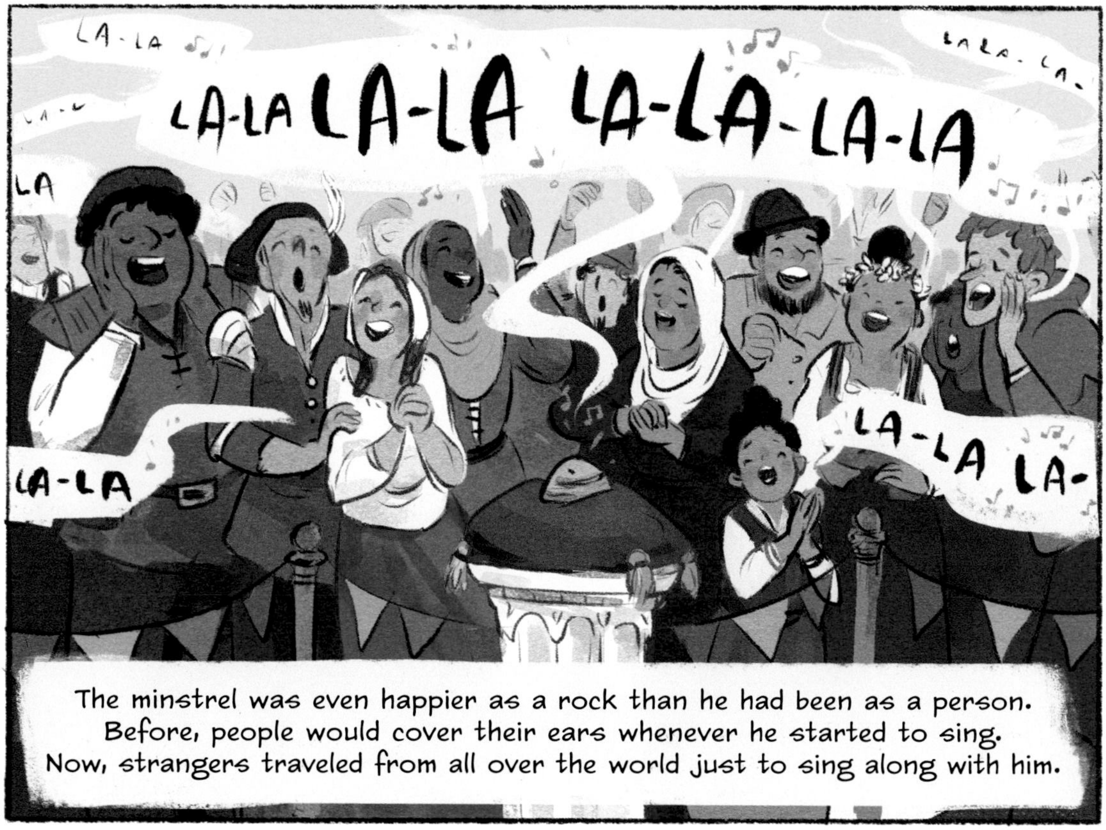
LA-LA
LA-LA LA-LA LA-LA-LA-LA
LA
LA-LA
LA-LA LA-
The minstrel was even happier as a rock than he had been as a person. Before, people would cover their ears whenever he started to sing. Now, strangers traveled from all over the world just to sing along with him.

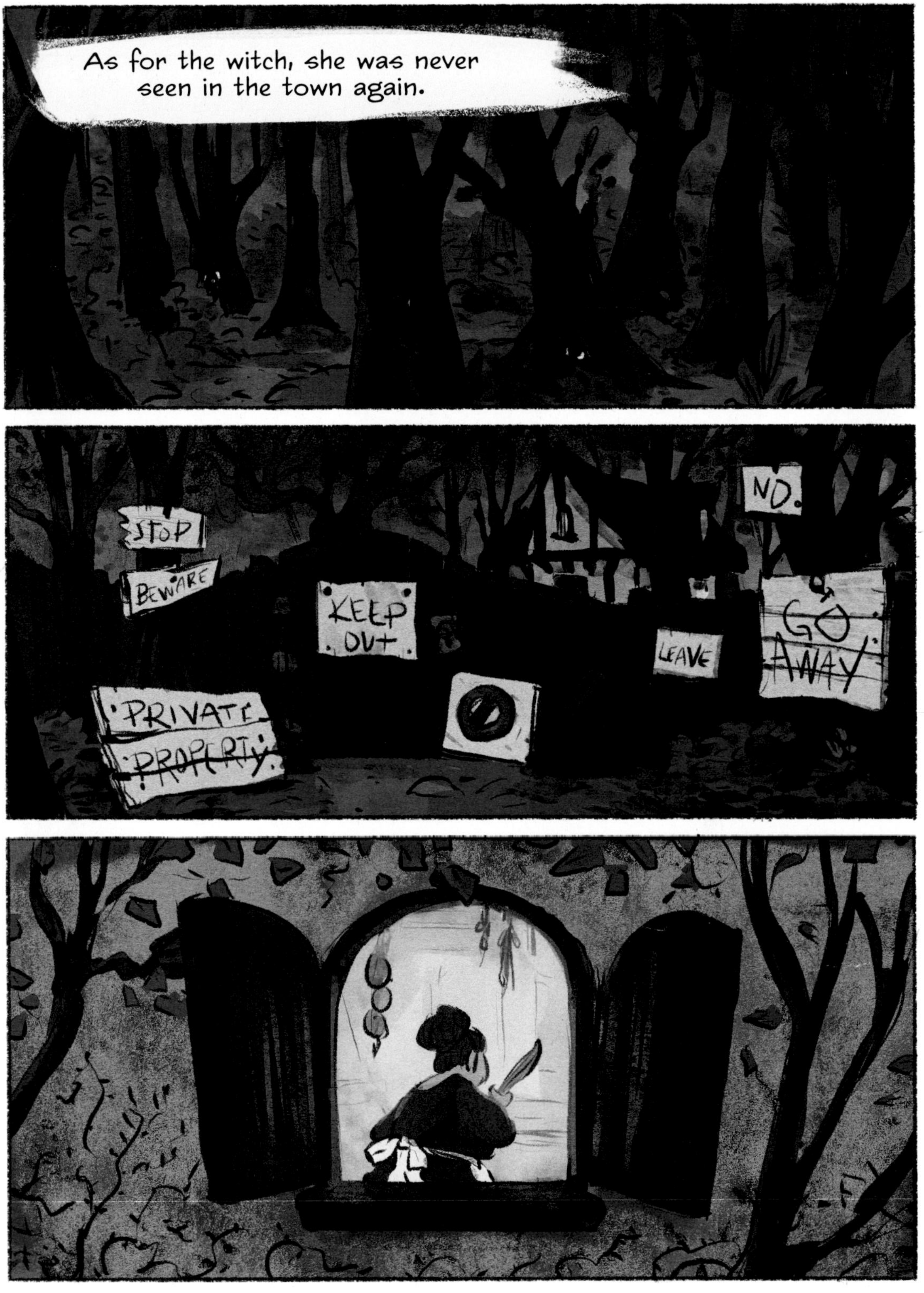

As for the witch, she was never seen in the town again.
STOP
BEWARE
KEEP OUT
NO.
LEAVE
GO AWAY
PRIVATE PROPERTY

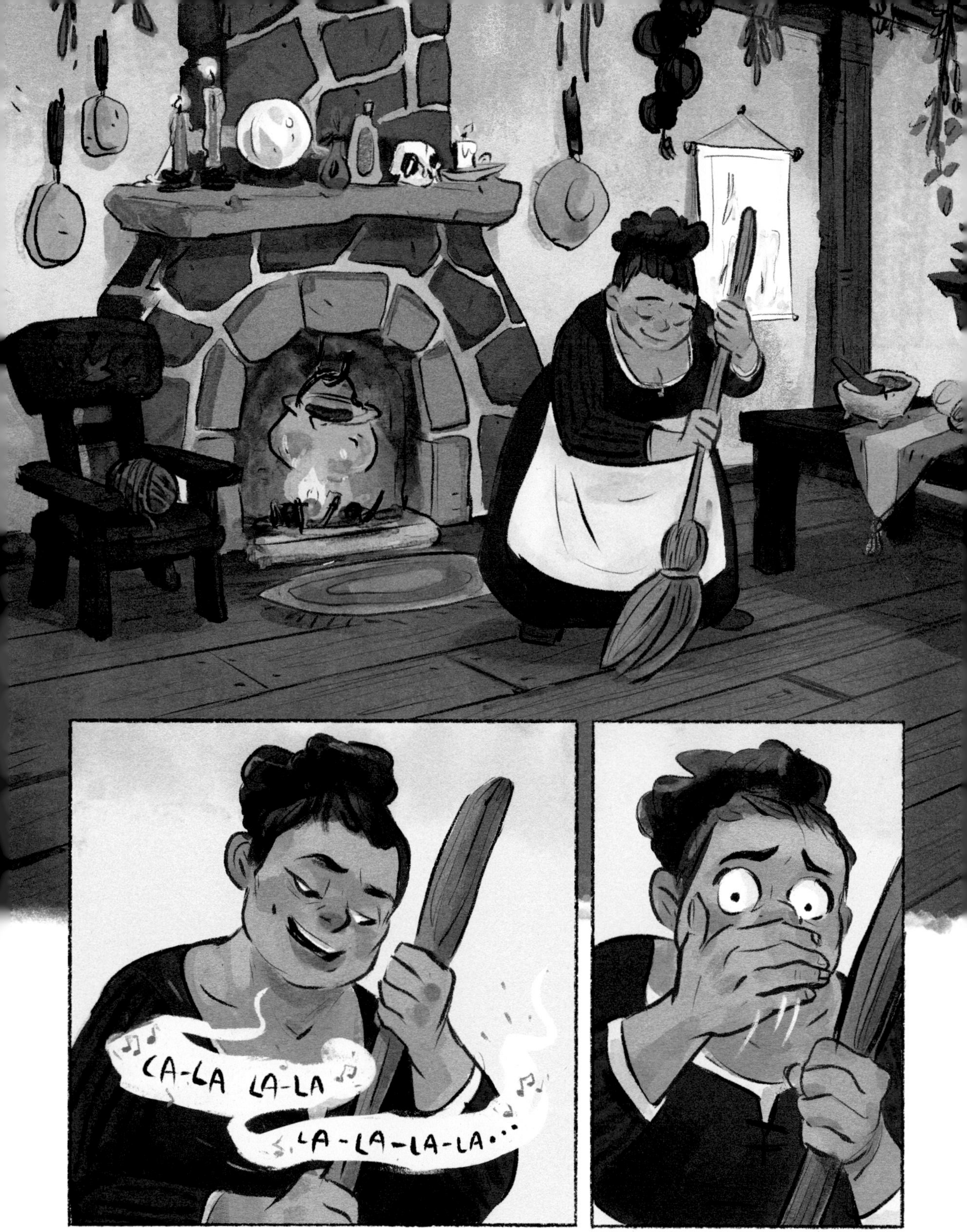
LA-LA LA-LA
LA-LA-LA-LA...

THE SORCERER'S NEW PET

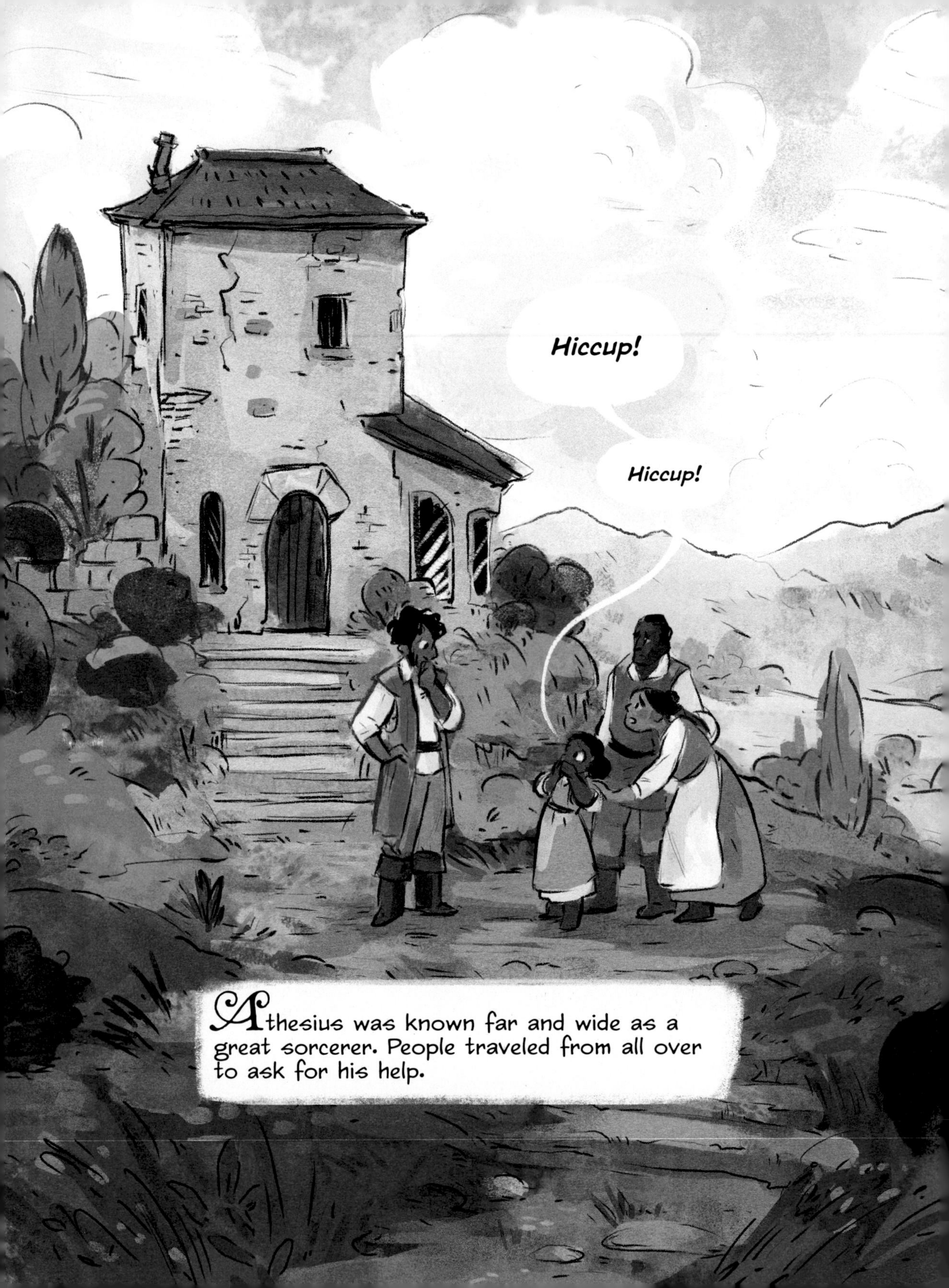
Hiccup!
Hiccup!
Athesius was known far and wide as a great sorcerer. People traveled from all over to ask for his help.

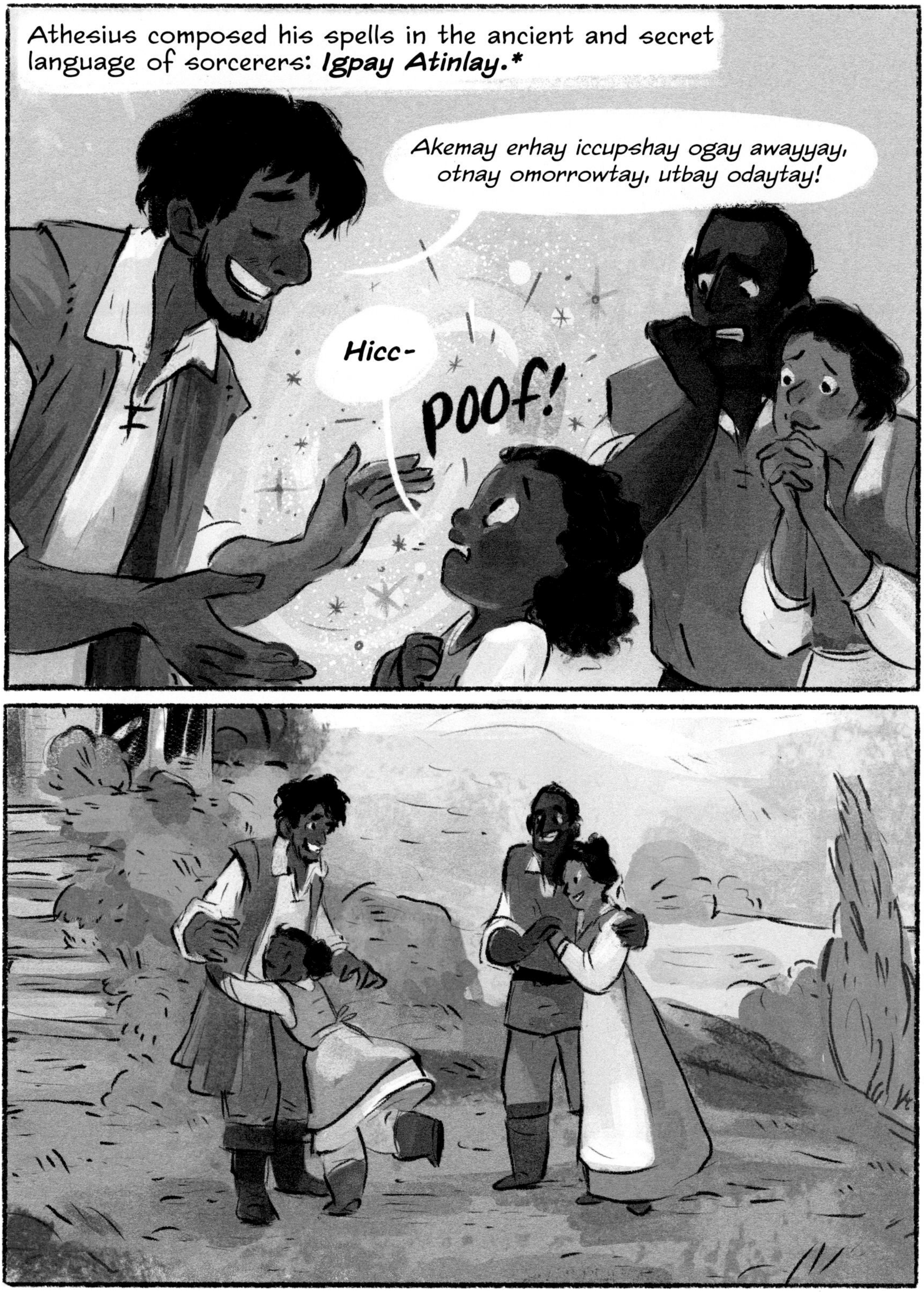
Athesius composed his spells in the ancient and secret language of sorcerers: ***Igpay Atinlay.****
Akemay erhay iccupshay ogay awayyay, otnay omorrowtay, utbay odaytay!
Hicc-
poof!

**Pig Latin*

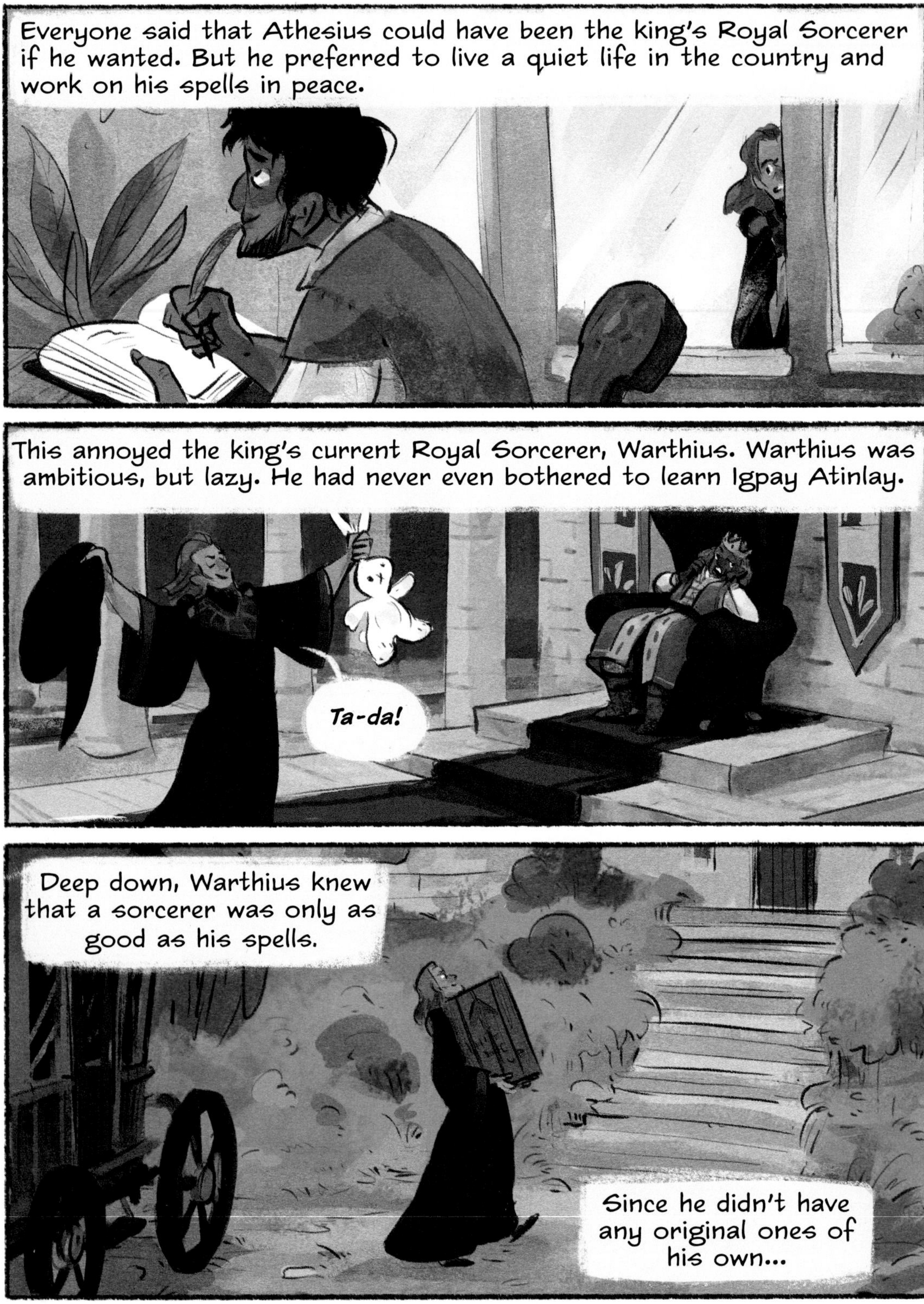
Everyone said that Athesius could have been the king's Royal Sorcerer if he wanted. But he preferred to live a quiet life in the country and work on his spells in peace.
This annoyed the king's current Royal Sorcerer, Warthius. Warthius was ambitious, but lazy. He had never even bothered to learn Igpay Atinlay.
Ta-da!
Deep down, Warthius knew that a sorcerer was only as good as his spells.
Since he didn't have any original ones of his own...

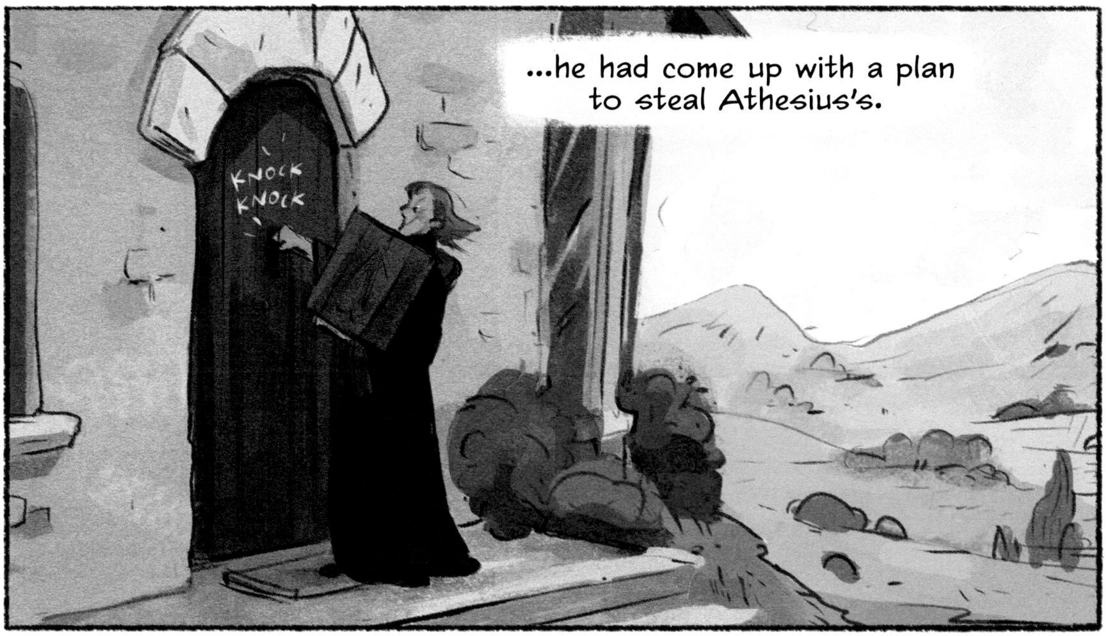
...he had come up with a plan to steal Athesius's.
KNOCK KNOCK

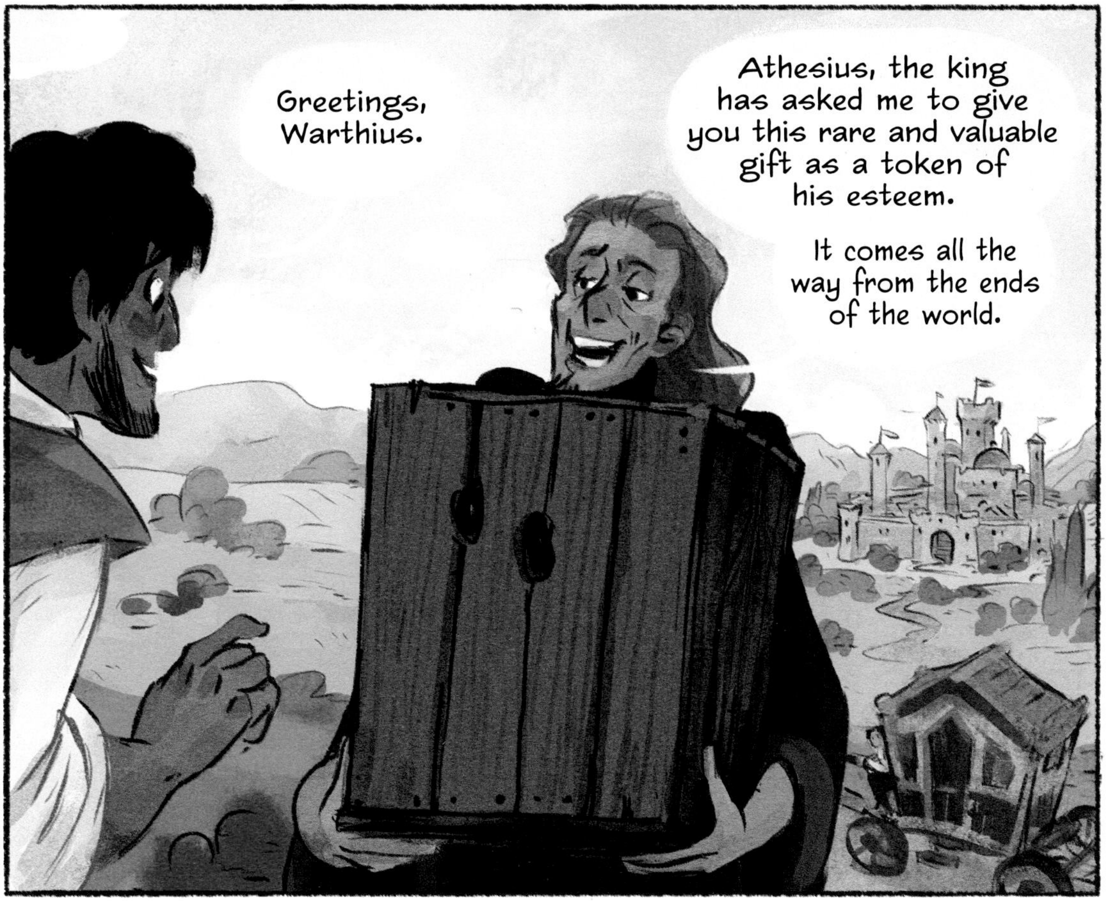
Greetings, Warthius.
Athesius, the king has asked me to give you this rare and valuable gift as a token of his esteem.
It comes all the way from the ends of the world.

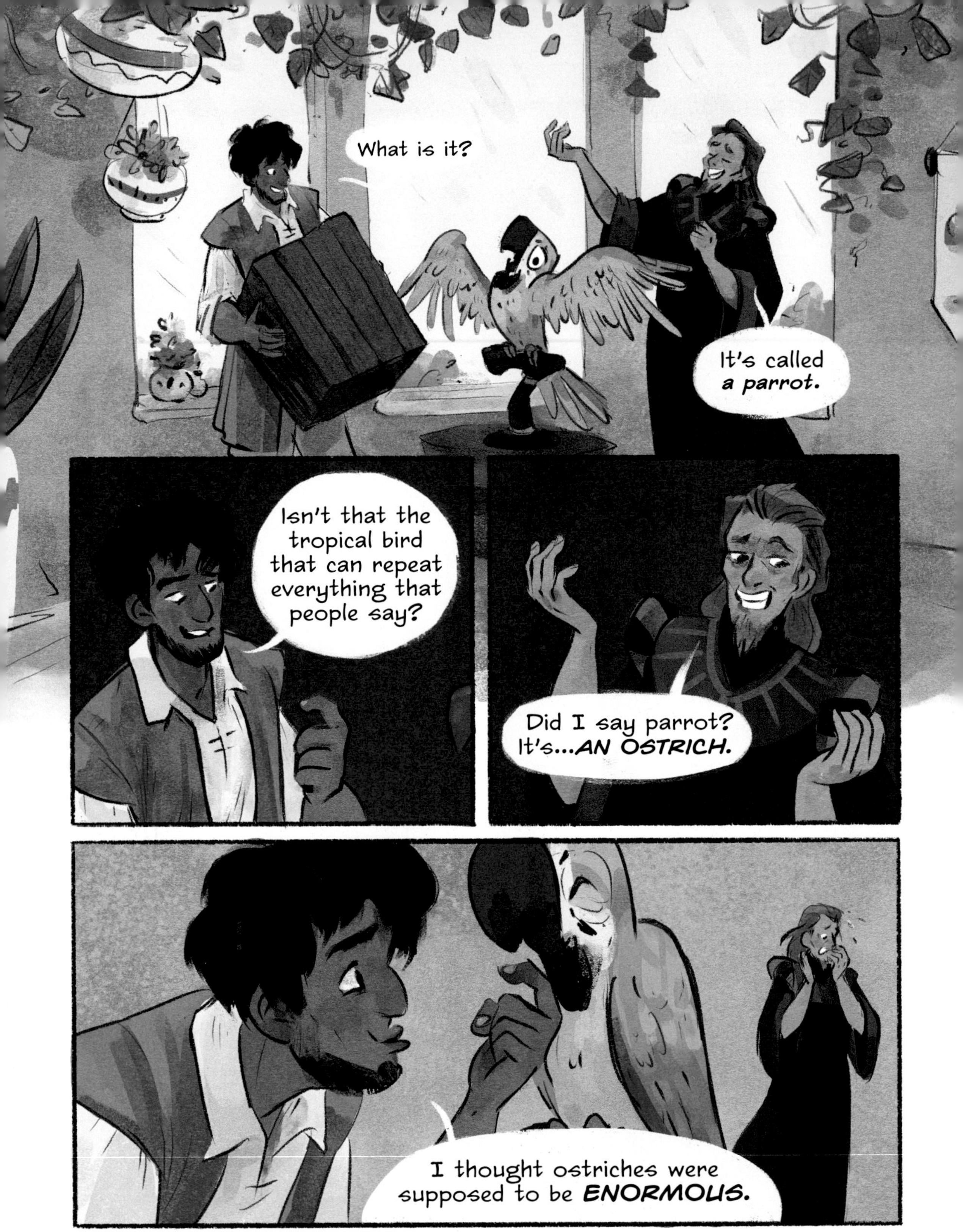
What is it?
It's called a parrot.
Isn't that the tropical bird that can repeat everything that people say?
Did I say parrot? It's...AN OSTRICH.
I thought ostriches were supposed to be ENORMOUS.

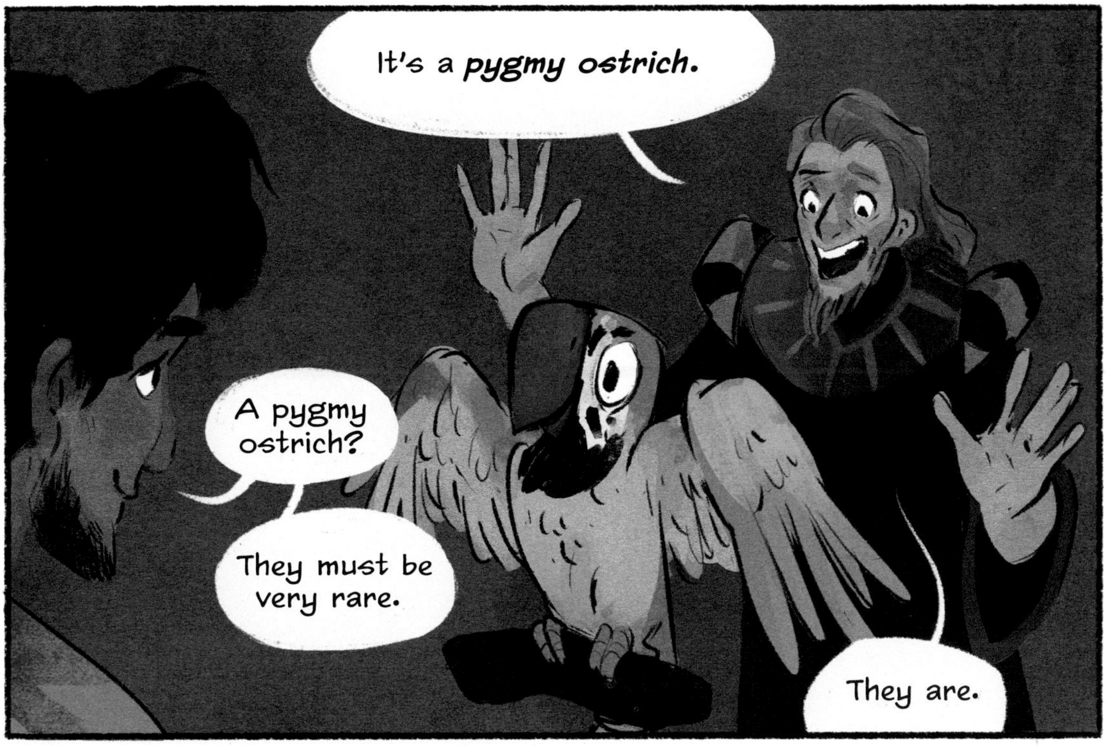
It's a **pygmy ostrich.**
A pygmy ostrich?
They must be very rare.
They are.

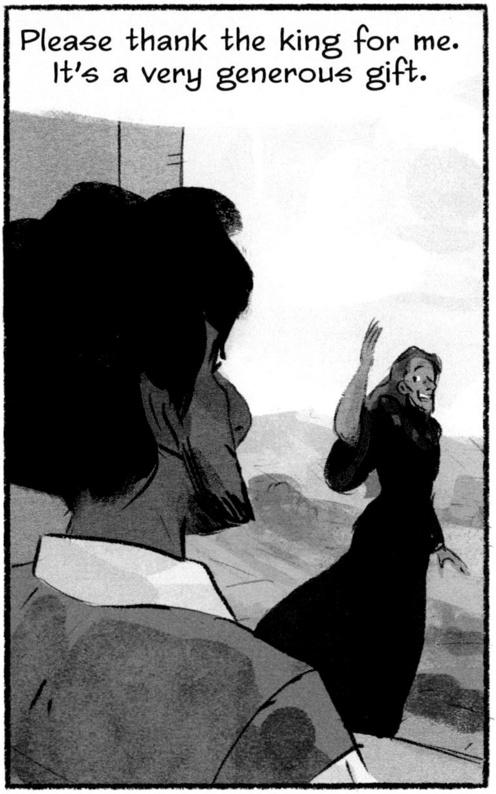
Please thank the king for me. It's a very generous gift.

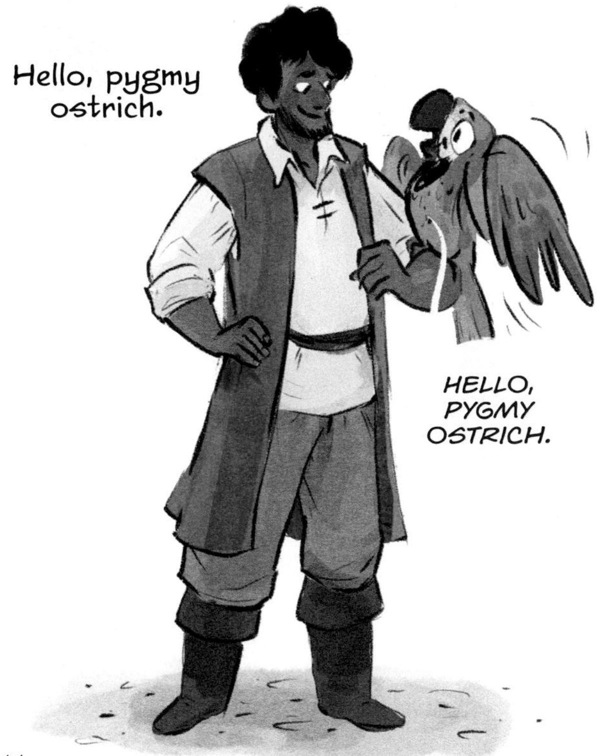
Hello, pygmy ostrich.
HELLO, PYGMY OSTRICH.

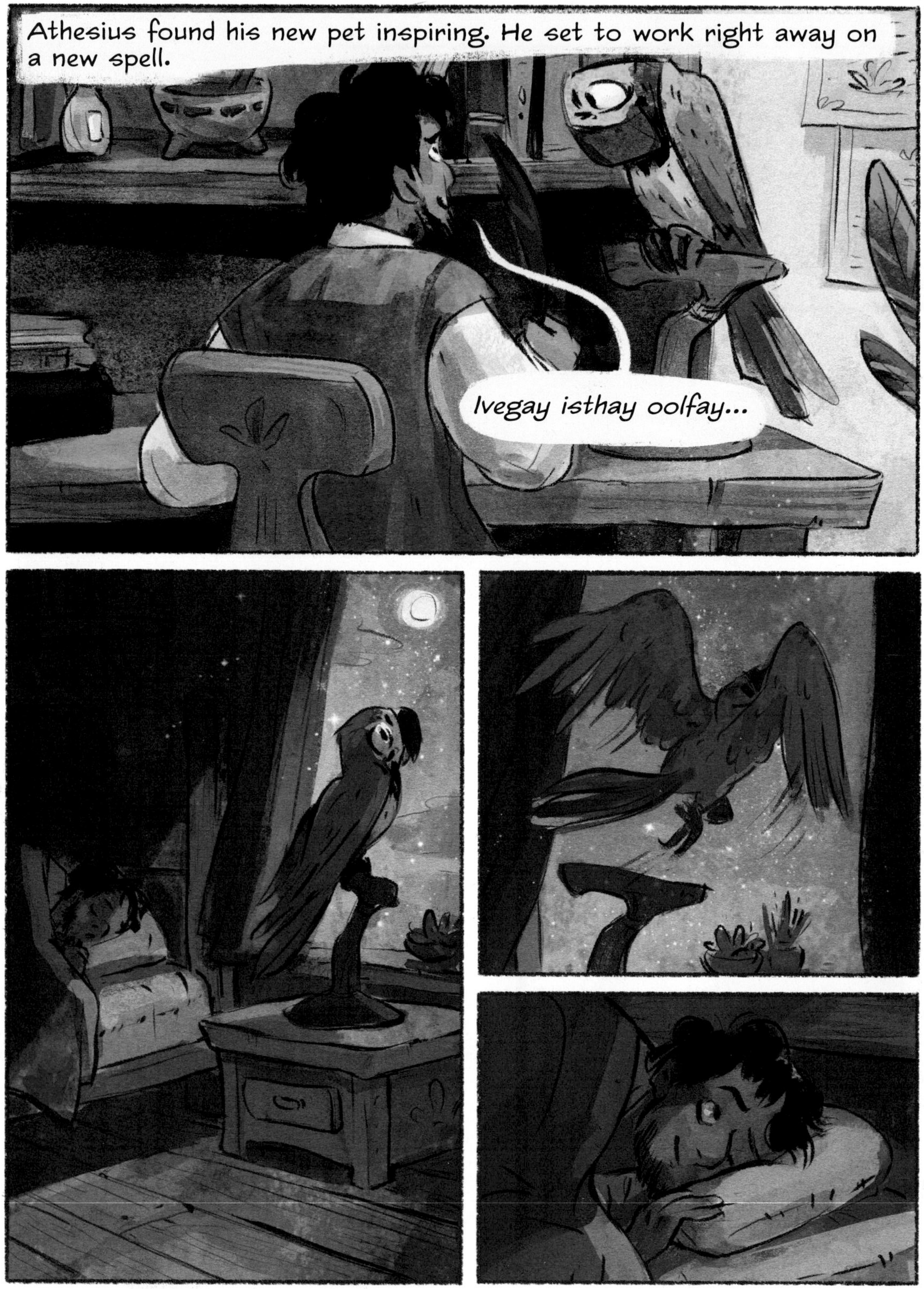
Athesius found his new pet inspiring. He set to work right away on a new spell.
Ivegay isthay oolfay...

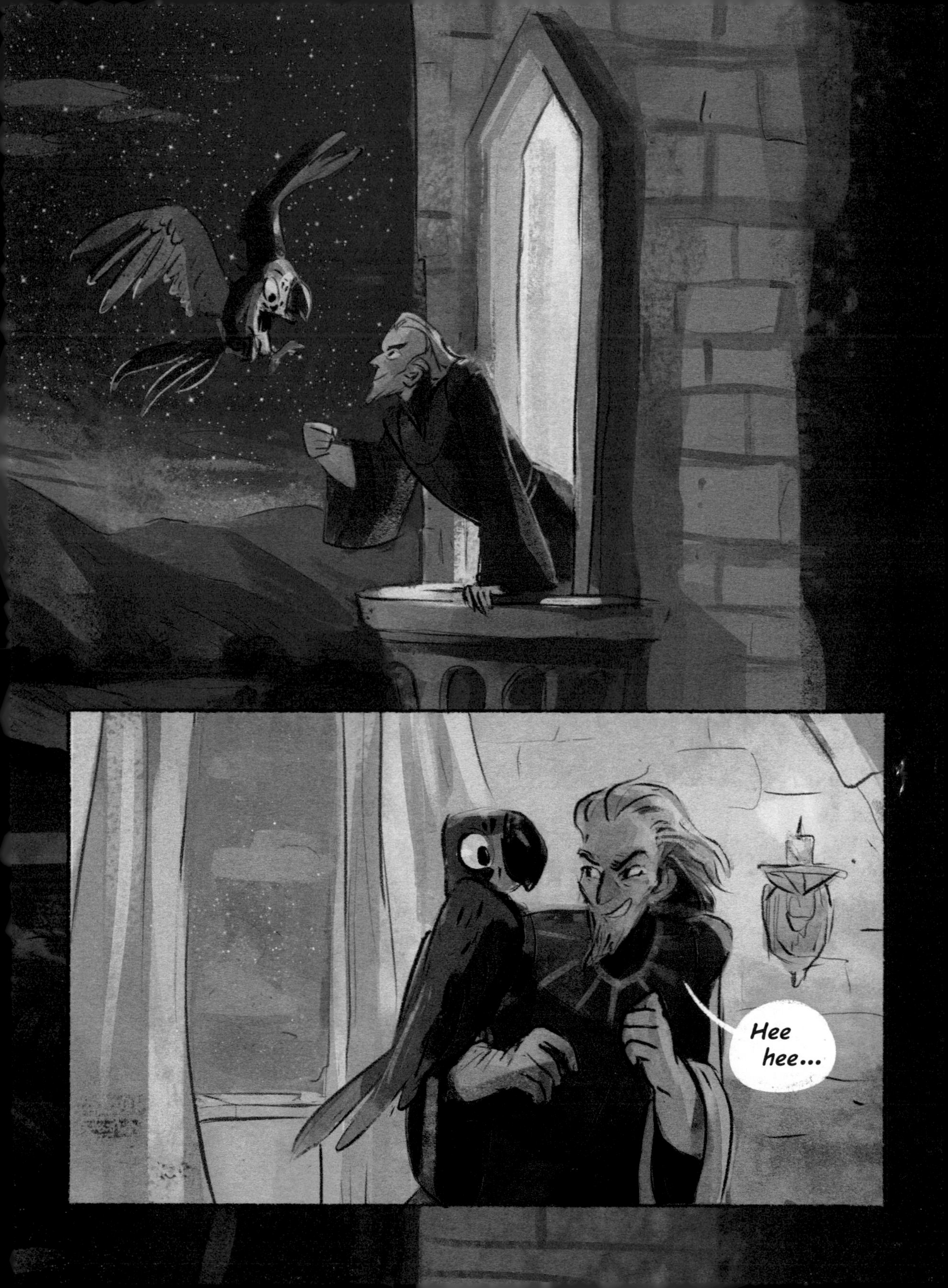
Hee hee...

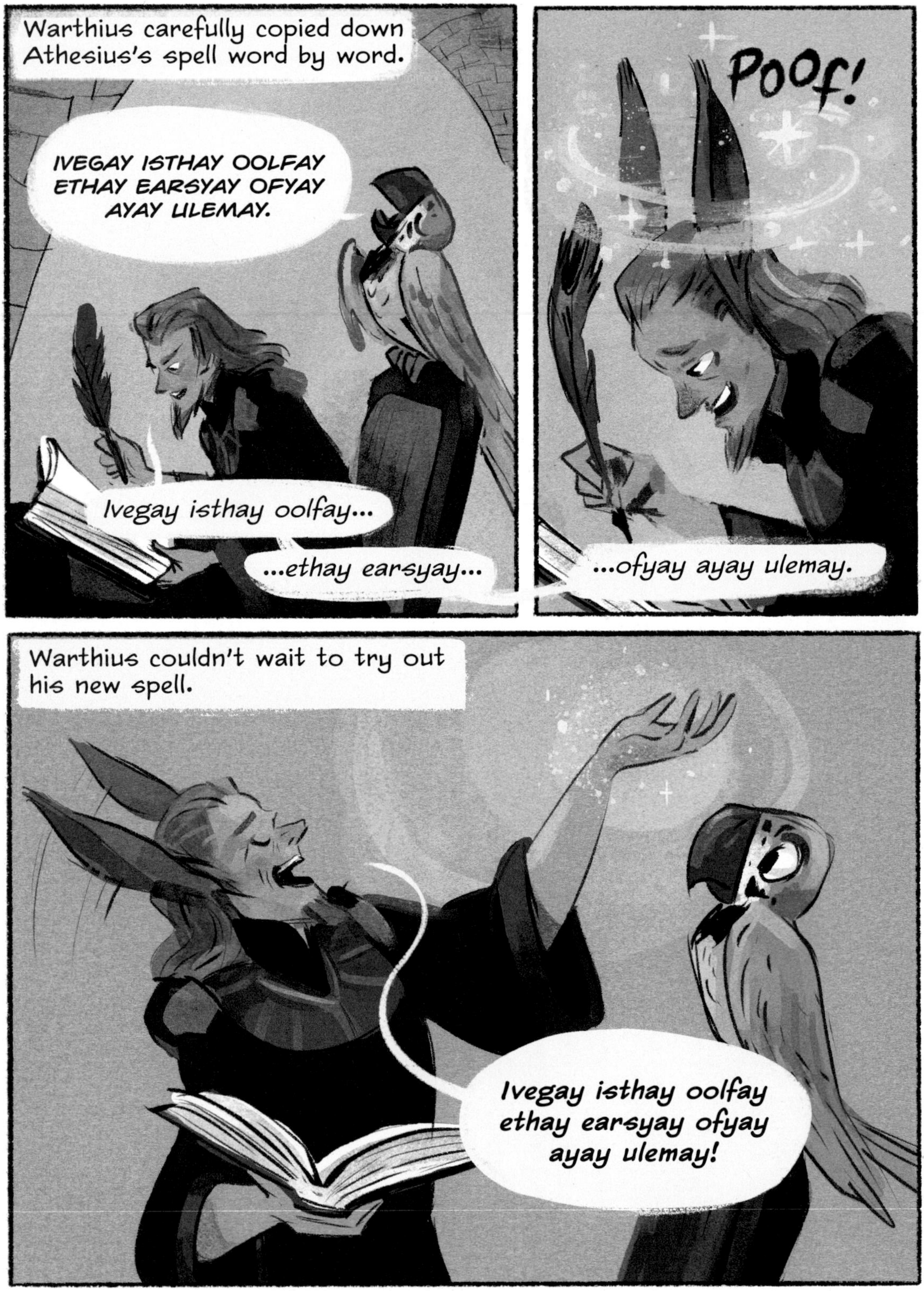
Warthius carefully copied down Athesius's spell word by word.
IVEGAY ISTHAY OOLFAY ETHAY EARSYAY OFYAY AYAY ULEMAY.
Ivegay isthay oolfay...
...ethay earsyay...
POOF!
...ofyay ayay ulemay.
Warthius couldn't wait to try out his new spell.
Ivegay isthay oolfay ethay earsyay ofyay ayay ulemay!

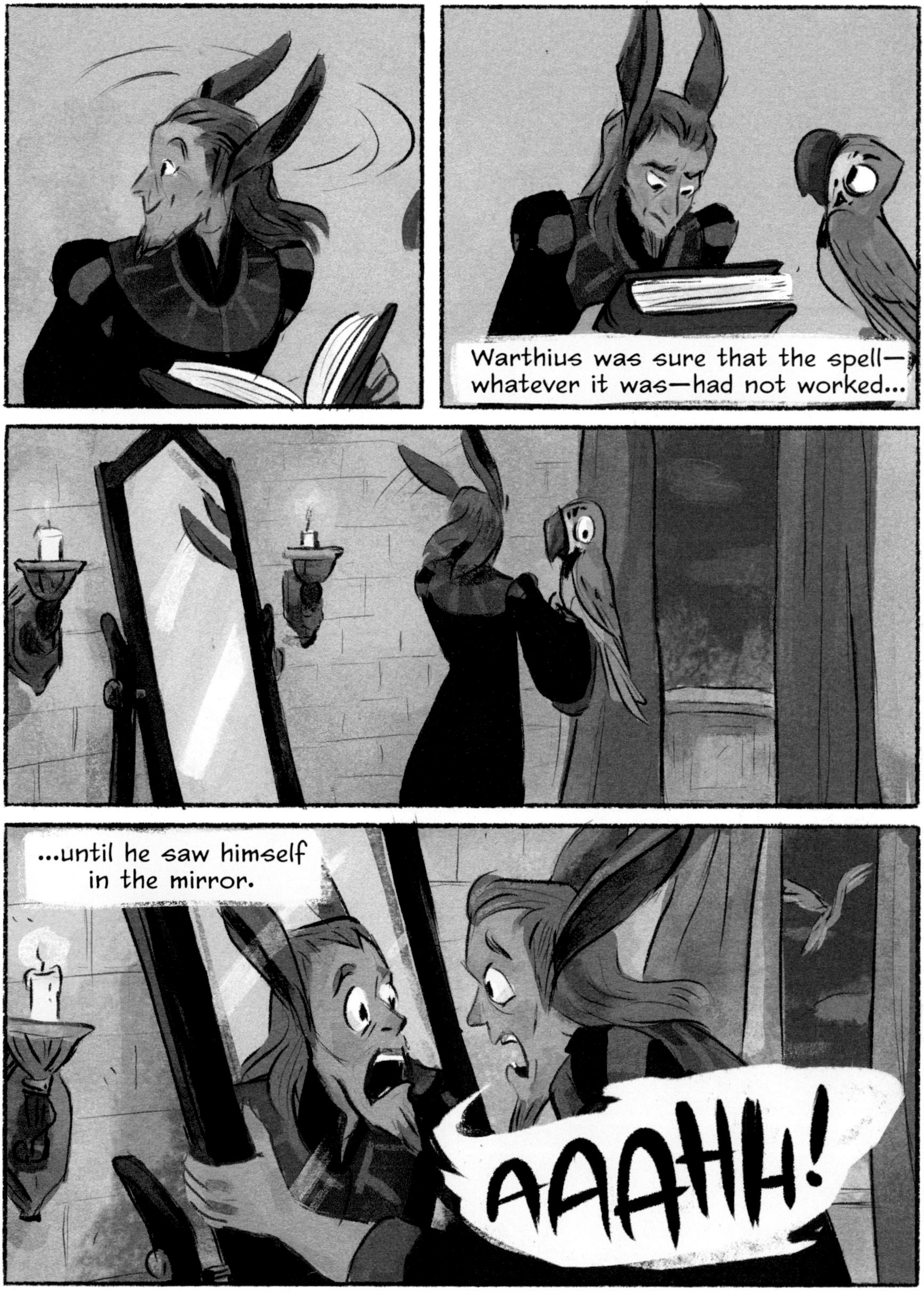
Warthius was sure that the spell—whatever it was—had not worked...
...until he saw himself in the mirror.
AAAHH!

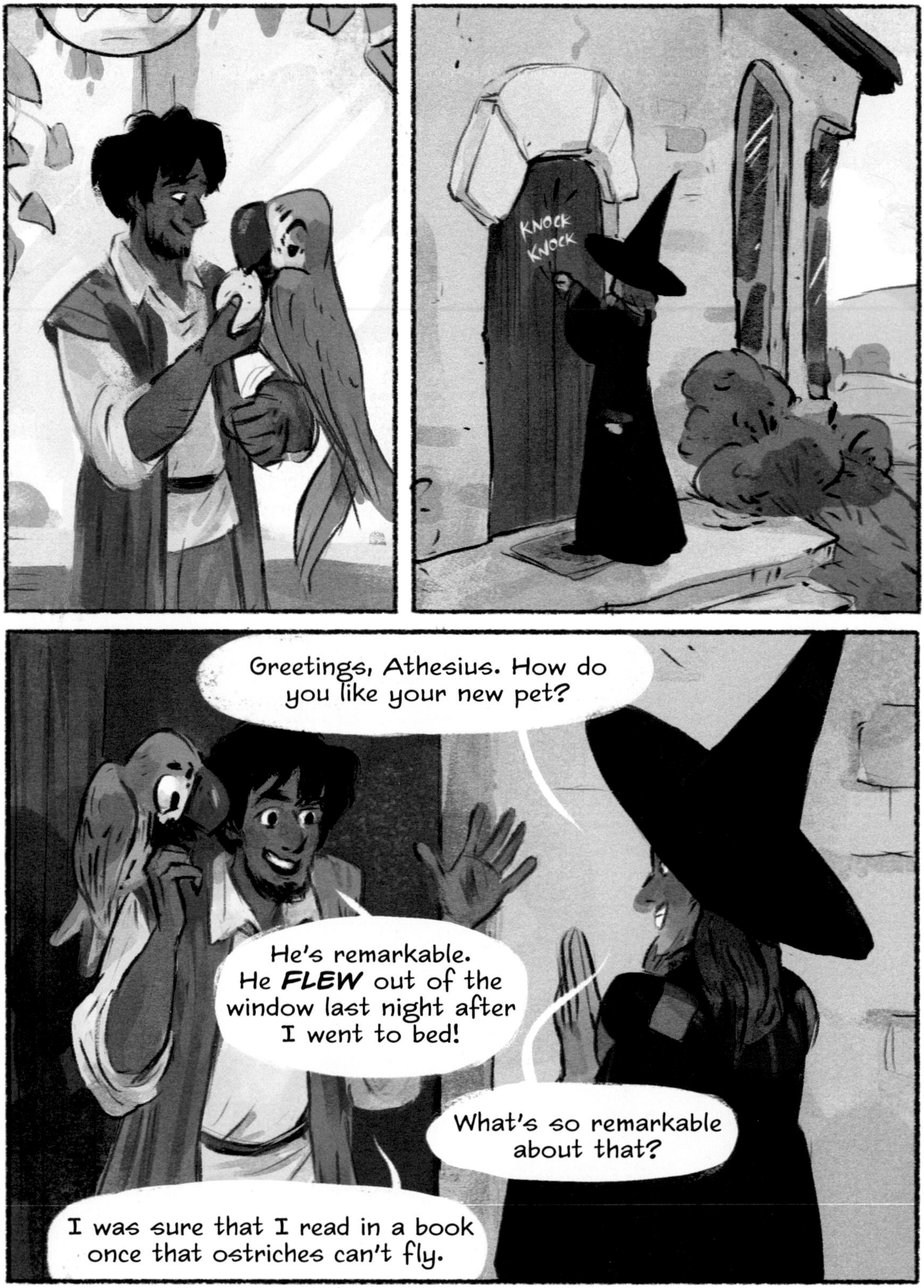
KNOCK KNOCK
Greetings, Athesius. How do you like your new pet?
He's remarkable. He **FLEW** out of the window last night after I went to bed!
What's so remarkable about that?
I was sure that I read in a book once that ostriches can't fly.

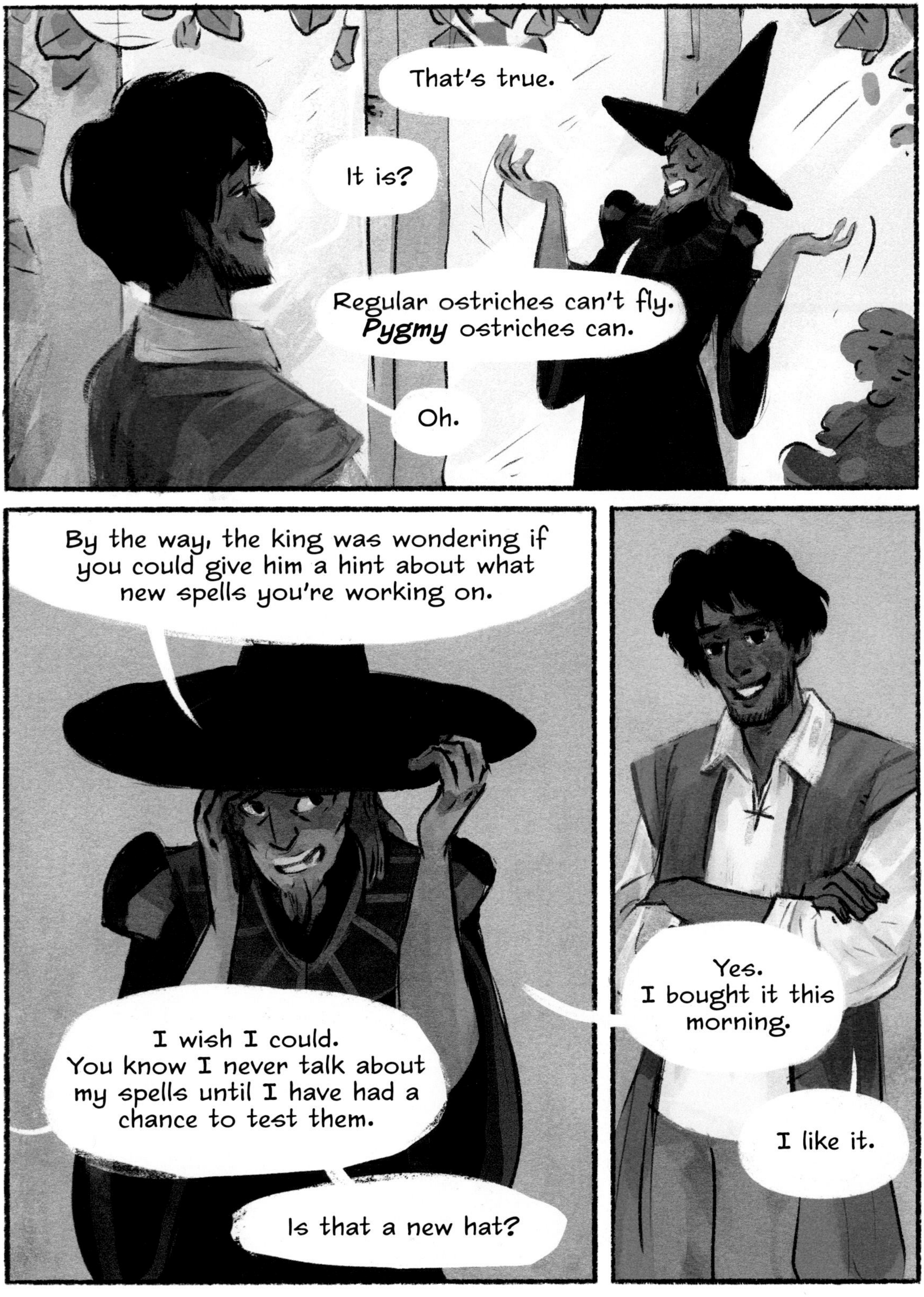
That's true.
It is?
Regular ostriches can't fly. *Pygmy* ostriches can.
Oh.
By the way, the king was wondering if you could give him a hint about what new spells you're working on.
I wish I could. You know I never talk about my spells until I have had a chance to test them.
Is that a new hat?
Yes. I bought it this morning.
I like it.

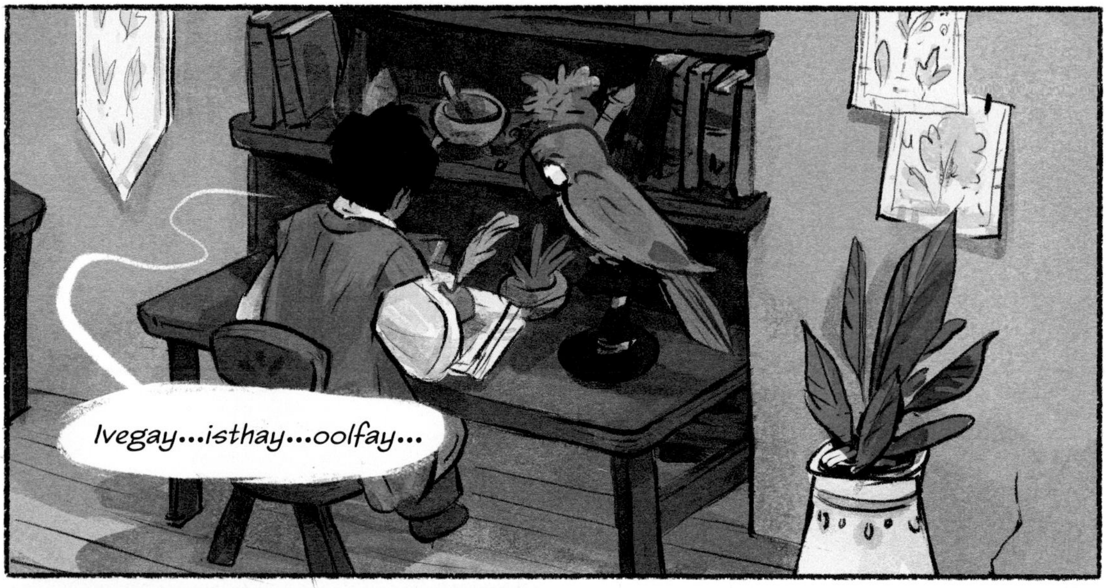
Ivegay...isthay...oolfay...

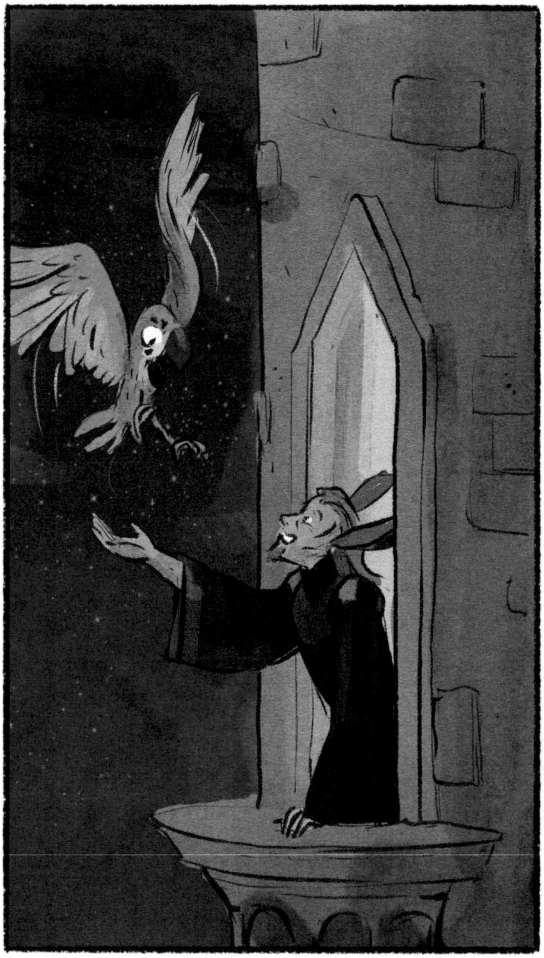

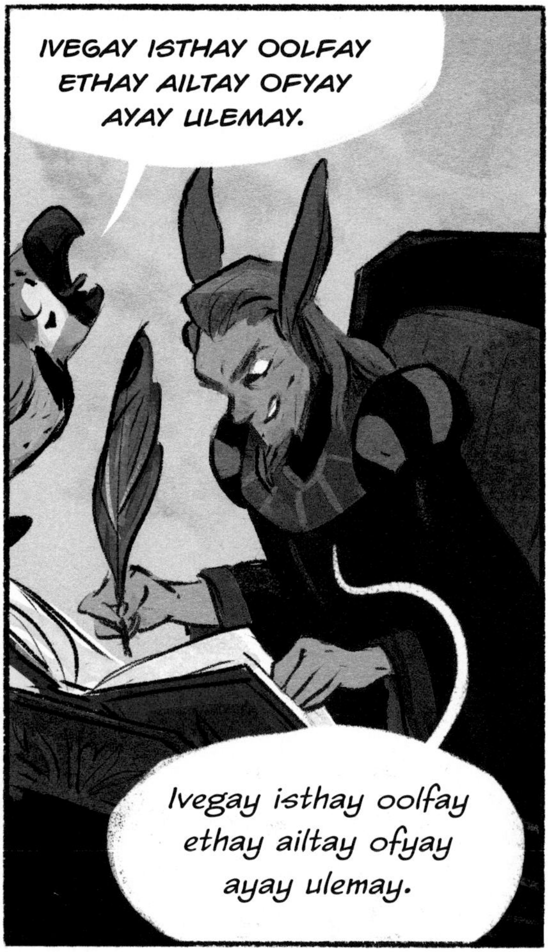
IVEGAY ISTHAY OOLFAY ETHAY AILTAY OFYAY AYAY ULEMAY.
Ivegay isthay oolfay ethay ailtay ofyay ayay ulemay.

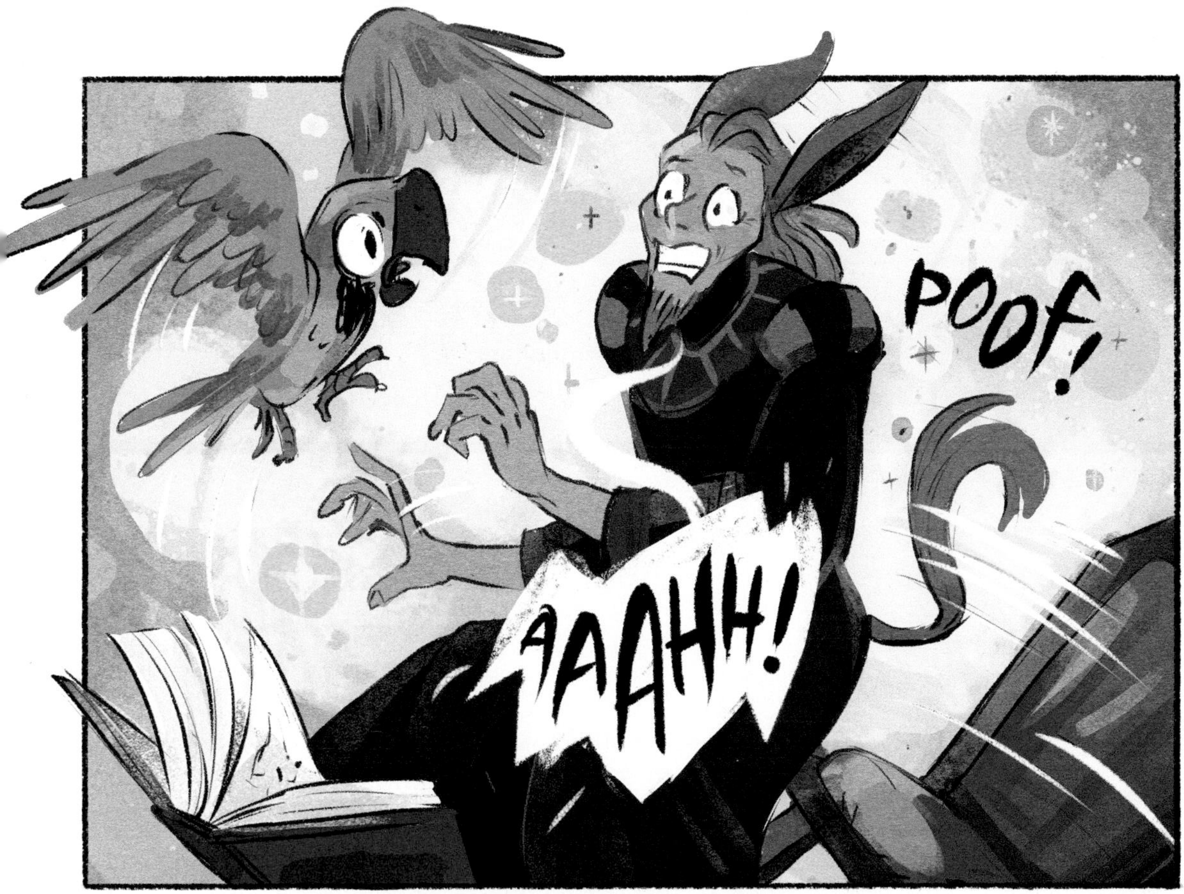
POOF!
AAAHH!

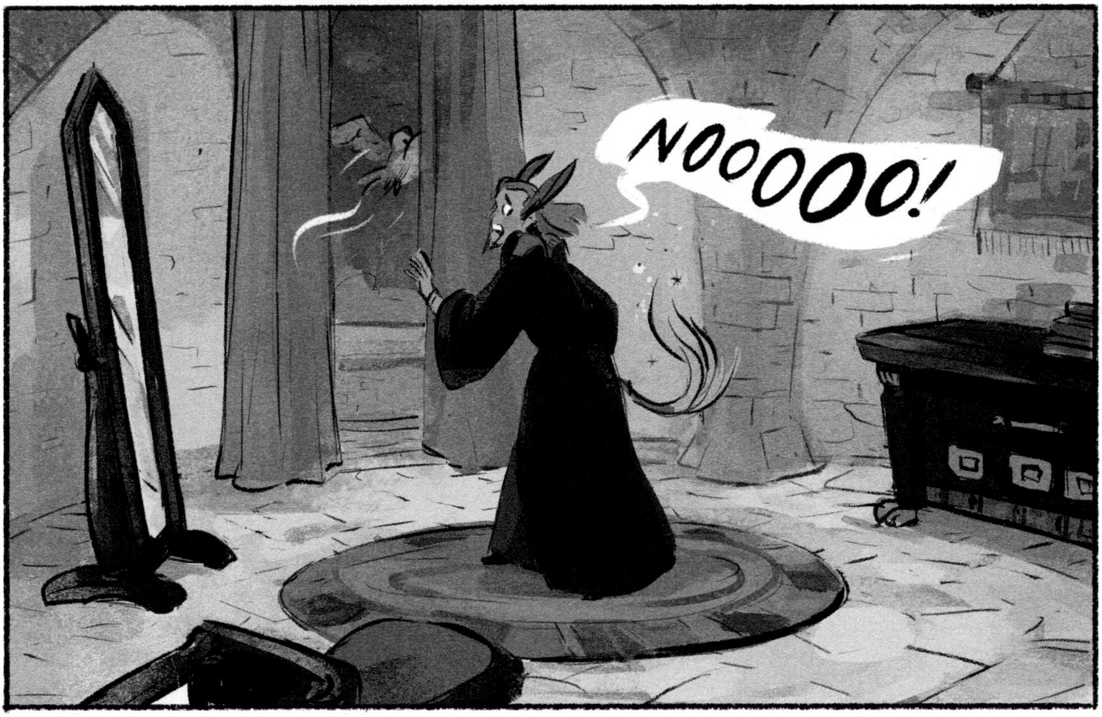
NOOOOO!

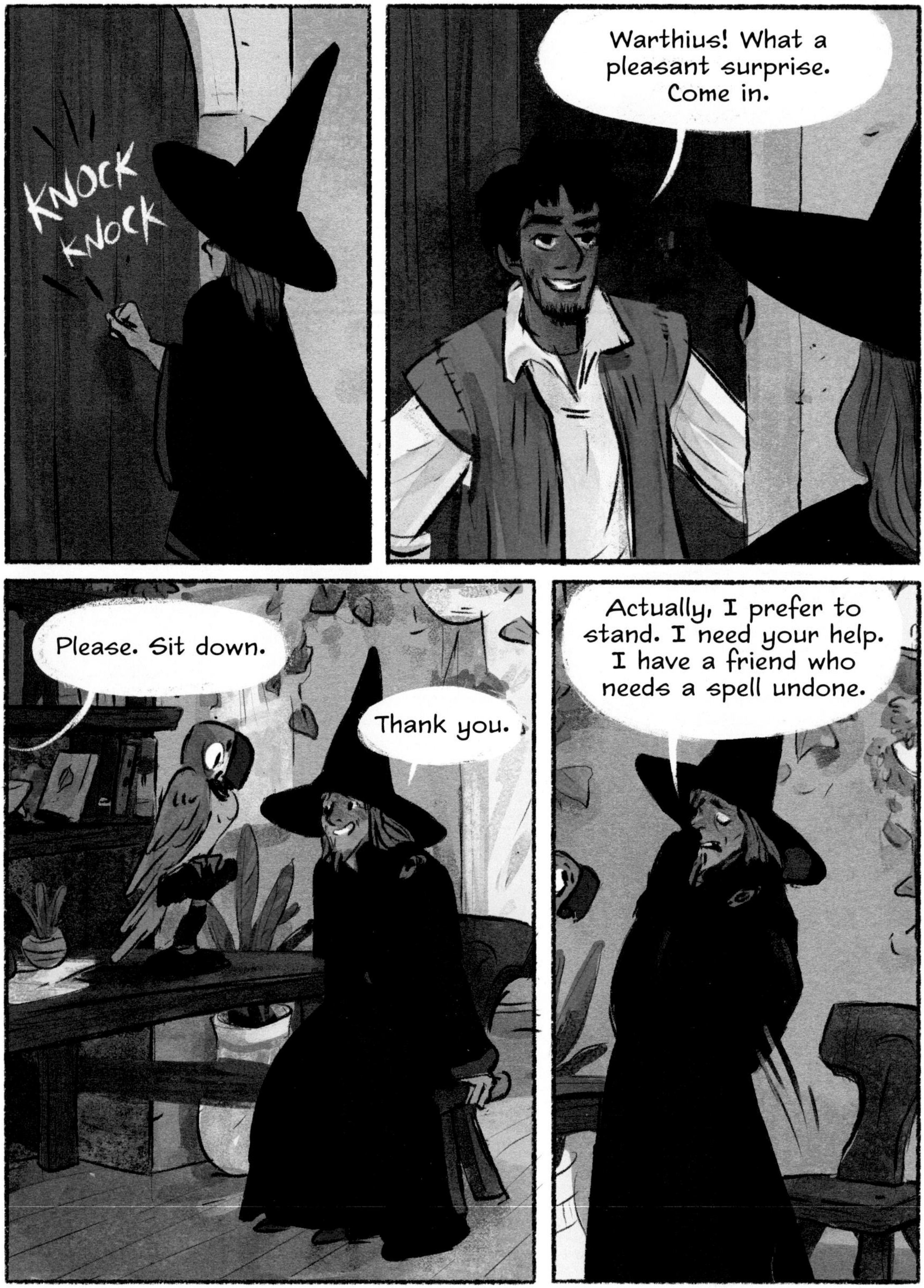
KNOCK
KNOCK
Warthius! What a pleasant surprise. Come in.
Please. Sit down.
Thank you.
Actually, I prefer to stand. I need your help. I have a friend who needs a spell undone.

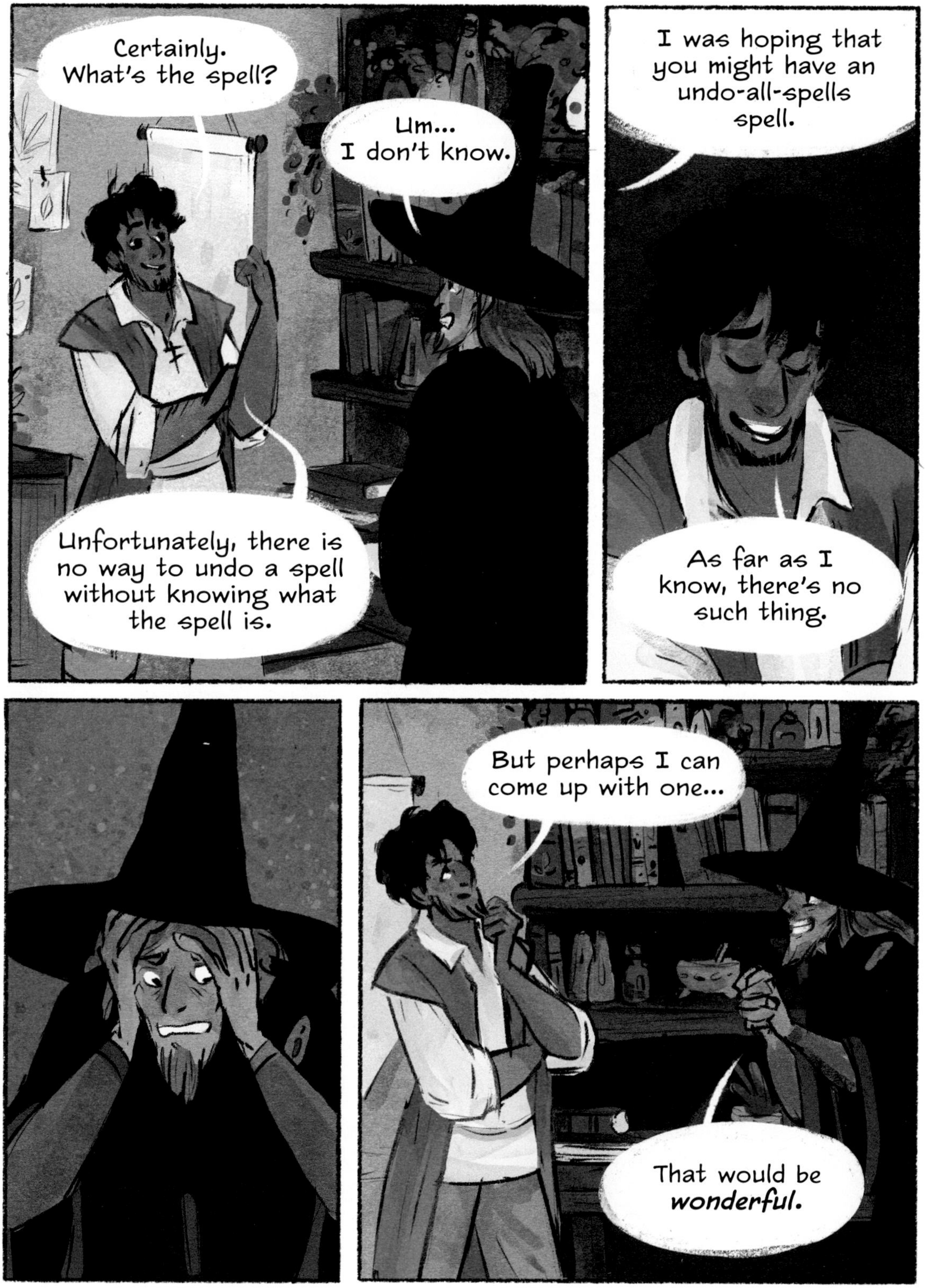
Certainly. What's the spell?
Um... I don't know.
Unfortunately, there is no way to undo a spell without knowing what the spell is.
I was hoping that you might have an undo-all-spells spell.
As far as I know, there's no such thing.
But perhaps I can come up with one...
That would be *wonderful*.

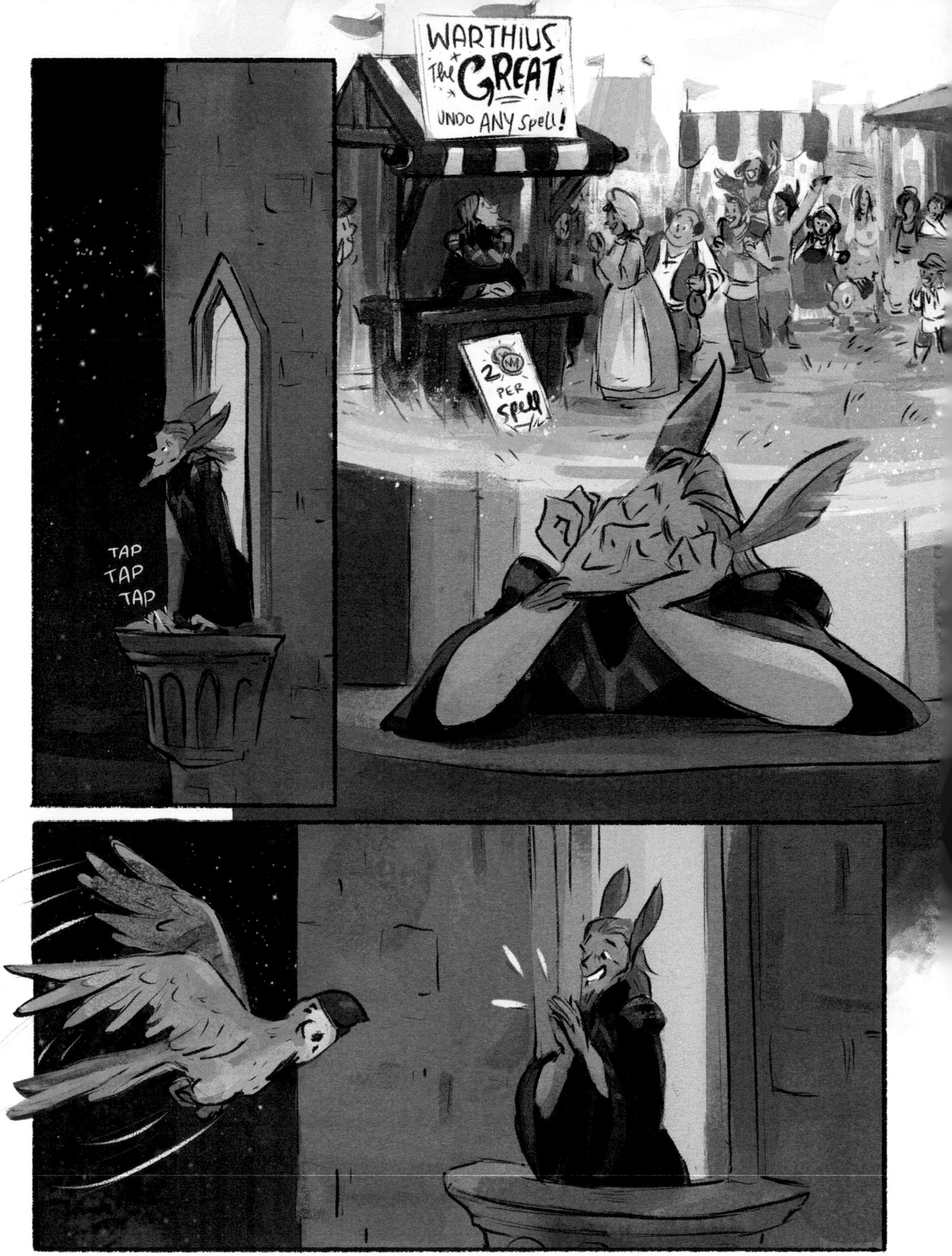
WARTHIUS the GREAT
UNDO ANY Spell!
2 PER Spell
TAP
TAP
TAP

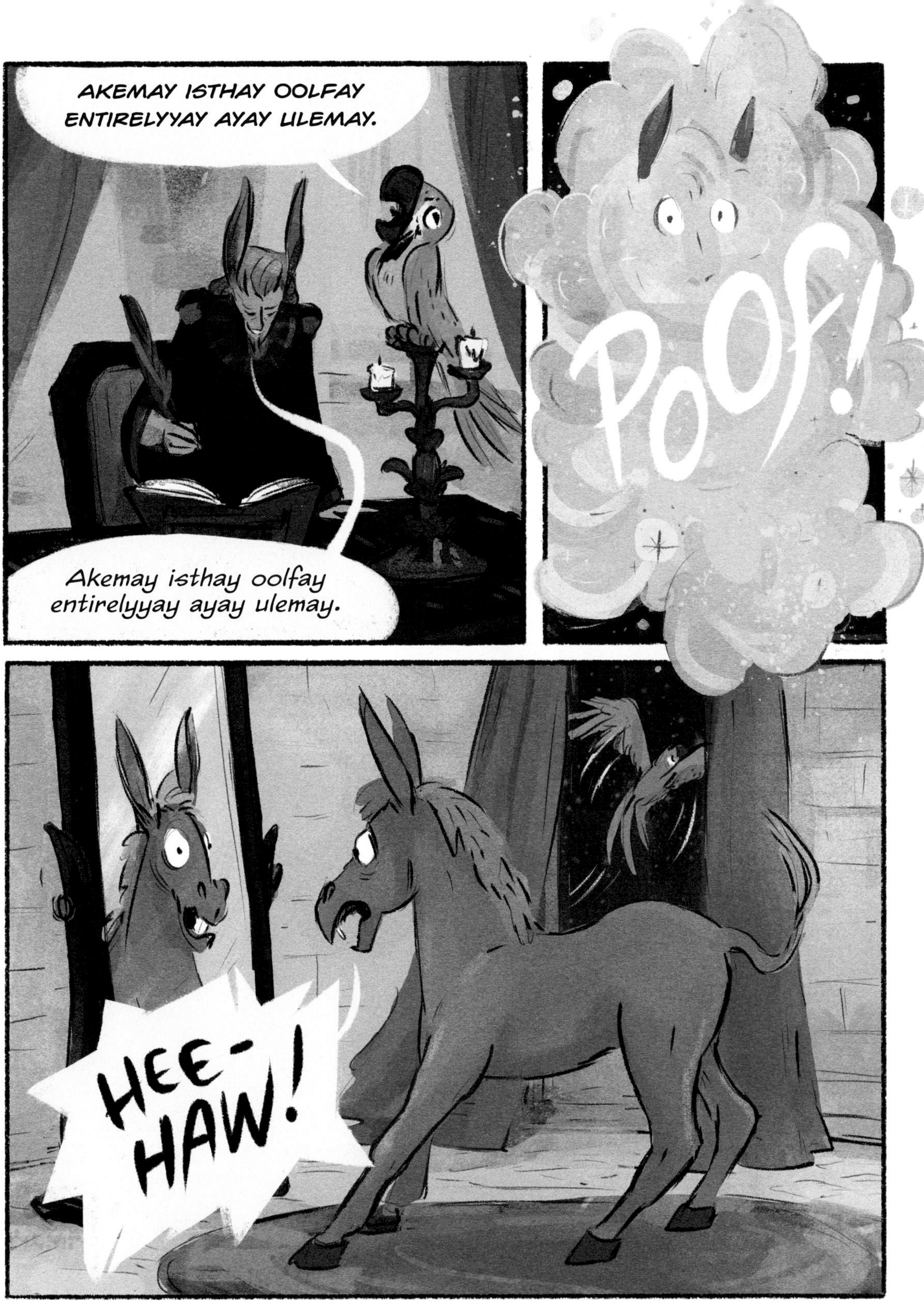
AKEMAY ISTHAY OOLFAY ENTIRELYYAY AYAY ULEMAY.
Akemay isthay oolfay entirelyyay ayay ulemay.
POOF!
HEE-HAW!

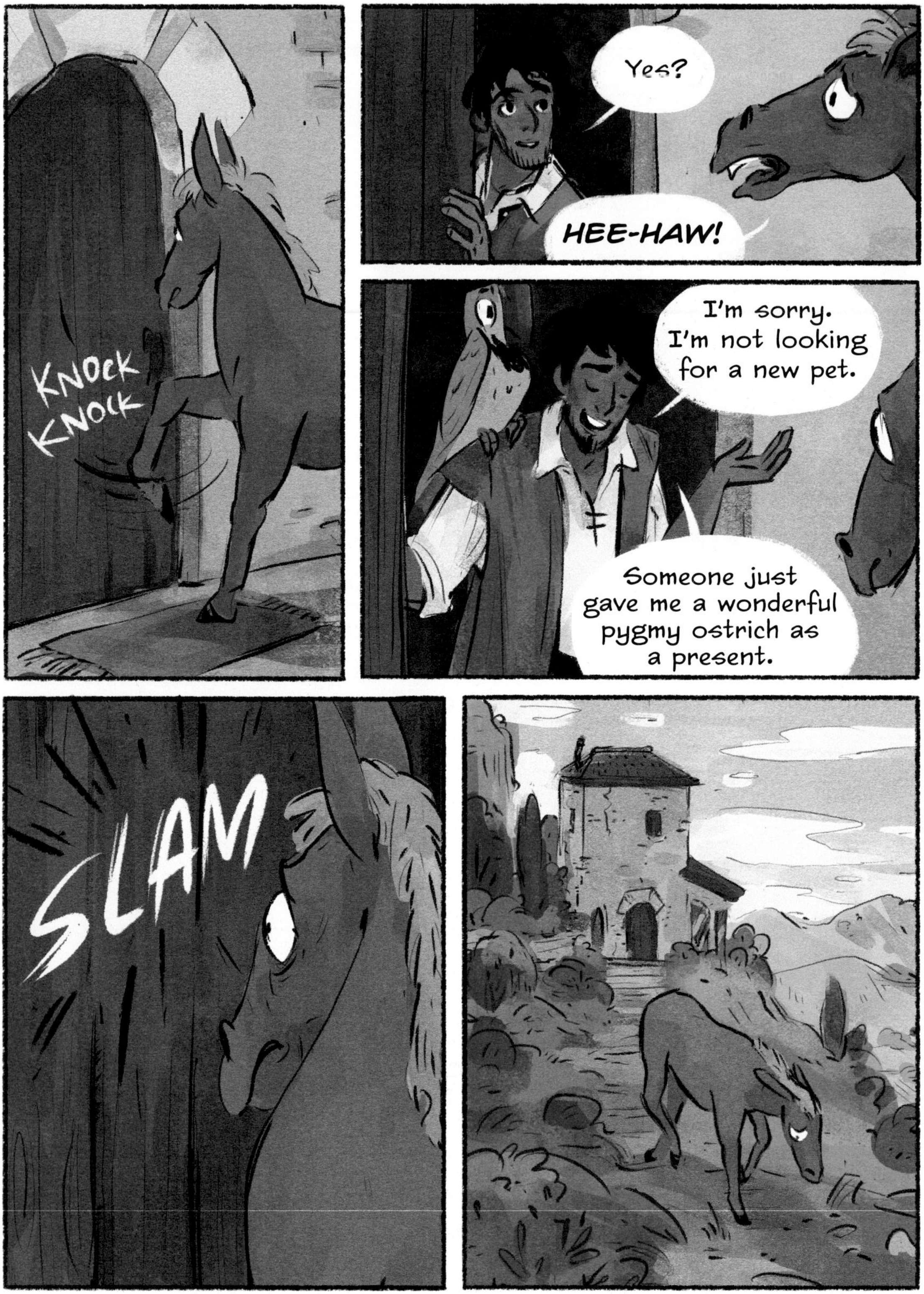
KNOCK KNOCK
Yes?
HEE-HAW!
I'm sorry. I'm not looking for a new pet.
Someone just gave me a wonderful pygmy ostrich as a present.
SLAM

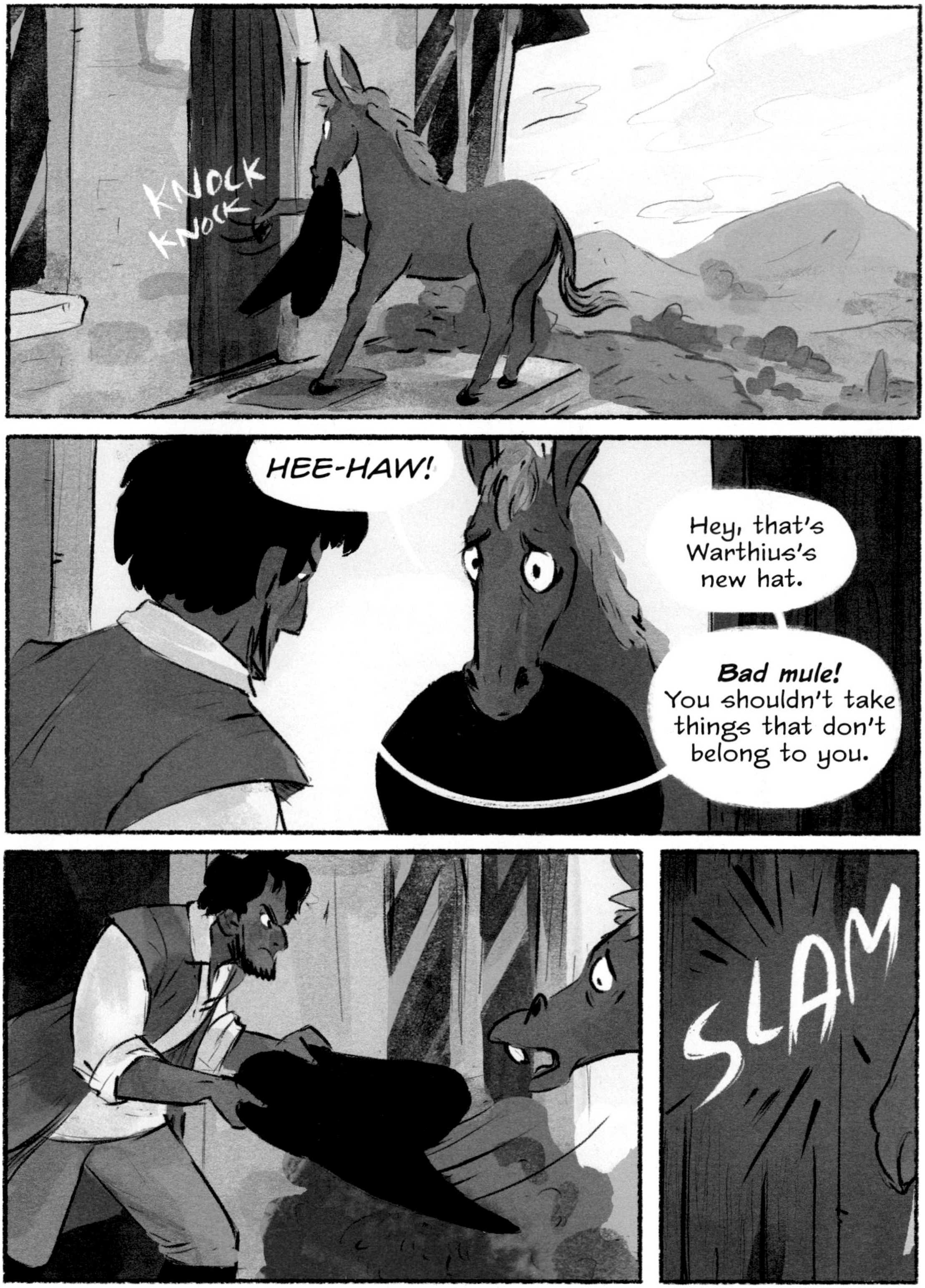
KNOCK
KNOCK
HEE-HAW!
Hey, that's Warthius's new hat.
Bad mule! You shouldn't take things that don't belong to you.
SLAM

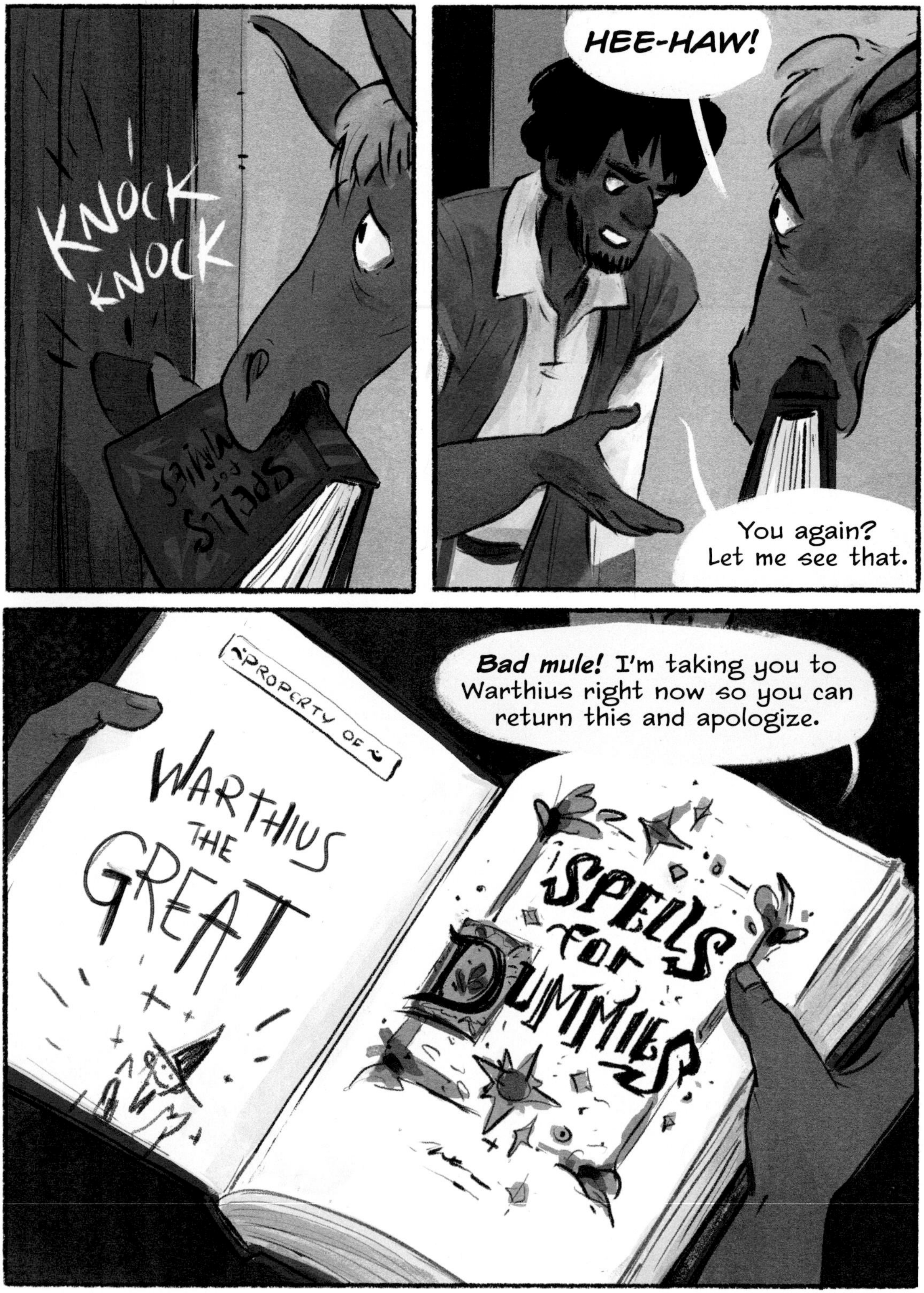
KNOCK KNOCK
SPELLS for DUMMIES
HEE-HAW!
You again? Let me see that.
PROPERTY OF
WARTHIUS THE GREAT
SPELLS for DUMMIES
Bad mule! I'm taking you to Warthius right now so you can return this and apologize.

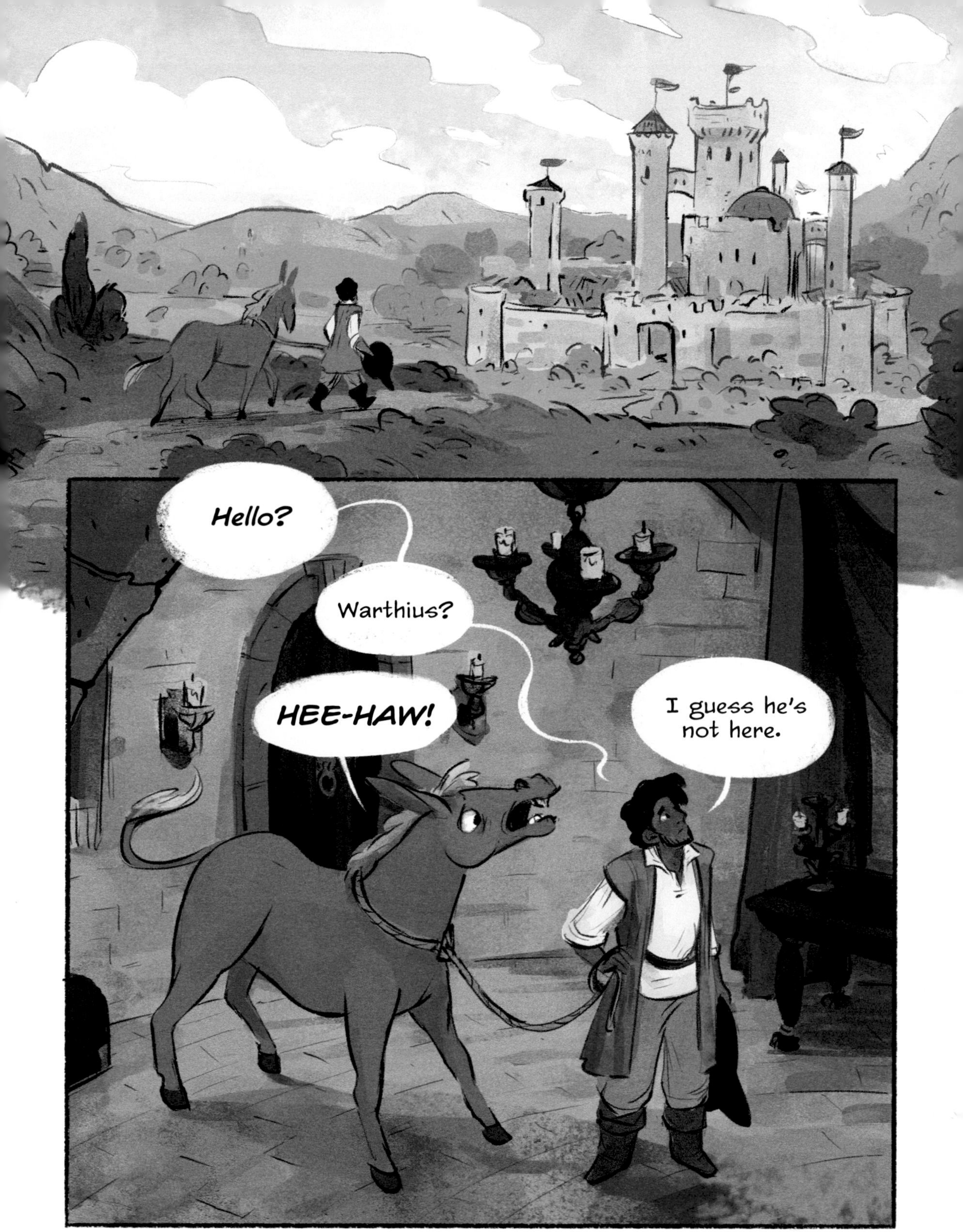
Hello?
Warthius?
HEE-HAW!
I guess he's not here.

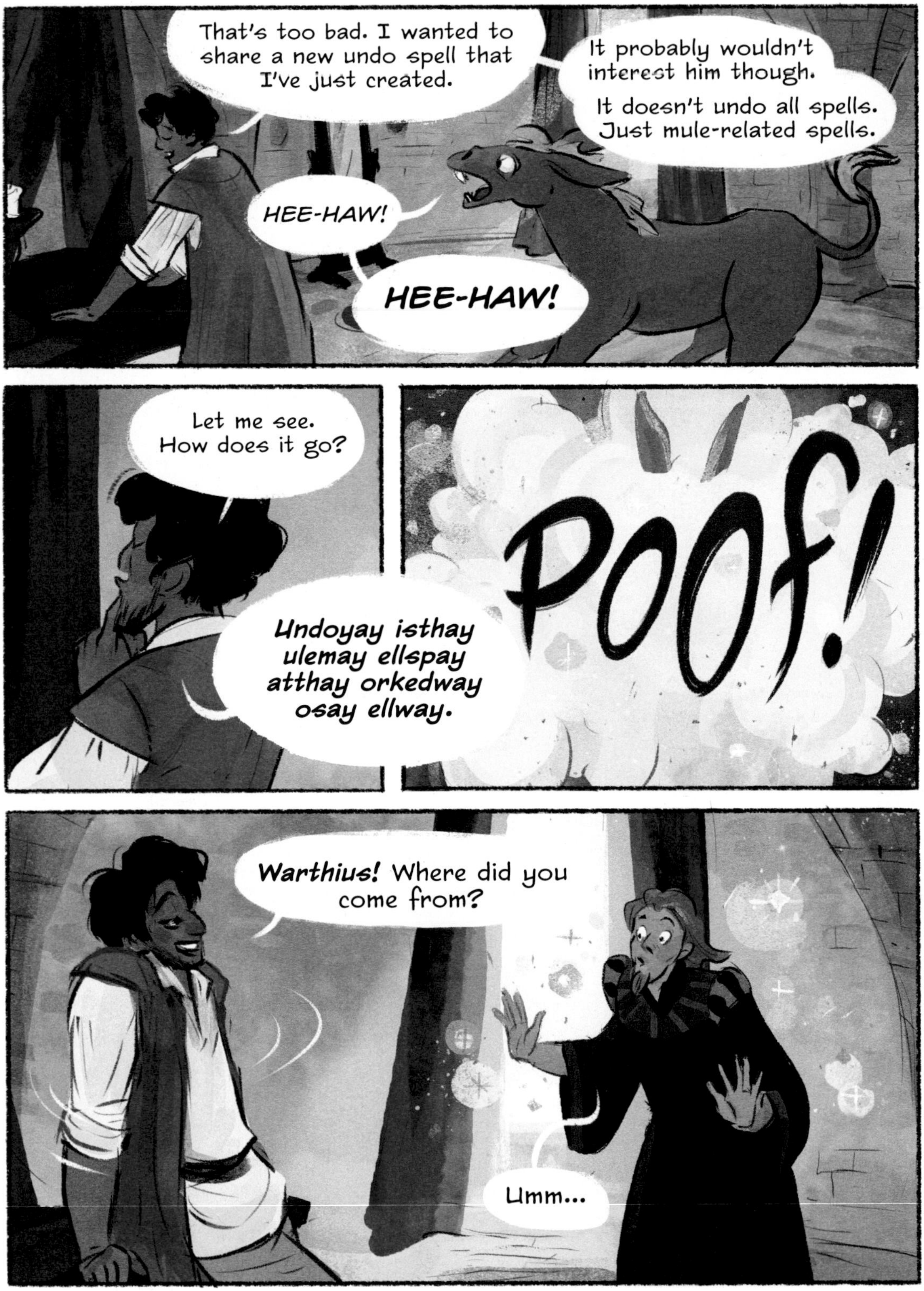
That's too bad. I wanted to share a new undo spell that I've just created.
It probably wouldn't interest him though.
It doesn't undo all spells. Just mule-related spells.
HEE-HAW!
HEE-HAW!
Let me see. How does it go?
Undoyay isthay ulemay ellspay atthay orkedway osay ellway.
POOF!
Warthius! Where did you come from?
Umm...

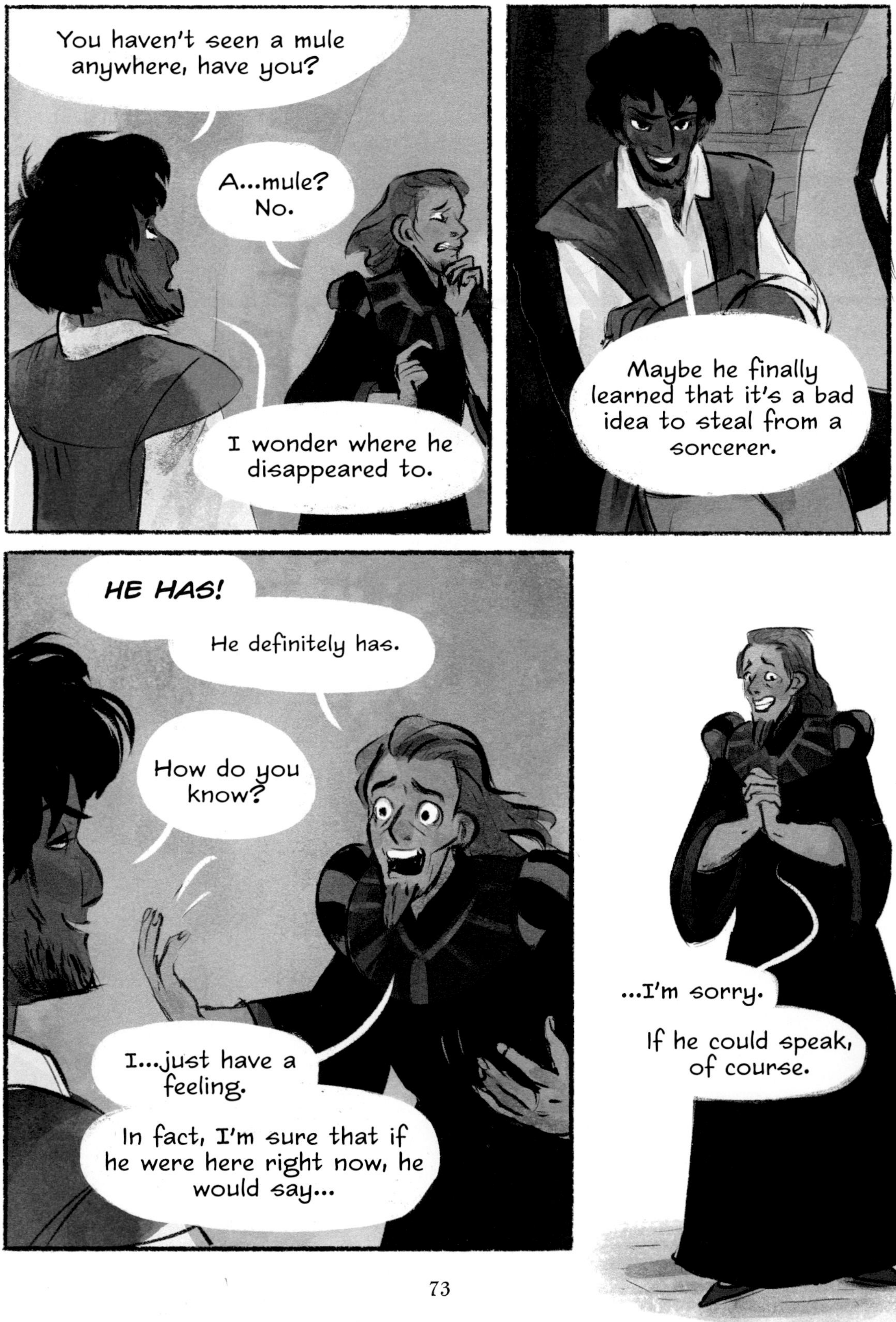

You haven't seen a mule anywhere, have you?
A...mule? No.
I wonder where he disappeared to.
Maybe he finally learned that it's a bad idea to steal from a sorcerer.
HE HAS!
He definitely has.
How do you know?
I...just have a feeling.
In fact, I'm sure that if he were here right now, he would say...
...I'm sorry.
If he could speak, of course.

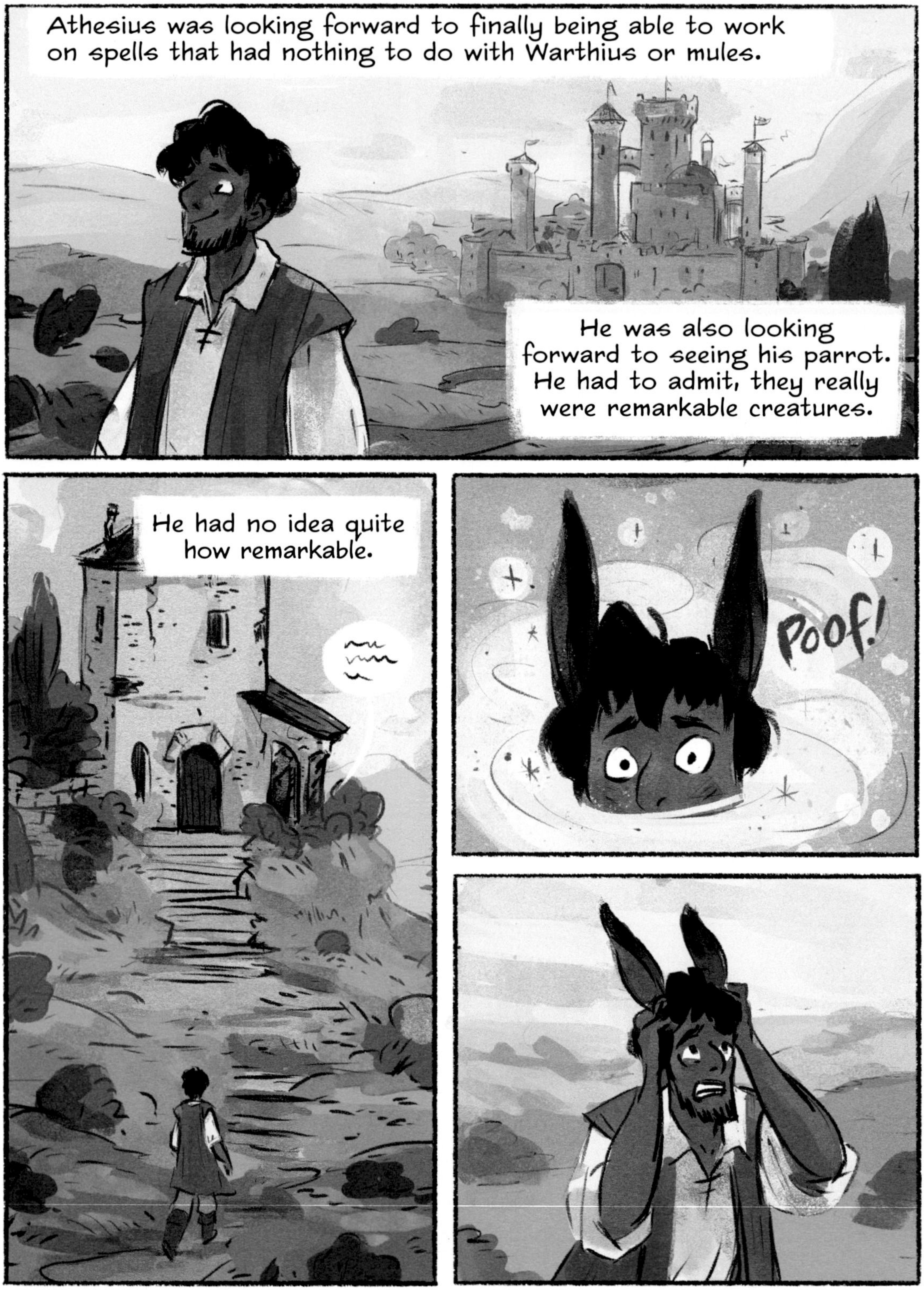
Athesius was looking forward to finally being able to work on spells that had nothing to do with Warthius or mules.
He was also looking forward to seeing his parrot. He had to admit, they really were remarkable creatures.
He had no idea quite how remarkable.
POOF!

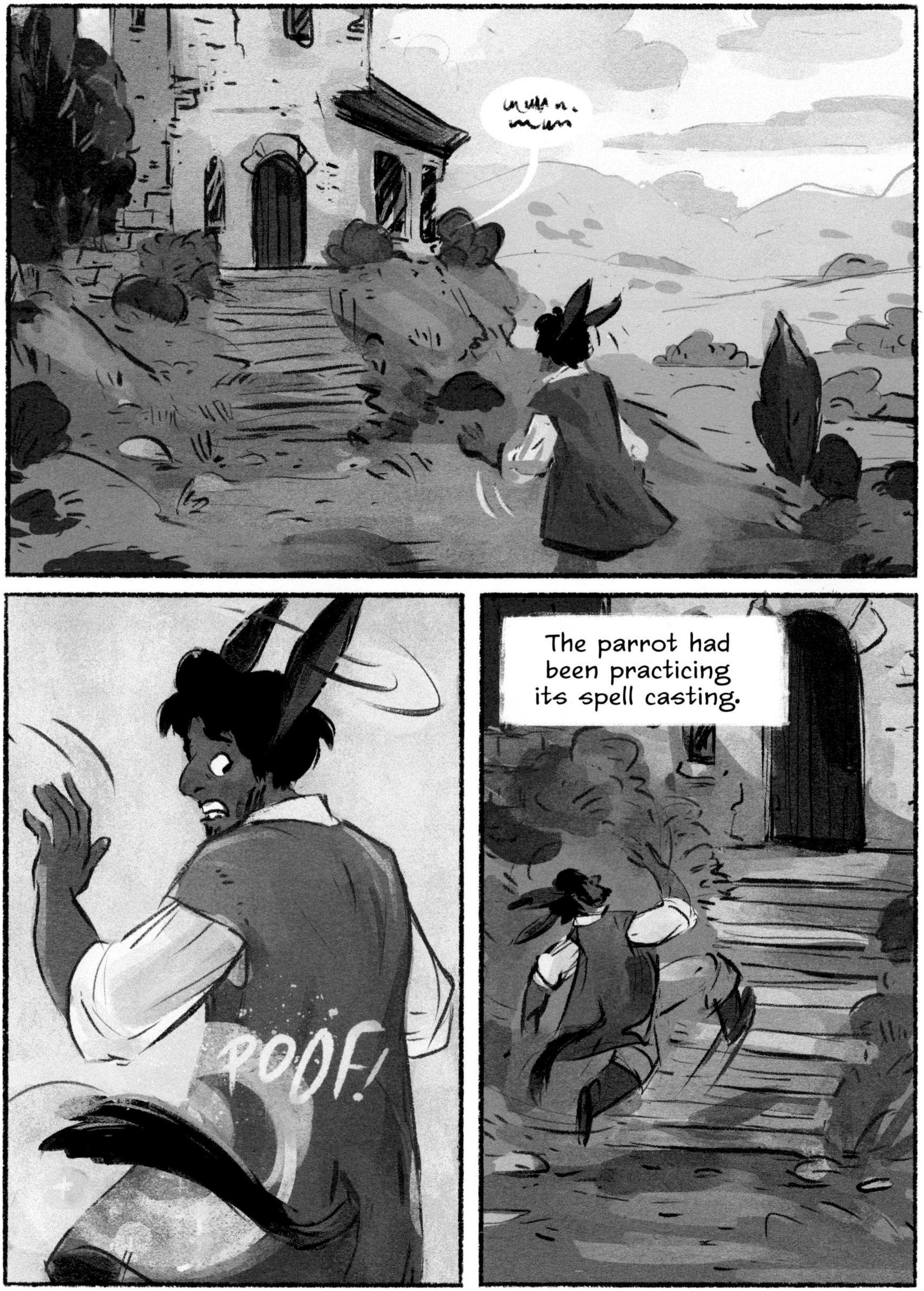
POOF!
The parrot had been practicing its spell casting.

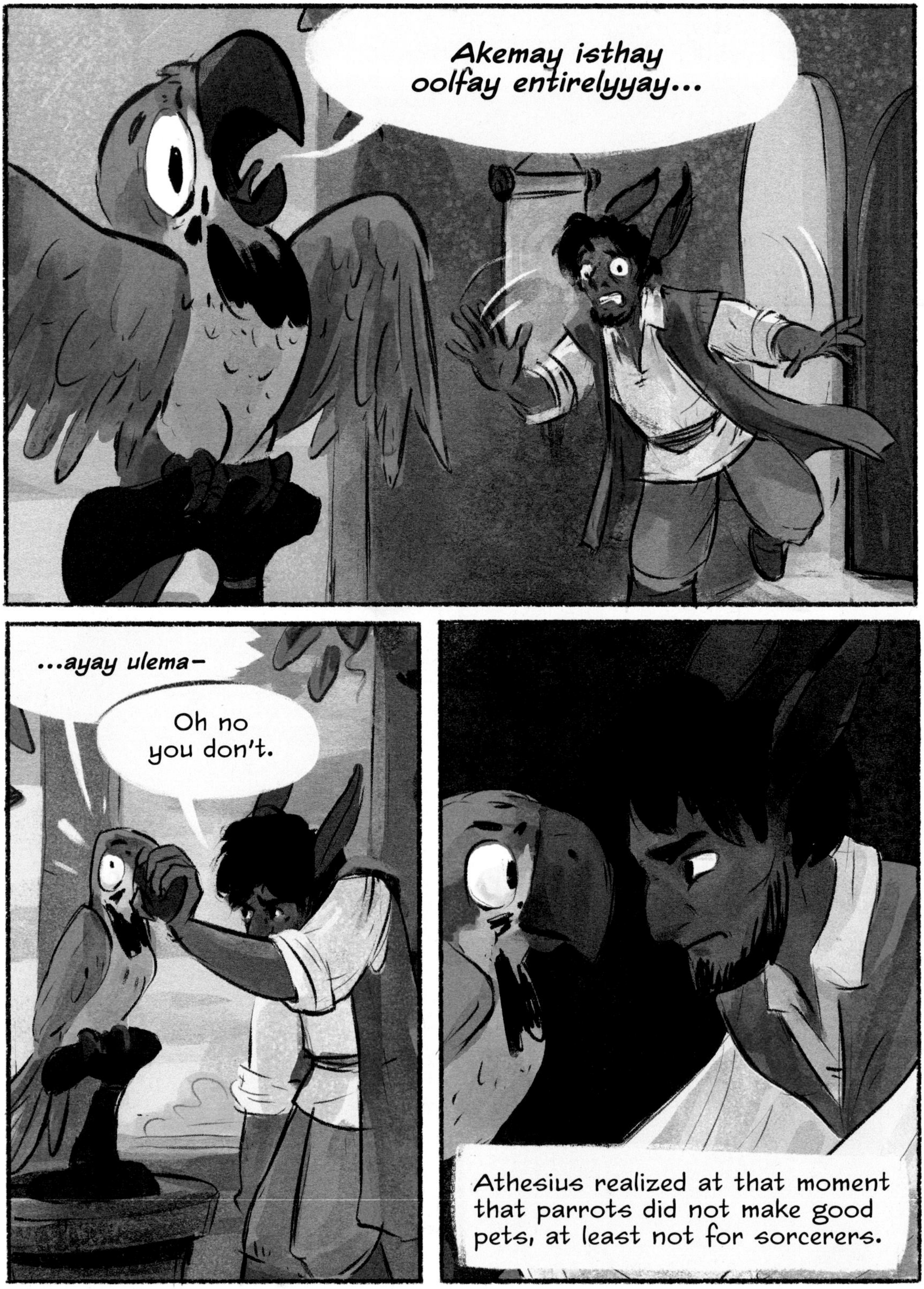
Akemay isthay oolfay entirelyyay...
...ayay ulema-
Oh no you don't.
Athesius realized at that moment that parrots did not make good pets, at least not for sorcerers.

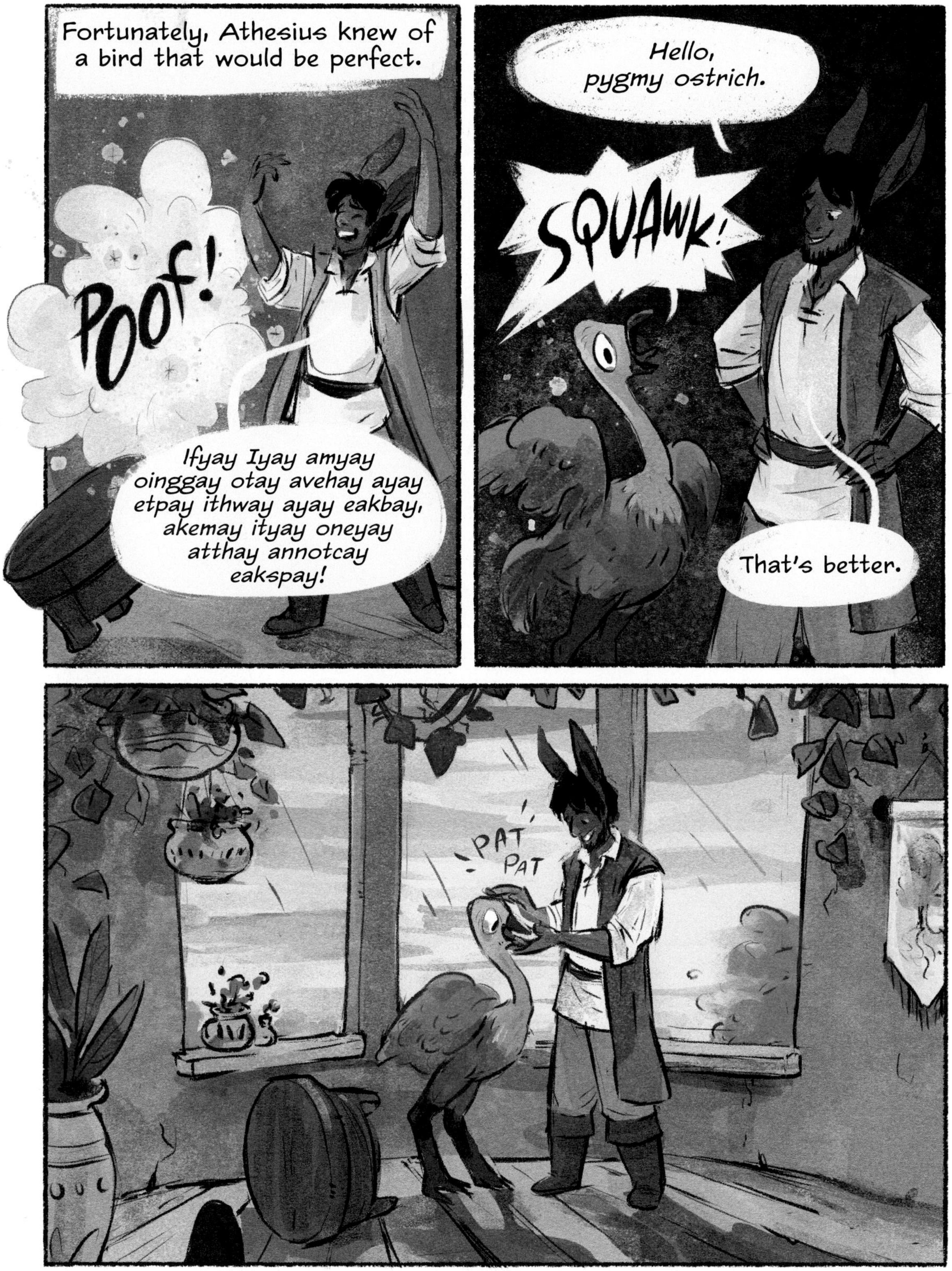
Fortunately, Athesius knew of a bird that would be perfect.
POOF!
Ifyay Iyay amyay oinggay otay avehay ayay etpay ithway ayay eakbay, akemay ityay oneyay atthay annotcay eakspay!
Hello, pygmy ostrich.
SQUAWK!
That's better.
PAT PAT

OGREISH ART

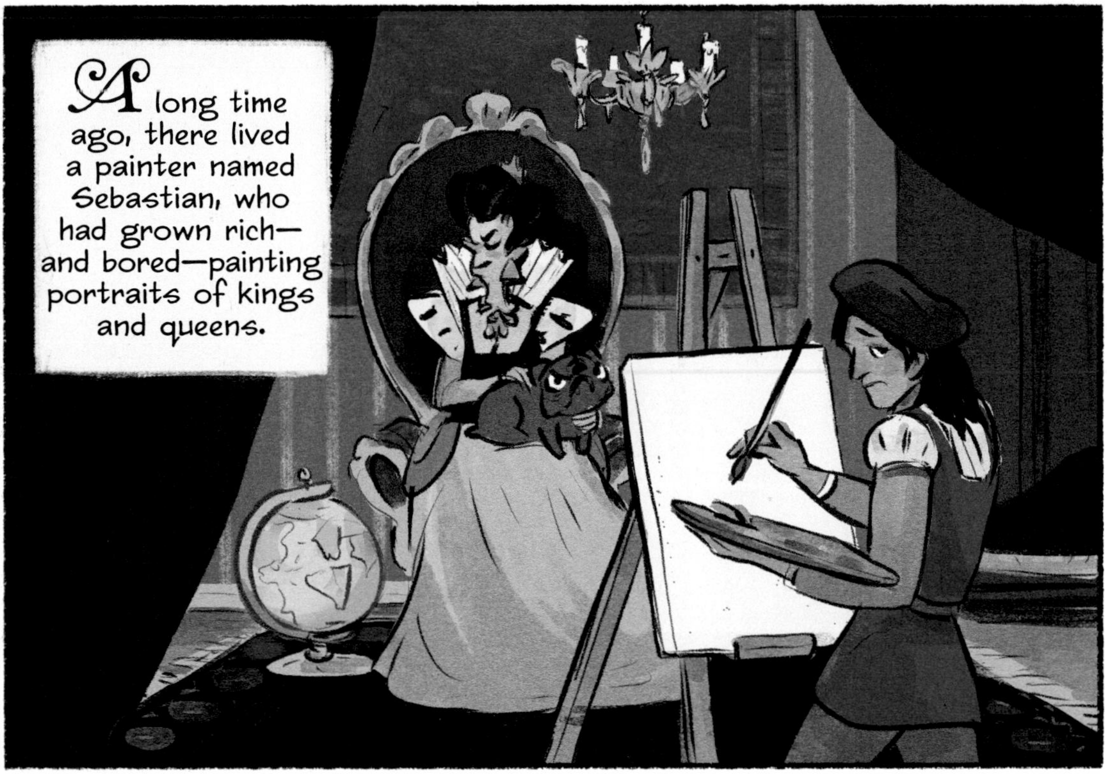
A long time ago, there lived a painter named Sebastian, who had grown rich—and bored—painting portraits of kings and queens.

It was said that he could make anyone, no matter how homely, as beautiful as the princes and princesses in storybooks.

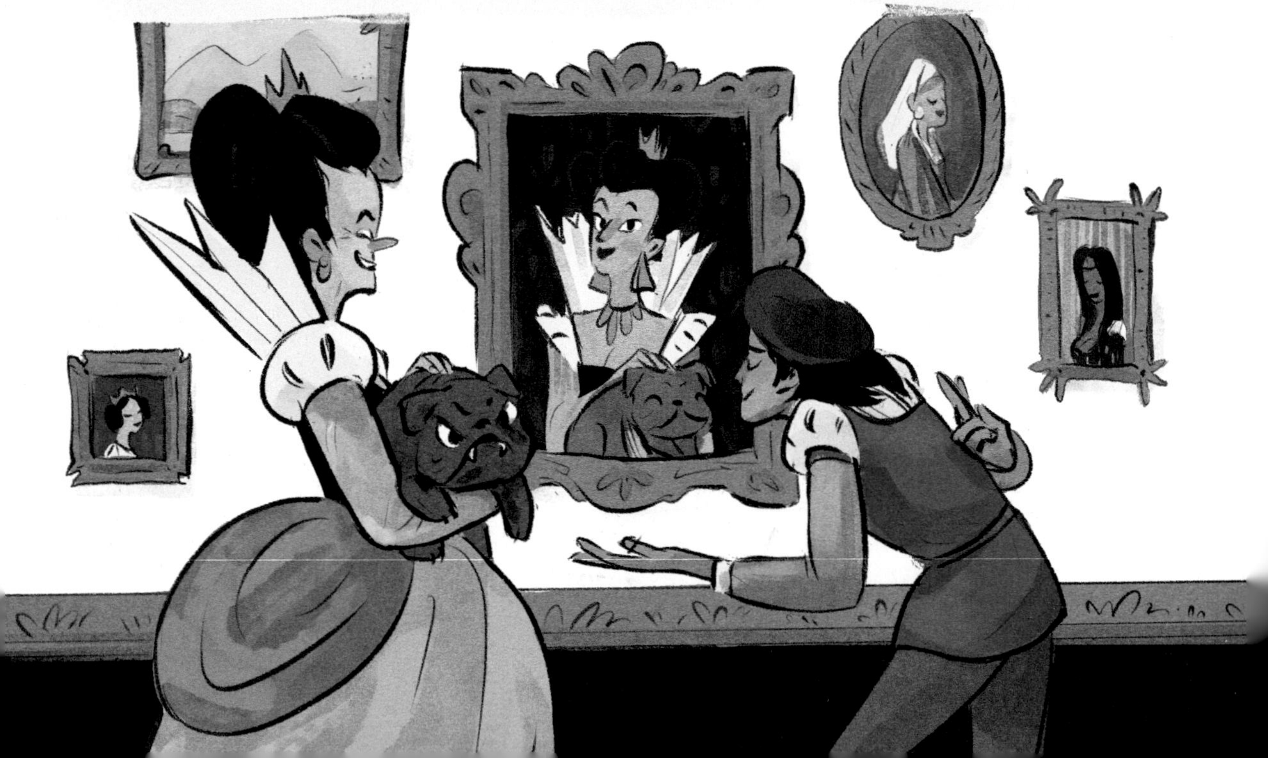

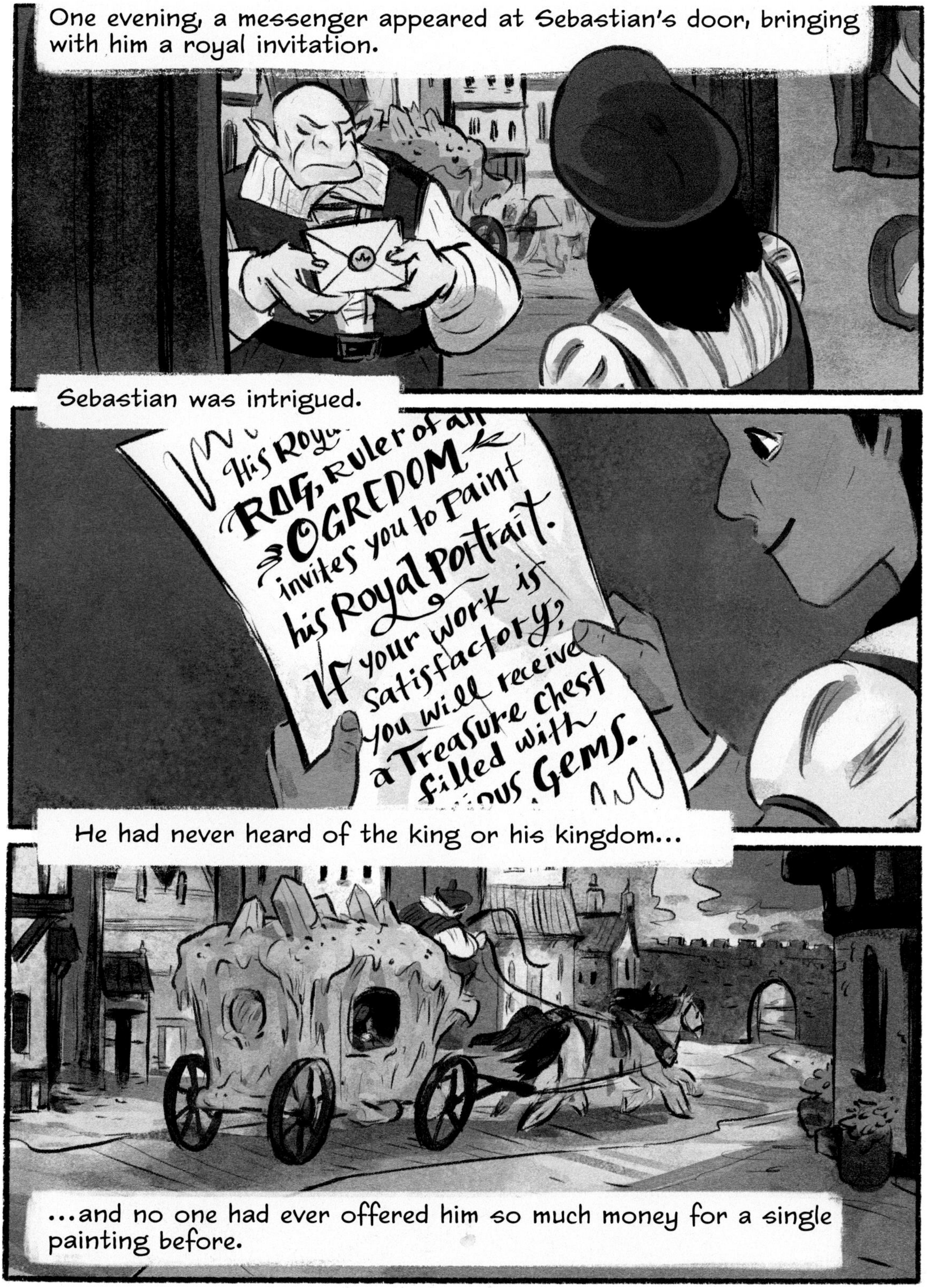
One evening, a messenger appeared at Sebastian's door, bringing with him a royal invitation.
Sebastian was intrigued.
ROG, ruler of
OGREDOM
invites you to paint
his Royal portrait.
If your work is
satisfactory,
you will receive
a Treasure chest
filled with
GEMS.
He had never heard of the king or his kingdom...
...and no one had ever offered him so much money for a single painting before.

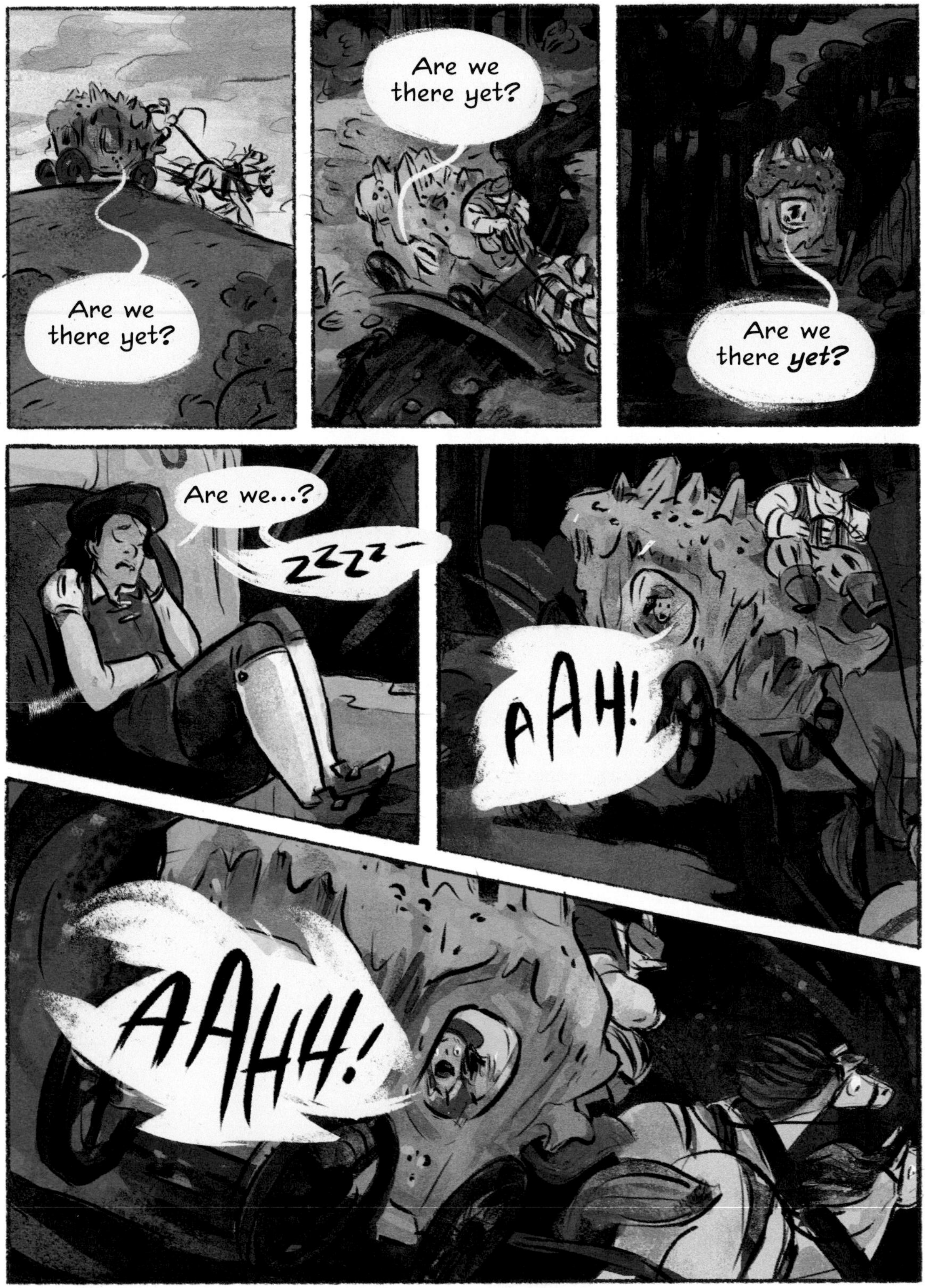
Are we there yet?
Are we there yet?
Are we there yet?
Are we...?
ZZZZ
AAH!
AAHH!

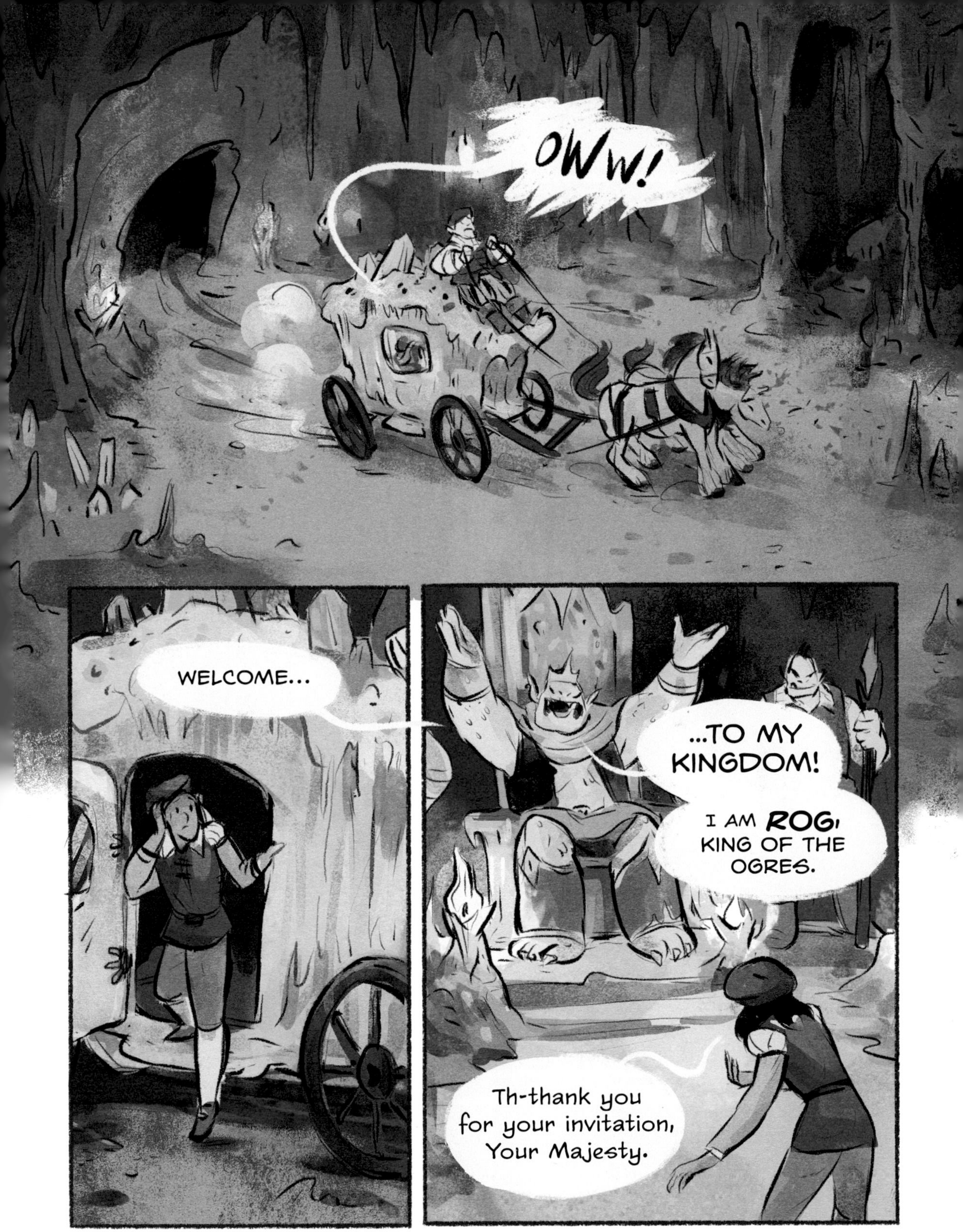
OWW!
WELCOME...
...TO MY KINGDOM!
I AM ROG, KING OF THE OGRES.
Th-thank you for your invitation, Your Majesty.

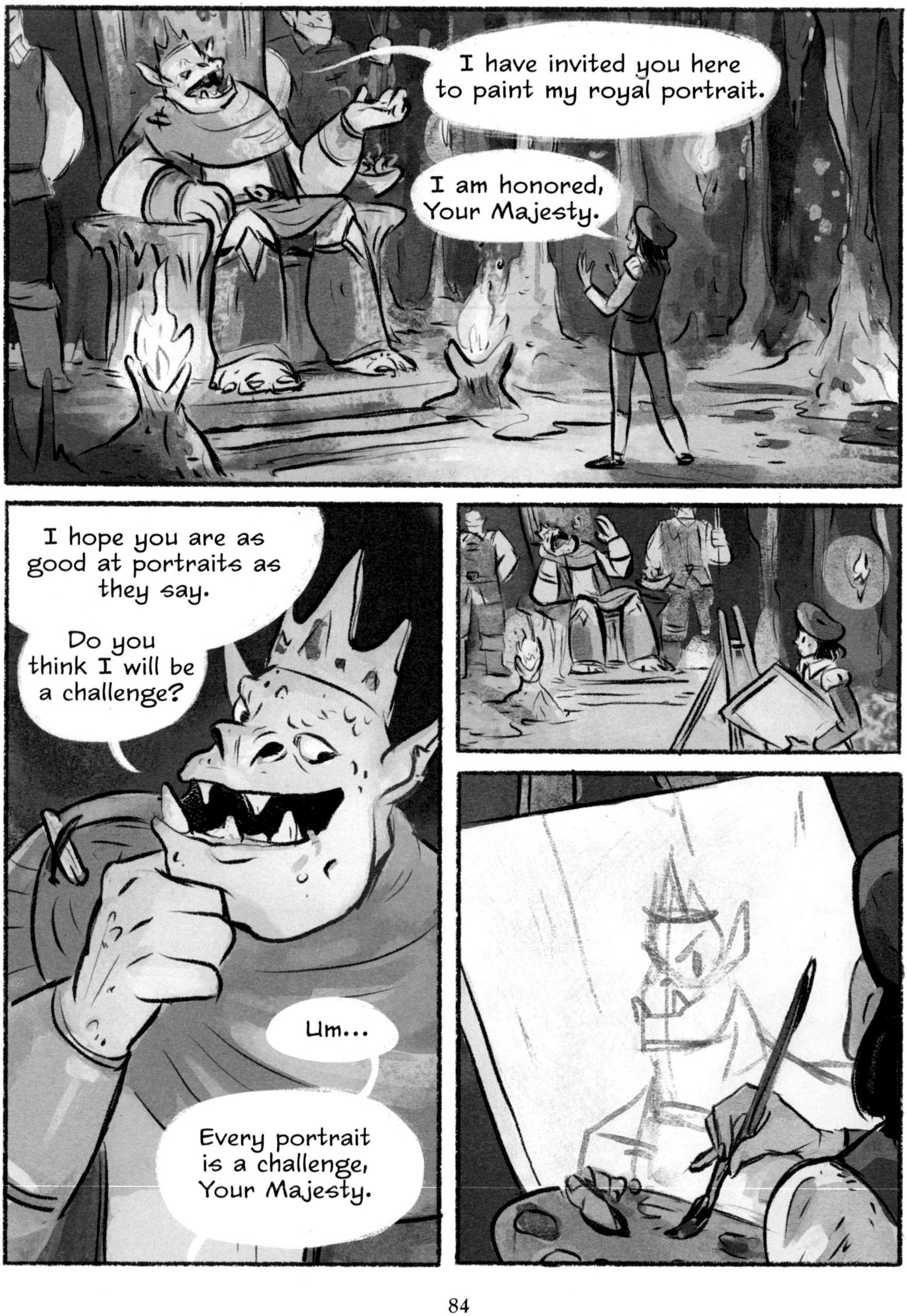
I have invited you here to paint my royal portrait.
I am honored, Your Majesty.
I hope you are as good at portraits as they say.
Do you think I will be a challenge?
Um...
Every portrait is a challenge, Your Majesty.

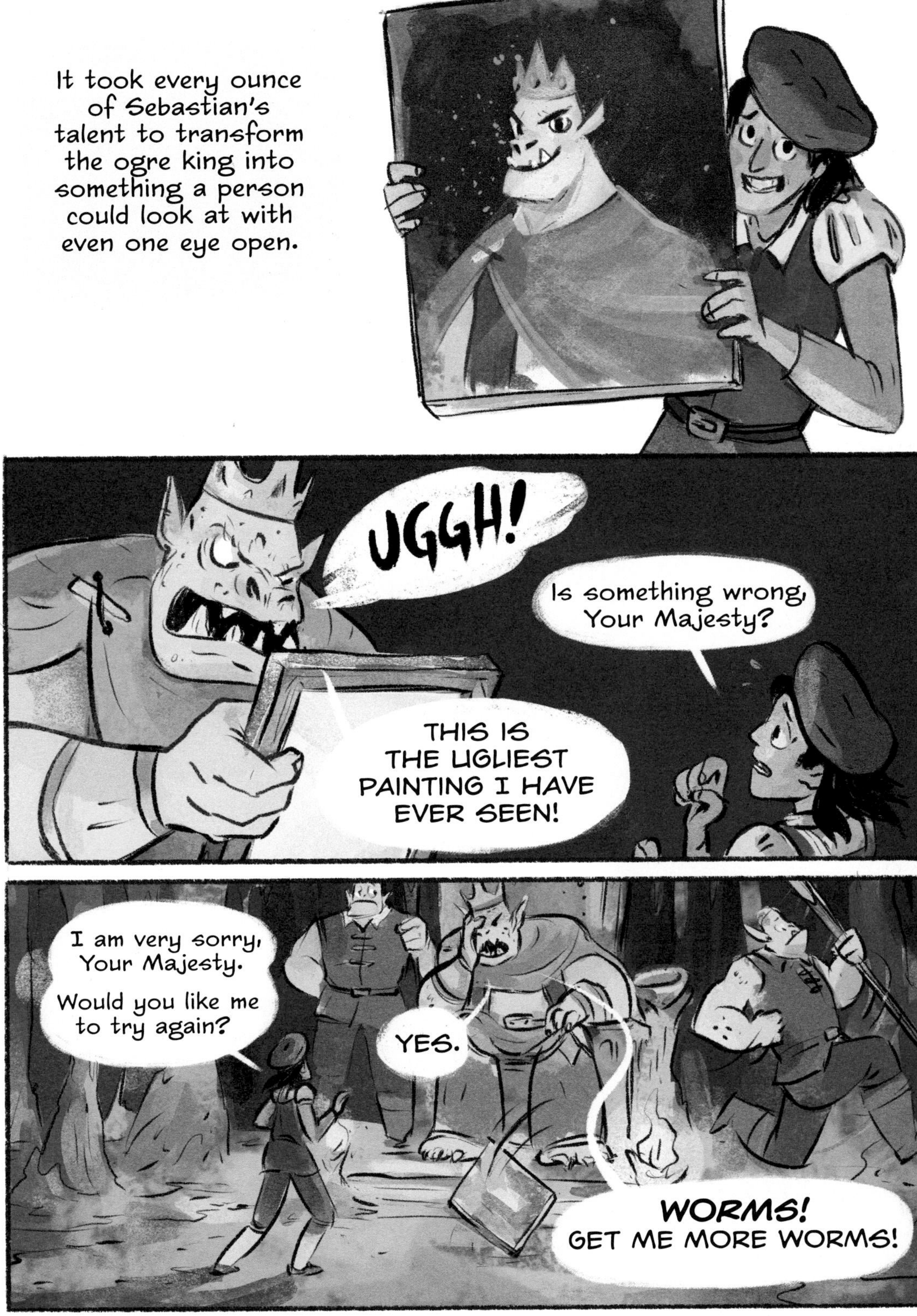
It took every ounce of Sebastian's talent to transform the ogre king into something a person could look at with even one eye open.
UGGH!
Is something wrong, Your Majesty?
THIS IS THE UGLIEST PAINTING I HAVE EVER SEEN!
I am very sorry, Your Majesty.
Would you like me to try again?
YES.
WORMS! GET ME MORE WORMS!

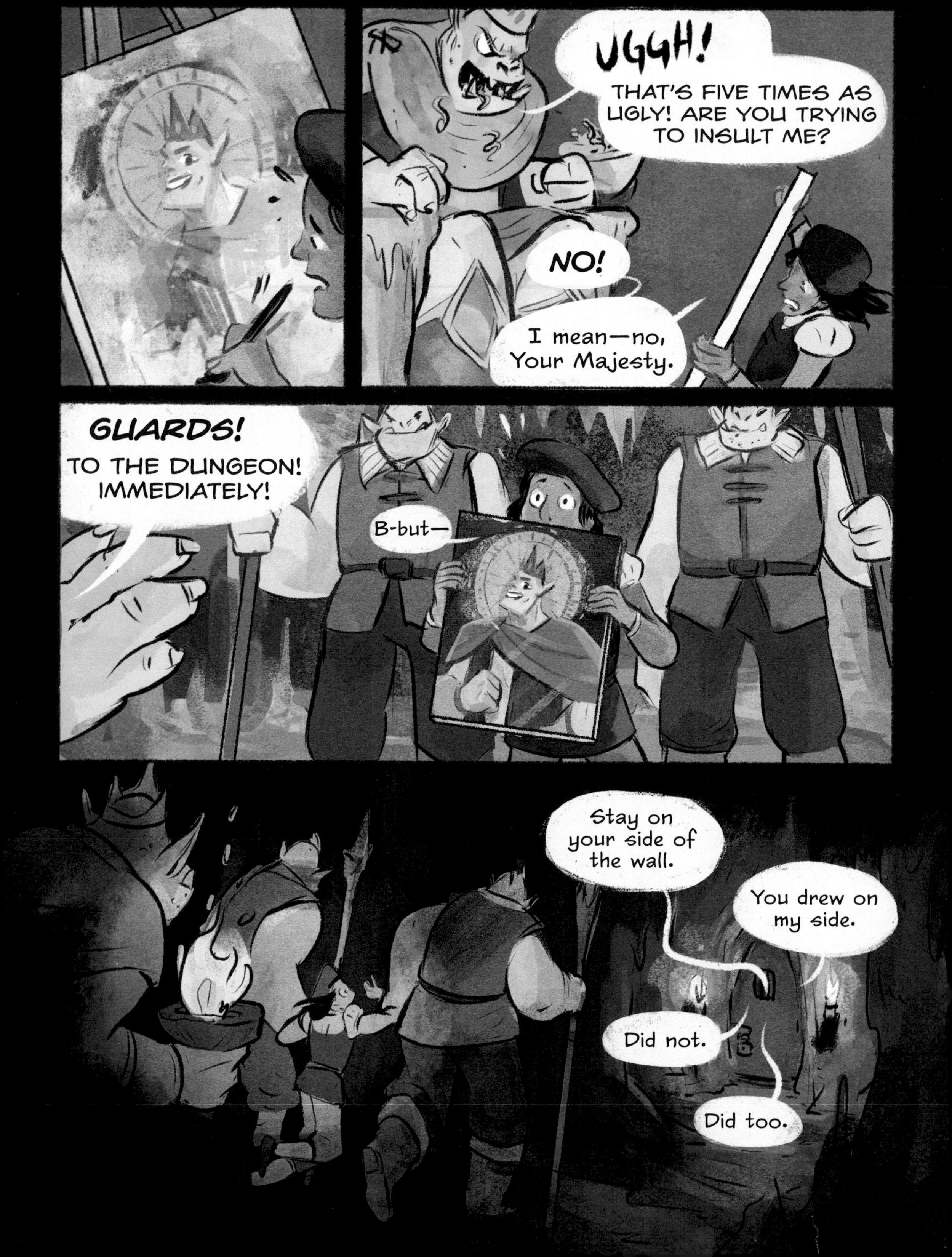
UGGH!
THAT'S FIVE TIMES AS UGLY! ARE YOU TRYING TO INSULT ME?
NO!
I mean—no, Your Majesty.
GUARDS!
TO THE DUNGEON! IMMEDIATELY!
B-but—
Stay on your side of the wall.
You drew on my side.
Did not.
Did too.

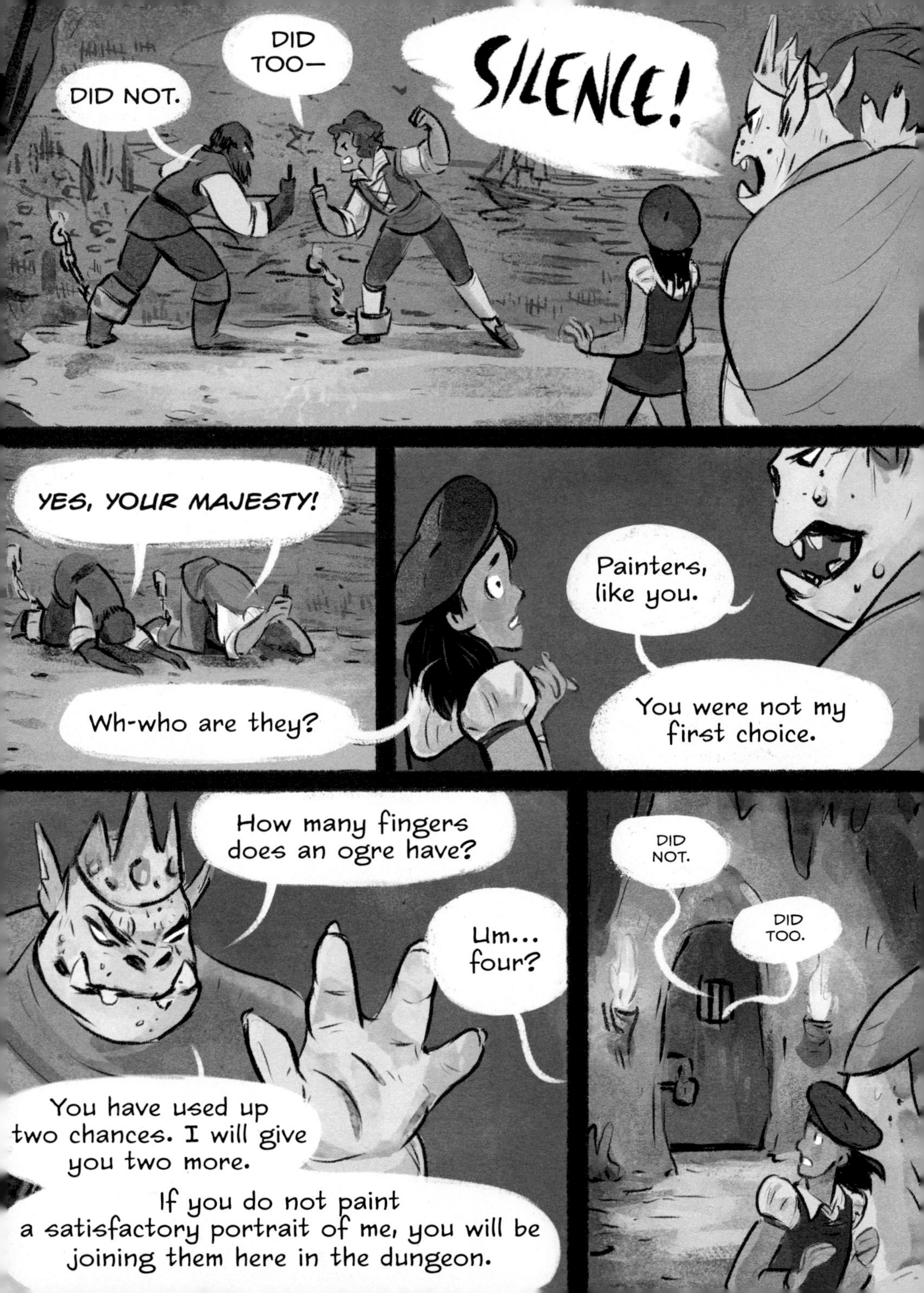
DID NOT.
DID TOO—
SILENCE!
YES, YOUR MAJESTY!
Wh-who are they?
Painters, like you.
You were not my first choice.
How many fingers does an ogre have?
Um... four?
You have used up two chances. I will give you two more.
If you do not paint a satisfactory portrait of me, you will be joining them here in the dungeon.
DID NOT.
DID TOO.

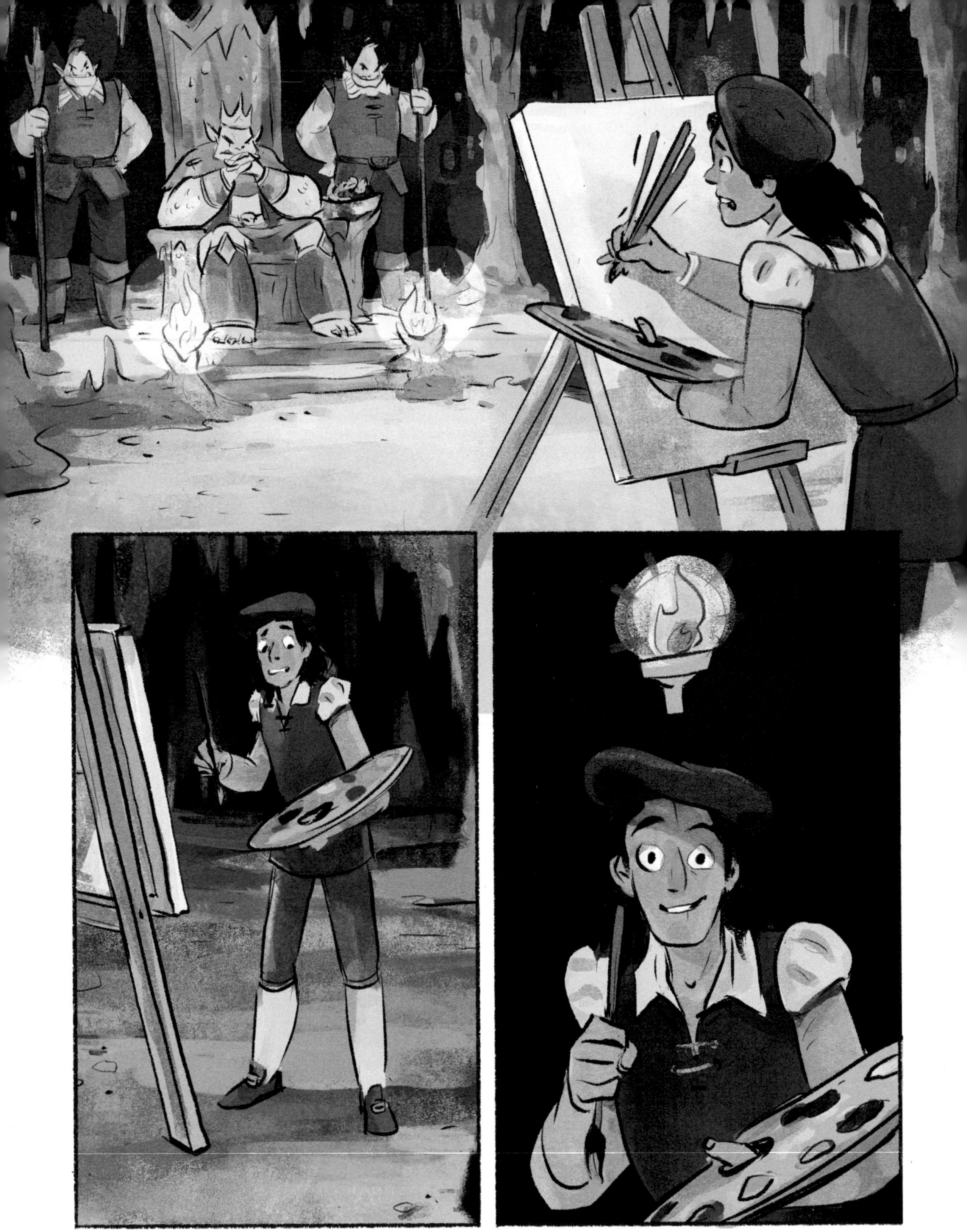

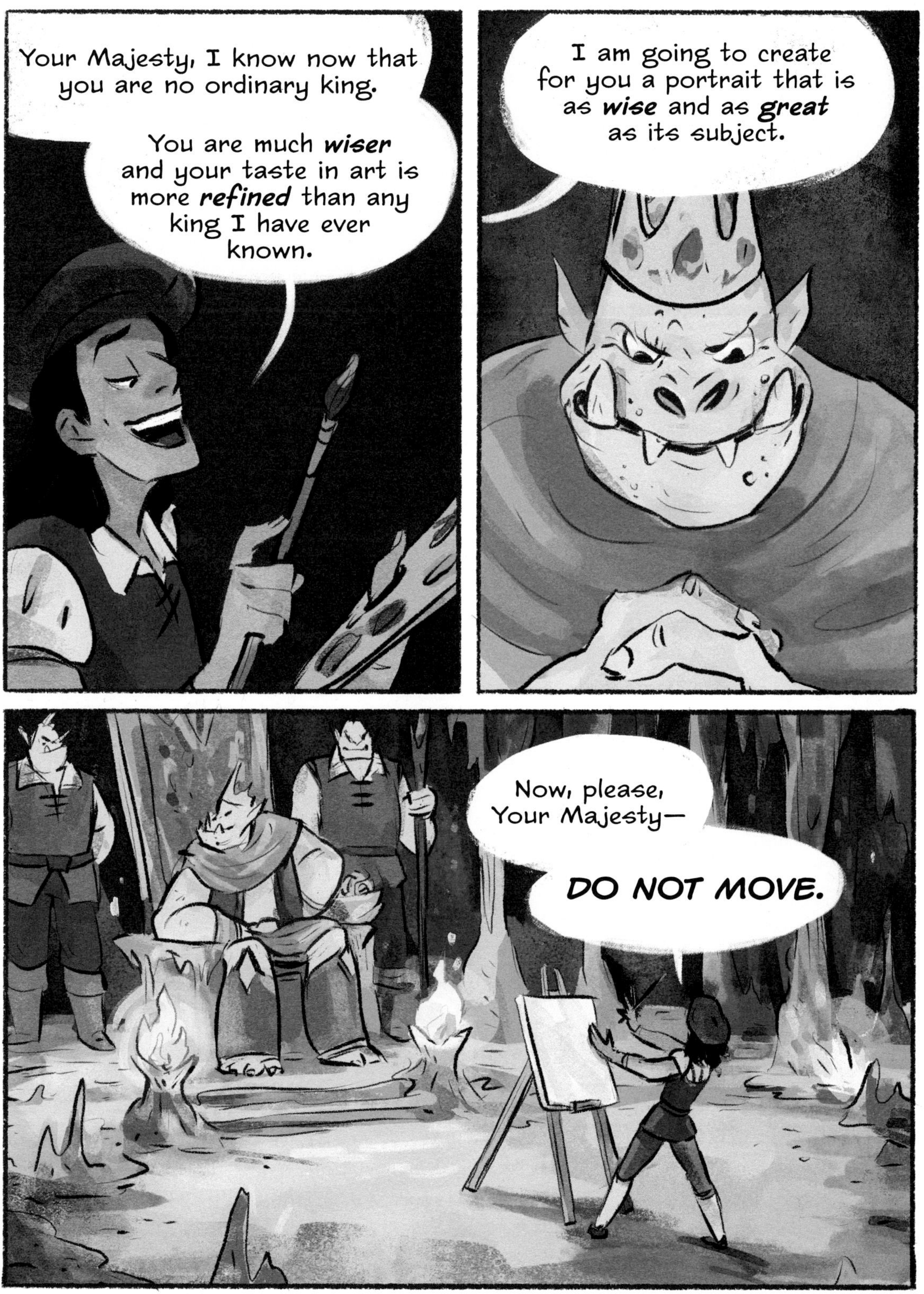
Your Majesty, I know now that you are no ordinary king.
You are much ***wiser*** and your taste in art is more ***refined*** than any king I have ever known.
I am going to create for you a portrait that is as ***wise*** and as ***great*** as its subject.
Now, please, Your Majesty—
DO NOT MOVE.

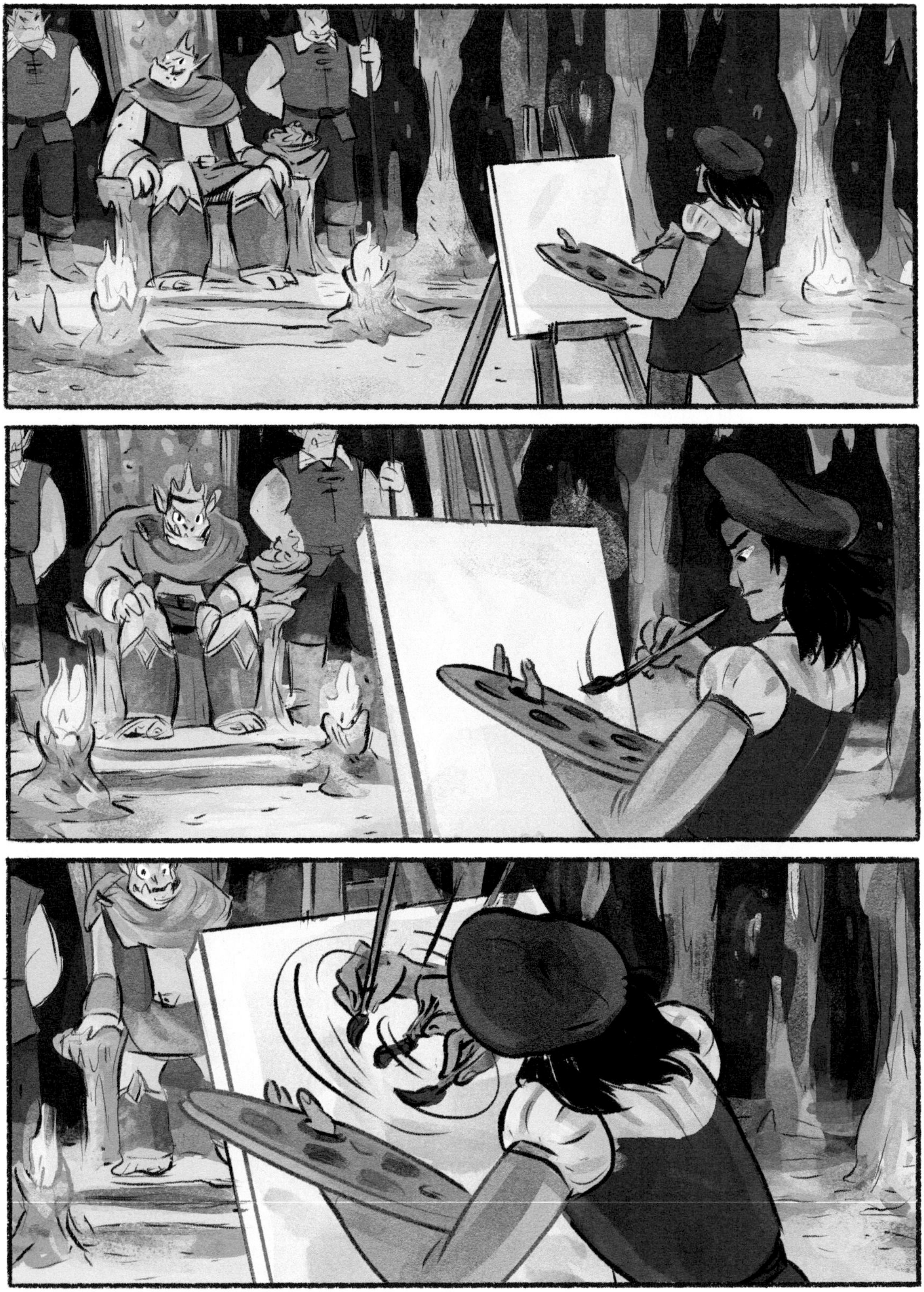

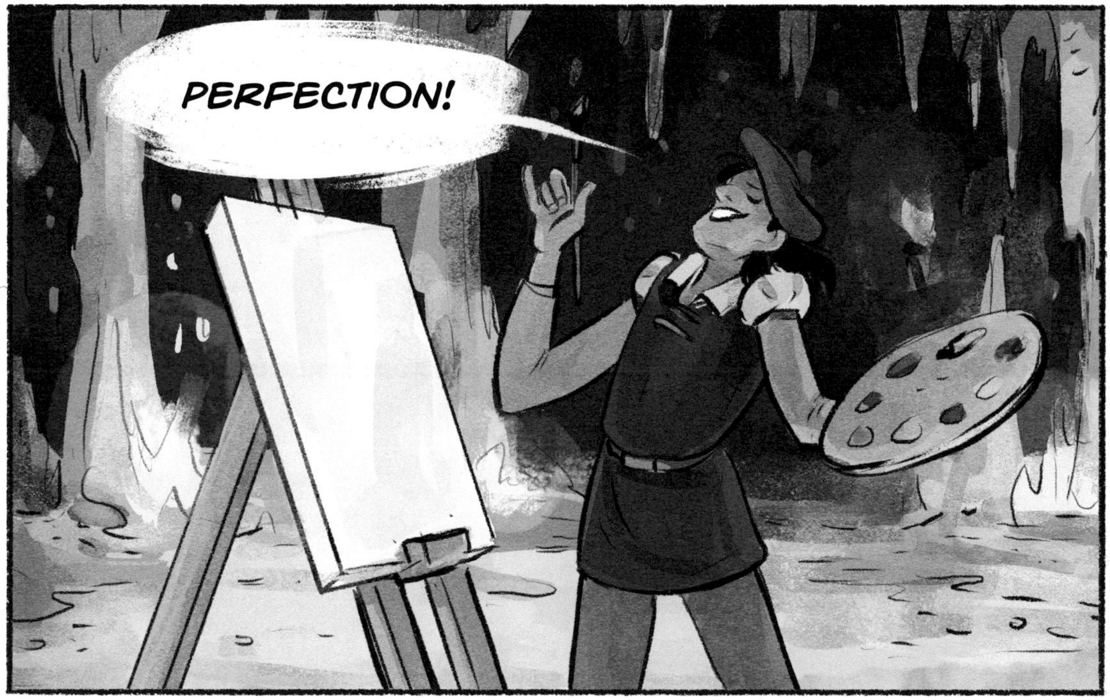
PERFECTION!

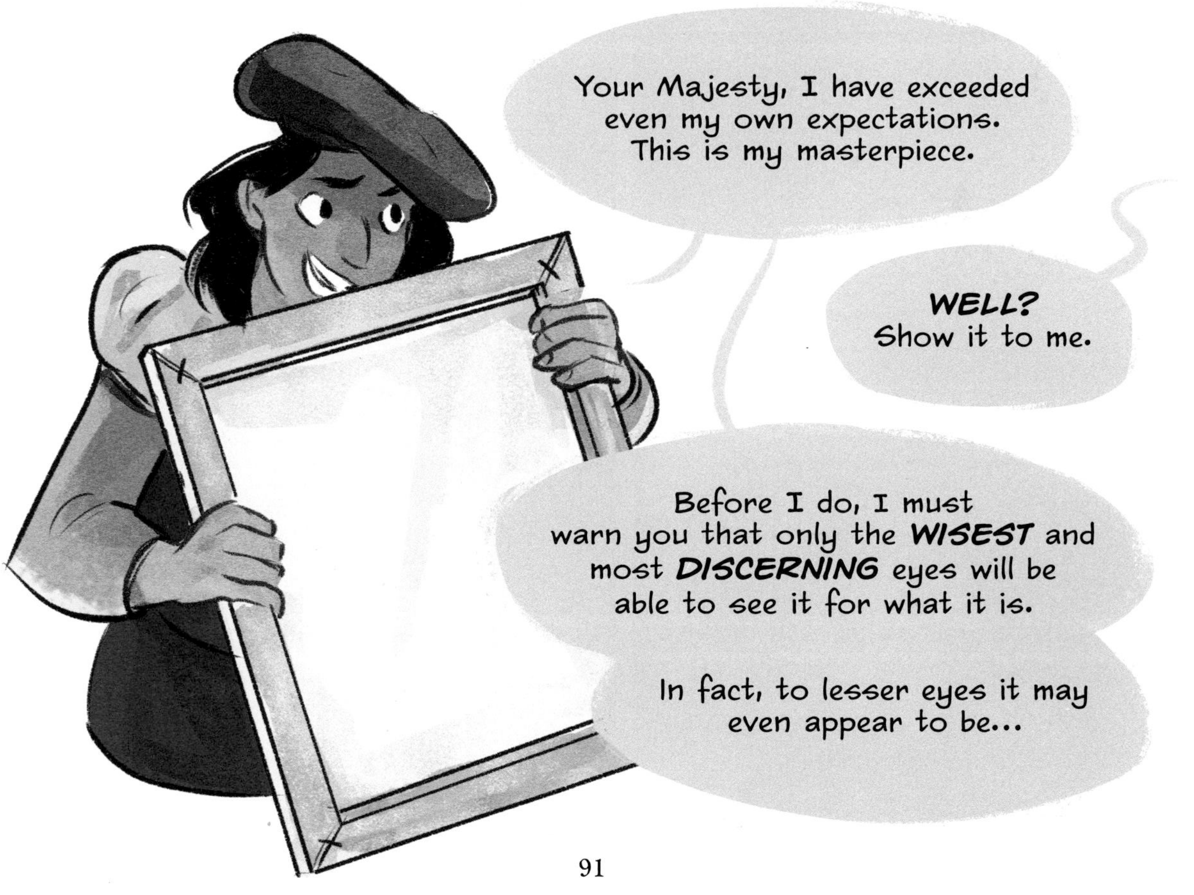
Your Majesty, I have exceeded even my own expectations. This is my masterpiece.
WELL? Show it to me.
Before I do, I must warn you that only the WISEST and most DISCERNING eyes will be able to see it for what it is.
In fact, to lesser eyes it may even appear to be...

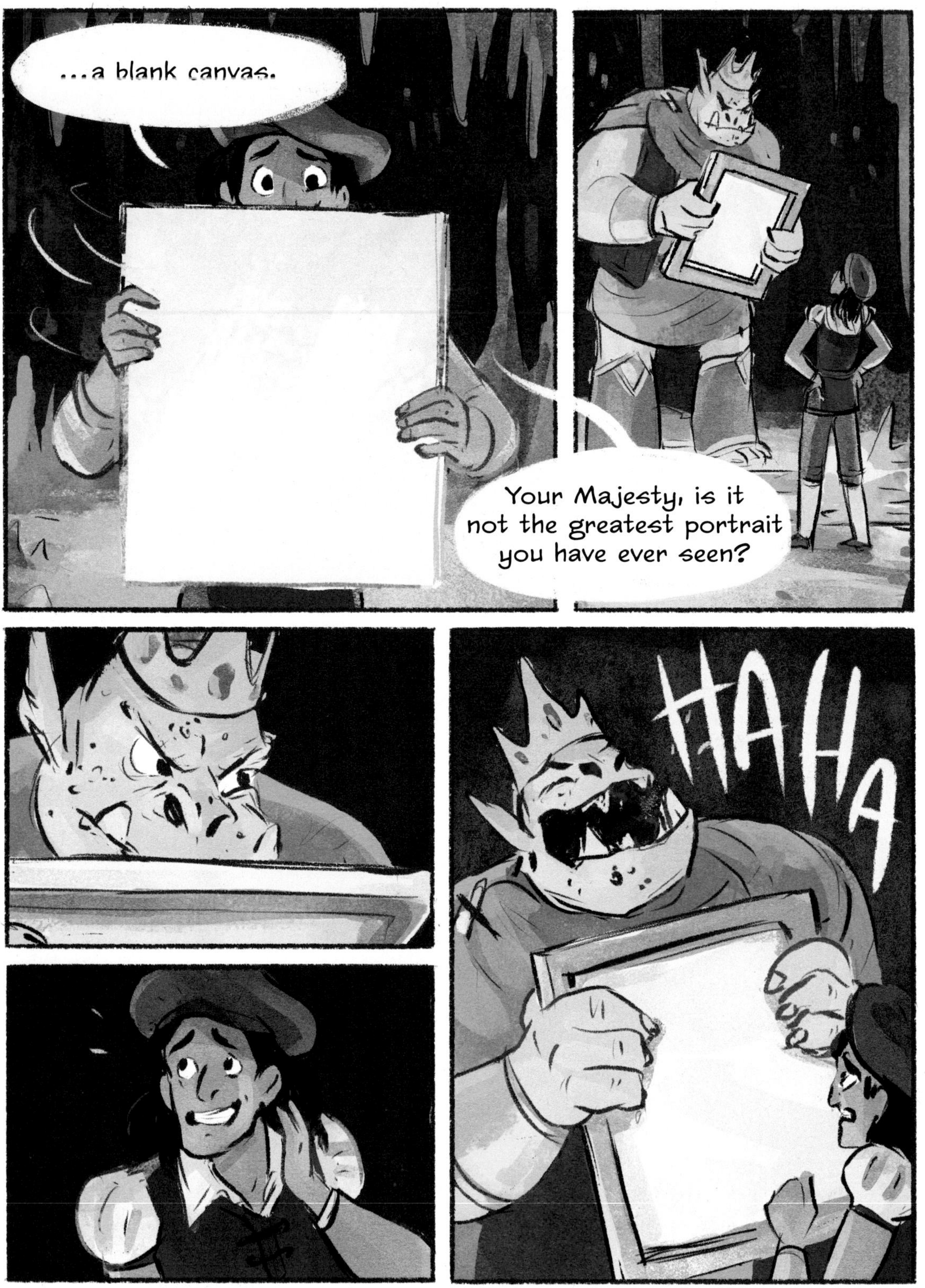
...a blank canvas.
Your Majesty, is it not the greatest portrait you have ever seen?
HAHAHA

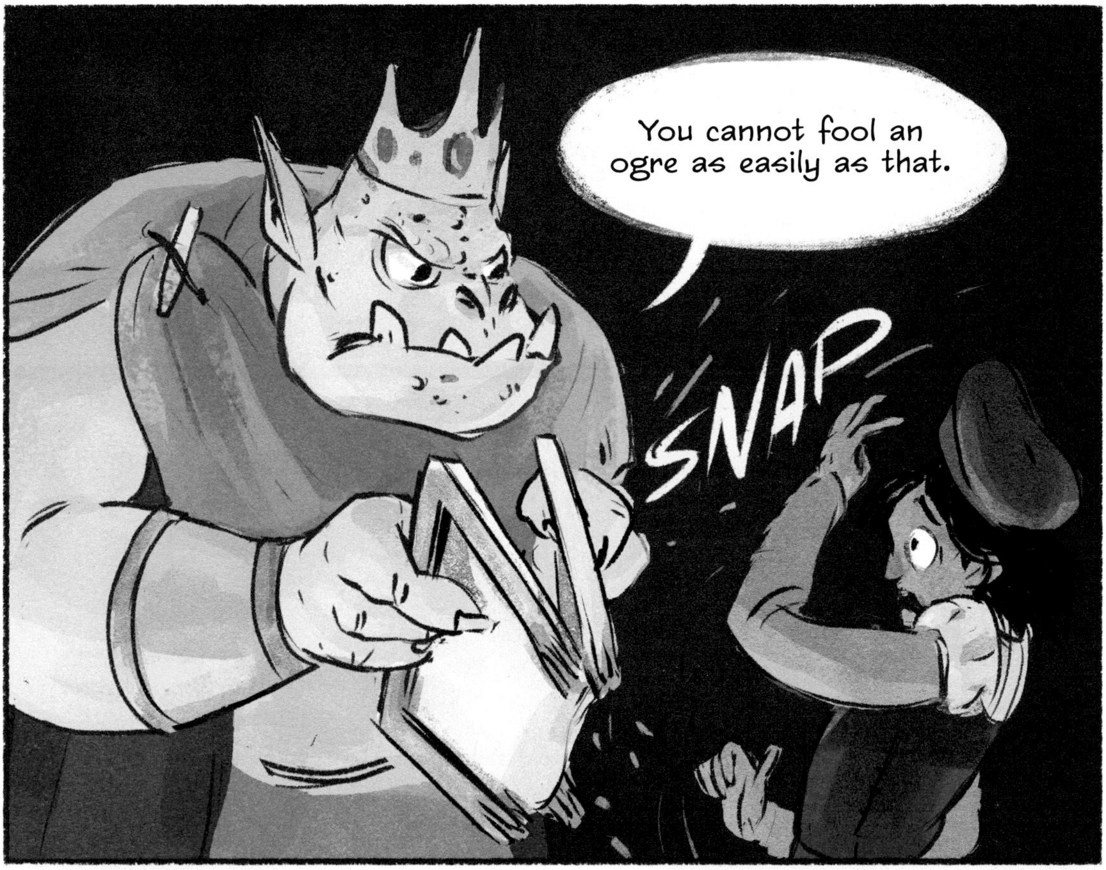
You cannot fool an ogre as easily as that.
SNAP

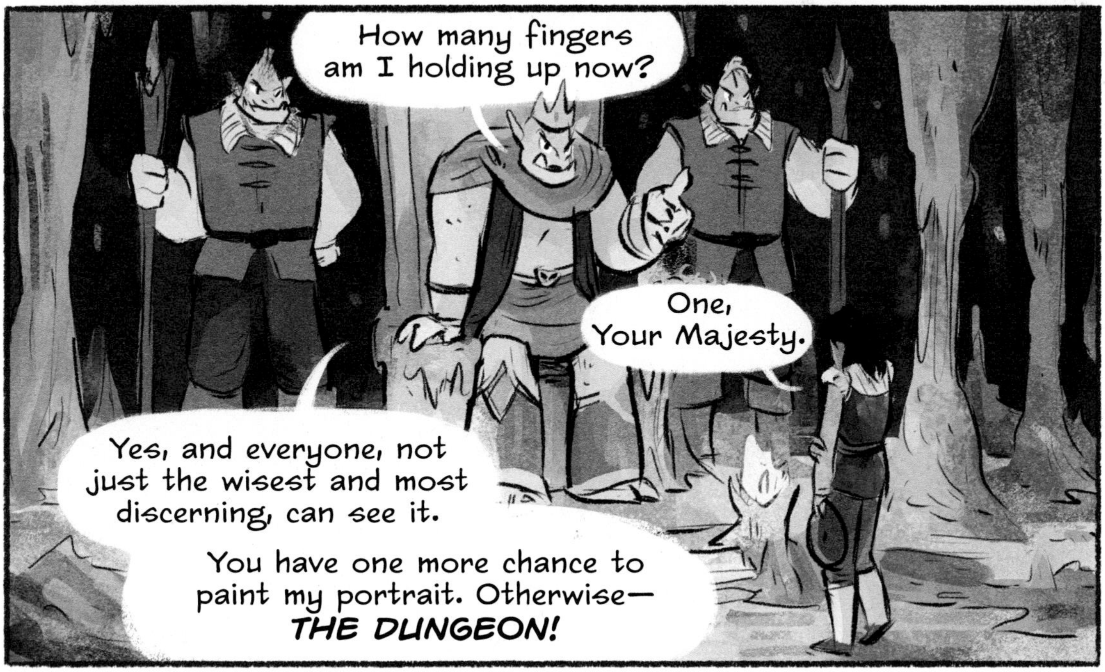
How many fingers am I holding up now?
One, Your Majesty.
Yes, and everyone, not just the wisest and most discerning, can see it.
You have one more chance to paint my portrait. Otherwise—
THE DUNGEON!

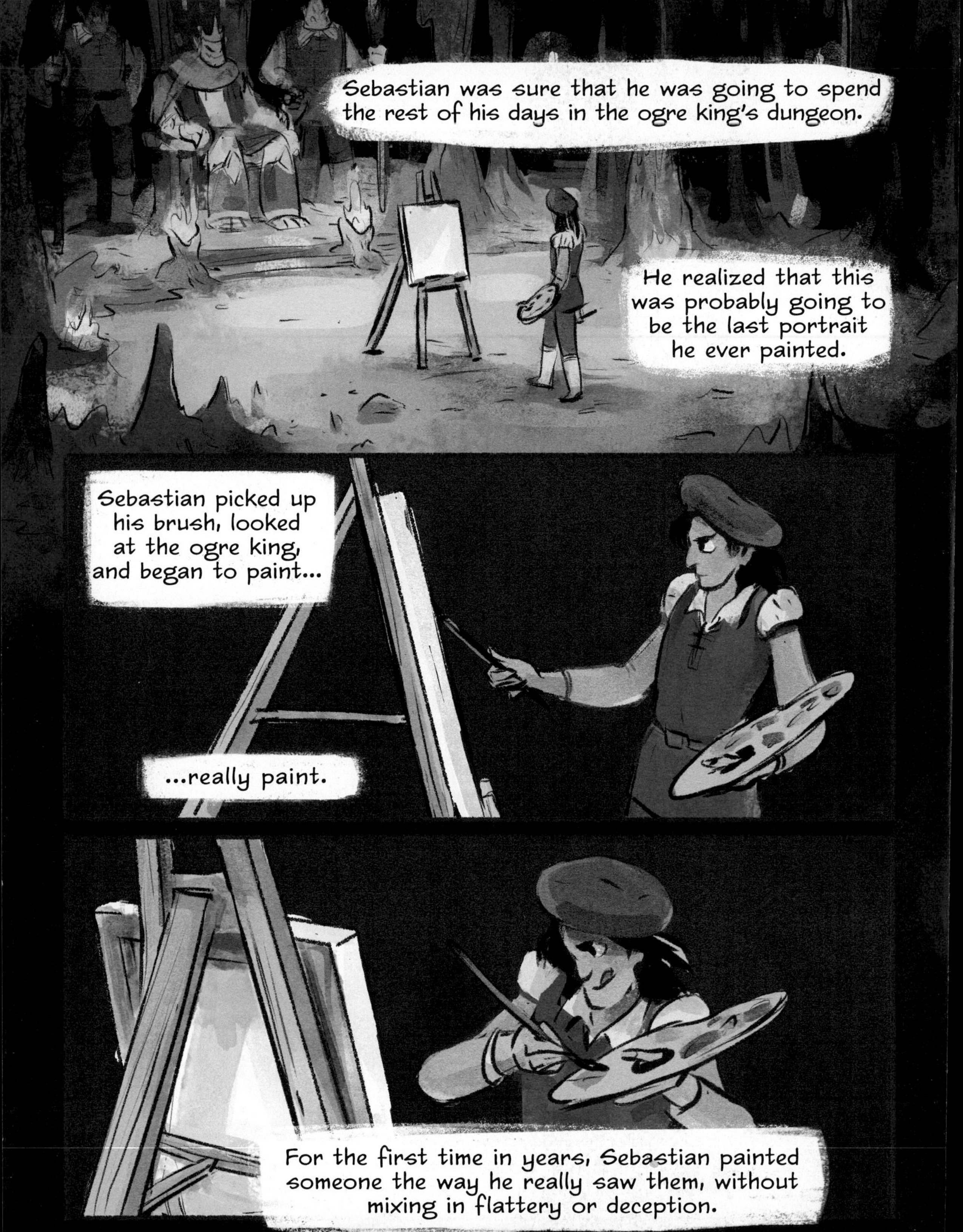
Sebastian was sure that he was going to spend the rest of his days in the ogre king's dungeon.
He realized that this was probably going to be the last portrait he ever painted.
Sebastian picked up his brush, looked at the ogre king, and began to paint...
...really paint.
For the first time in years, Sebastian painted someone the way he really saw them, without mixing in flattery or deception.

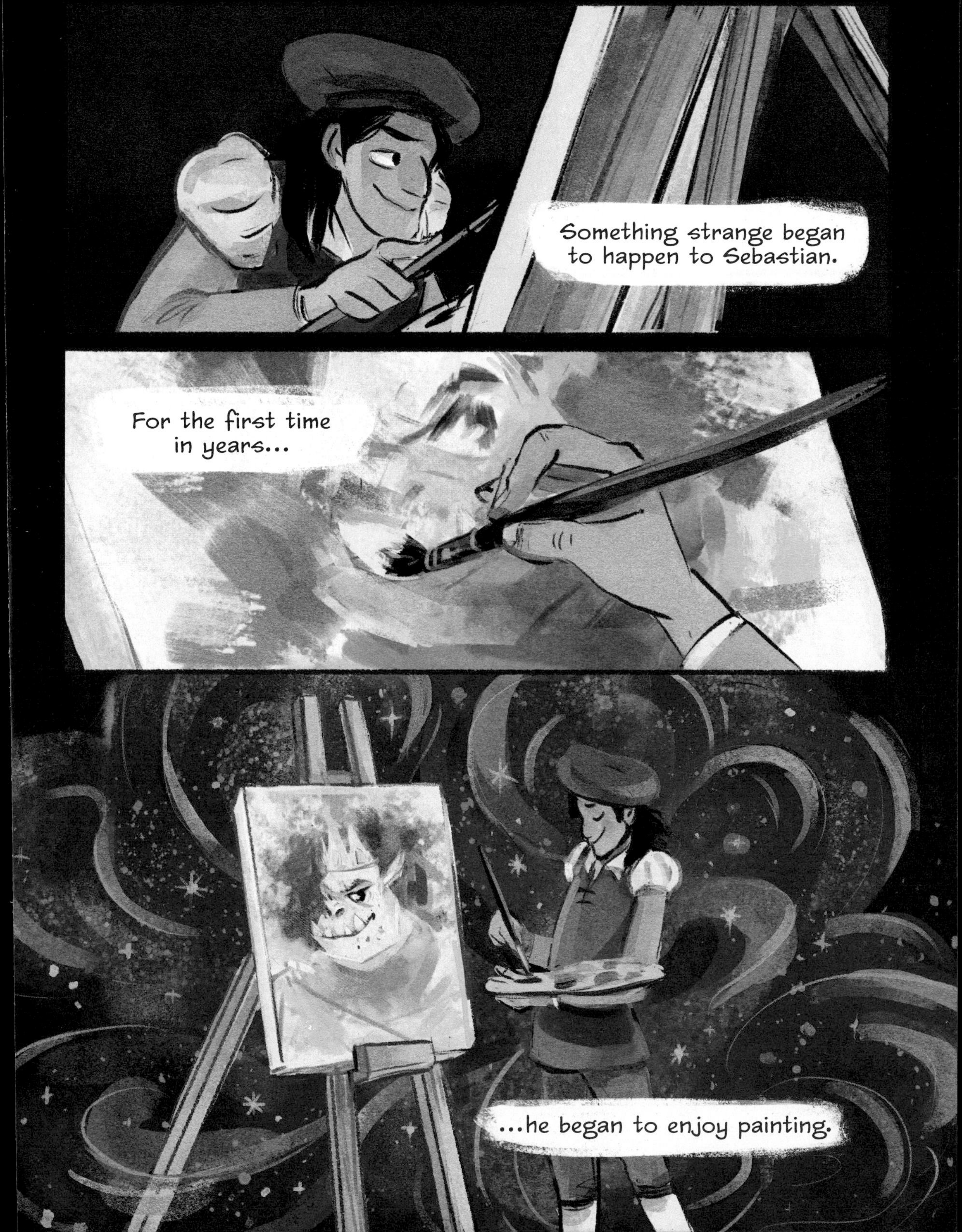
Something strange began to happen to Sebastian.
For the first time in years...
...he began to enjoy painting.

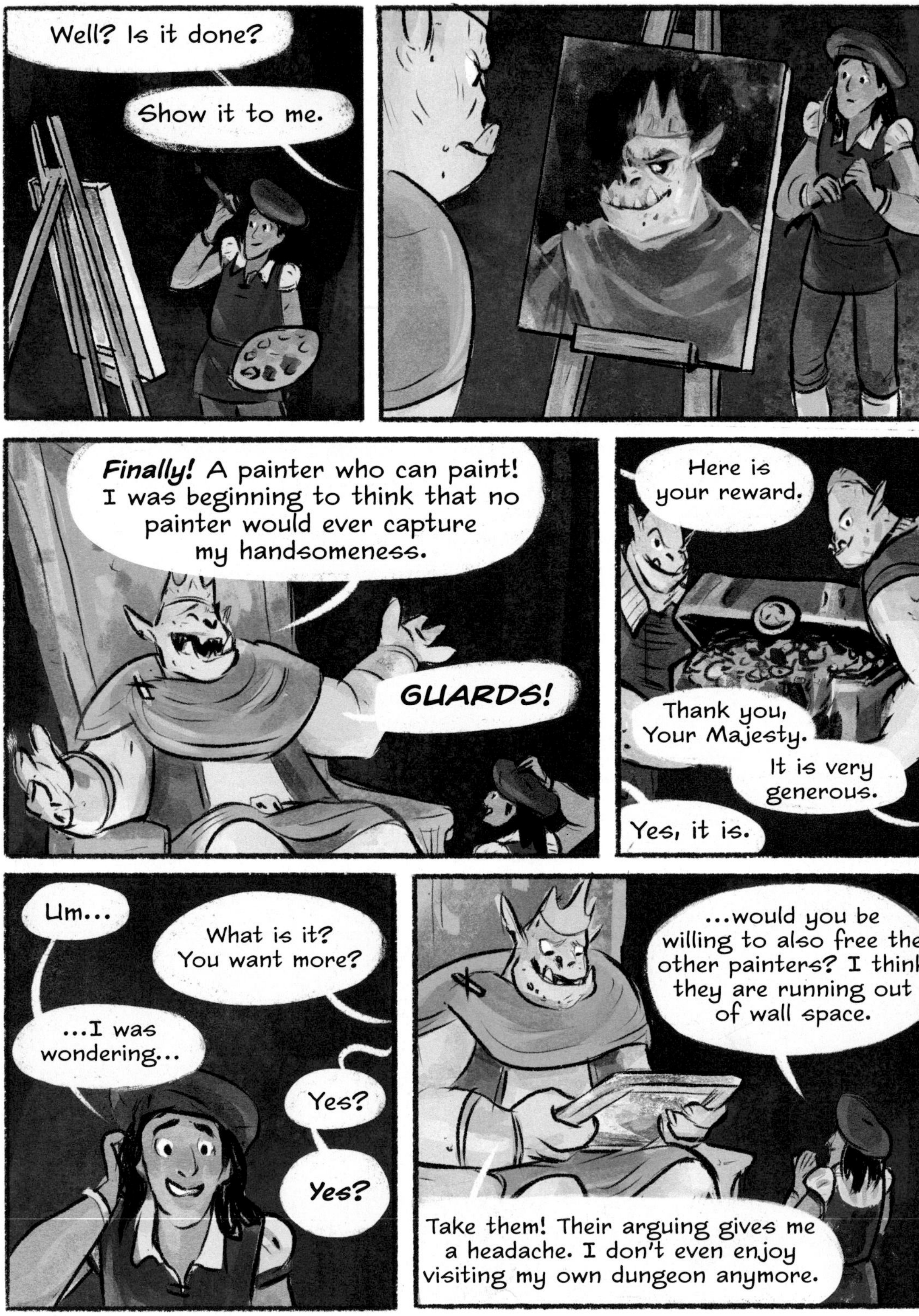
Well? Is it done?
Show it to me.
Finally! A painter who can paint! I was beginning to think that no painter would ever capture my handsomeness.
GUARDS!
Here is your reward.
Thank you, Your Majesty.
It is very generous.
Yes, it is.
Um...
What is it? You want more?
...I was wondering...
Yes?
Yes?
...would you be willing to also free the other painters? I think they are running out of wall space.
Take them! Their arguing gives me a headache. I don't even enjoy visiting my own dungeon anymore.

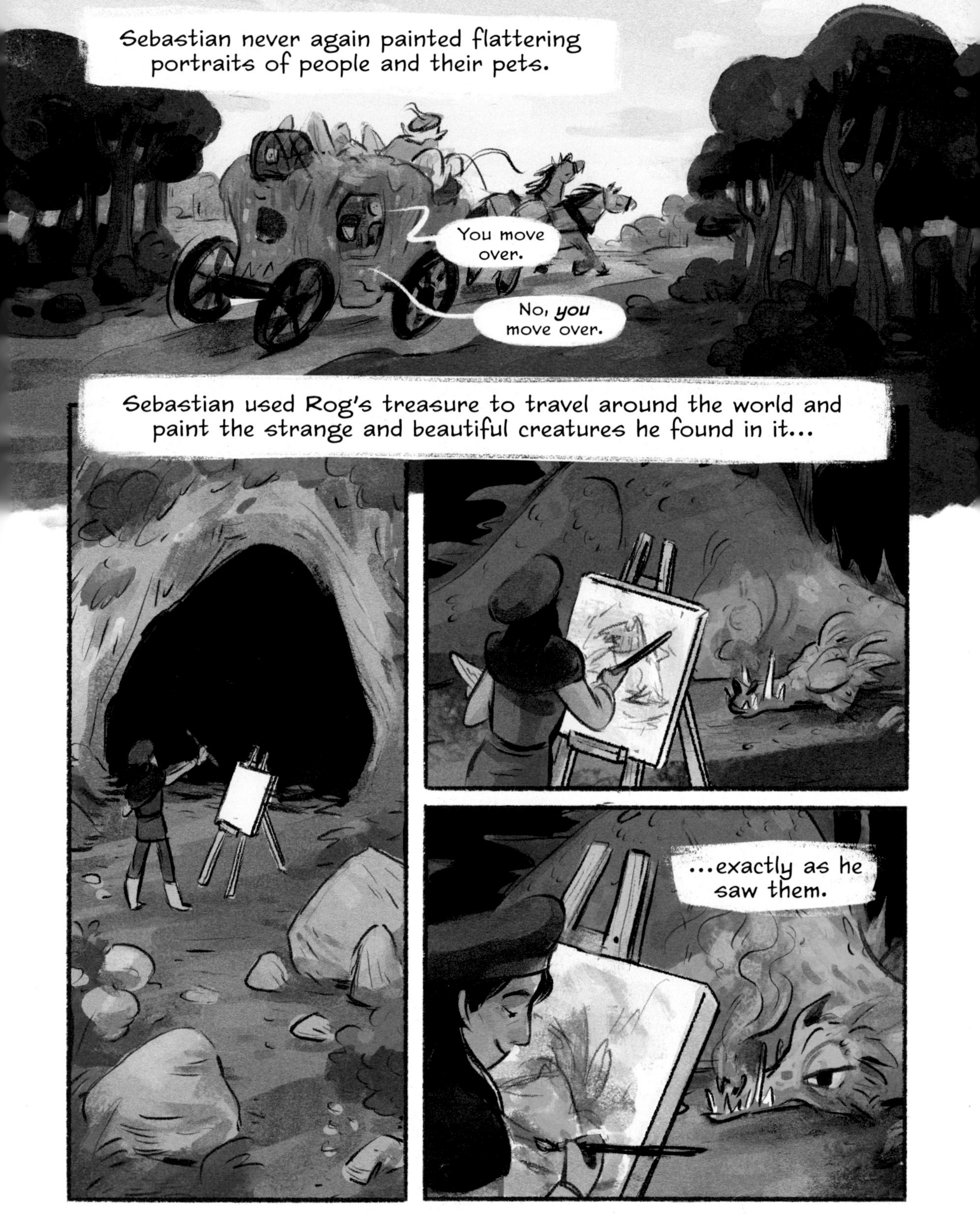
Sebastian never again painted flattering portraits of people and their pets.
You move over.
No, *you* move over.
Sebastian used Rog's treasure to travel around the world and paint the strange and beautiful creatures he found in it...
...exactly as he saw them.

Acknowledgments

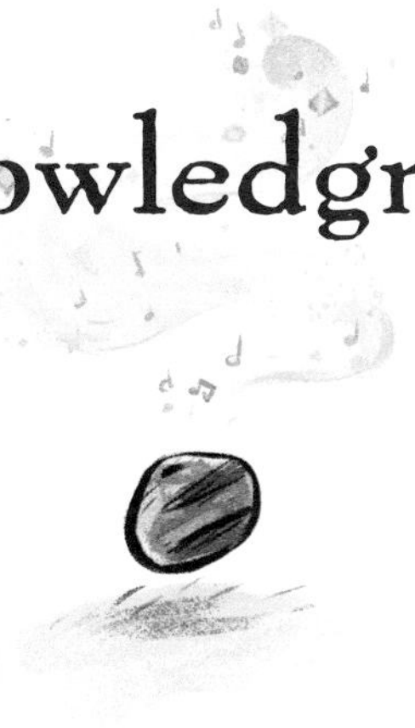

I would like to thank my mother, who kept my bookshelves well-stocked with fairy tales and folktales when I was a kid. I would also like to thank my wife, who has been there for me every step of the way (and there were many steps and it was a long way). Most of all, I would like to thank Wolf Pup and Beauty, who bring to each and every day a little bit of the magic of fairy tales.

—Nathaniel Lachenmeyer

Many thanks to the excellent team at First Second for turning our work into this real, finished book. Chris—thank you for your endlessly patient editing and encouragement. It's here! Calista, Nathanial—thanks for taking a chance on me. And always, forever, thank you to my family for the support and space you've given me to pursue this career and the opportunity to choose it.

—Simini Blocker

Character Designs

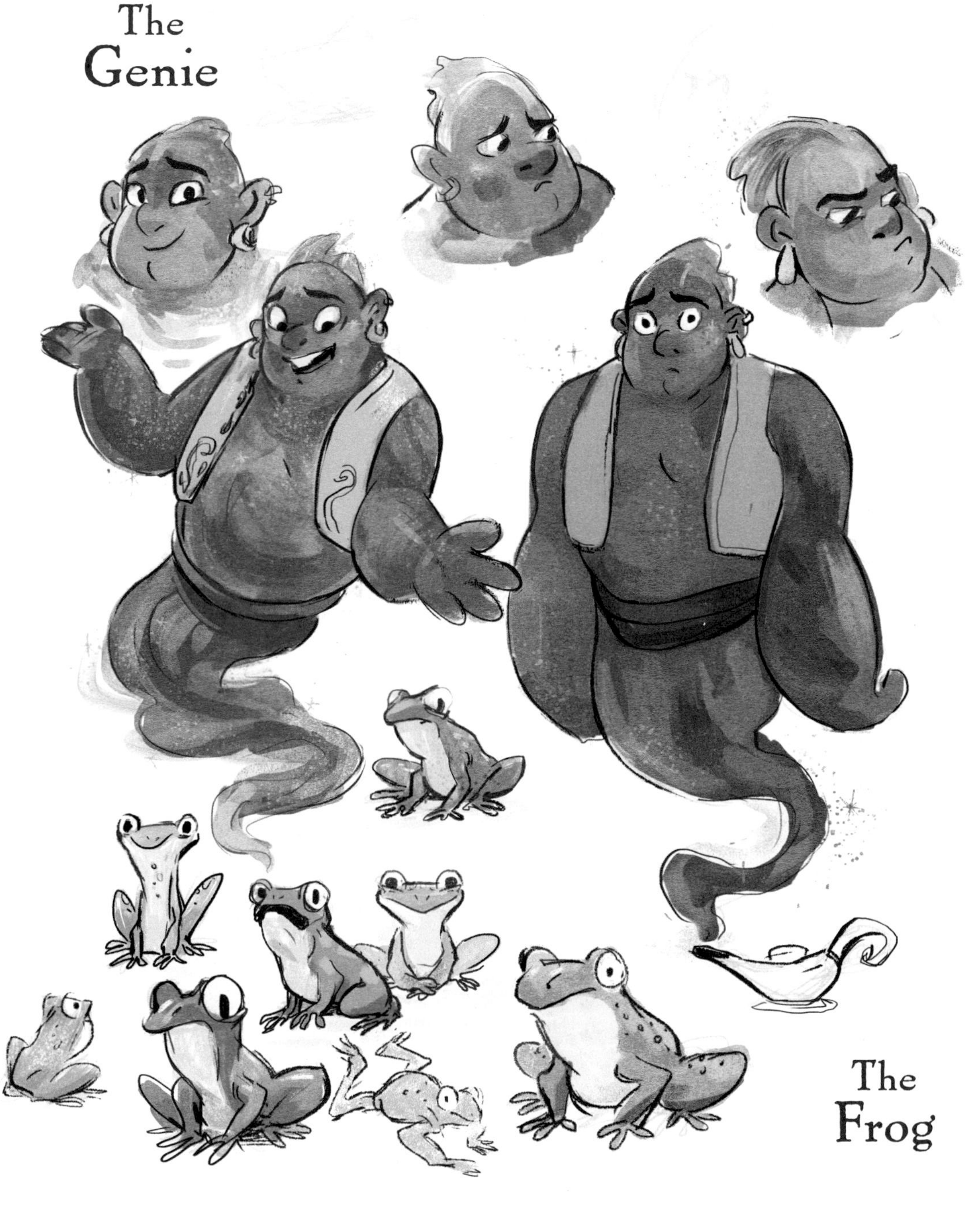
The Genie
The Frog

The Witch

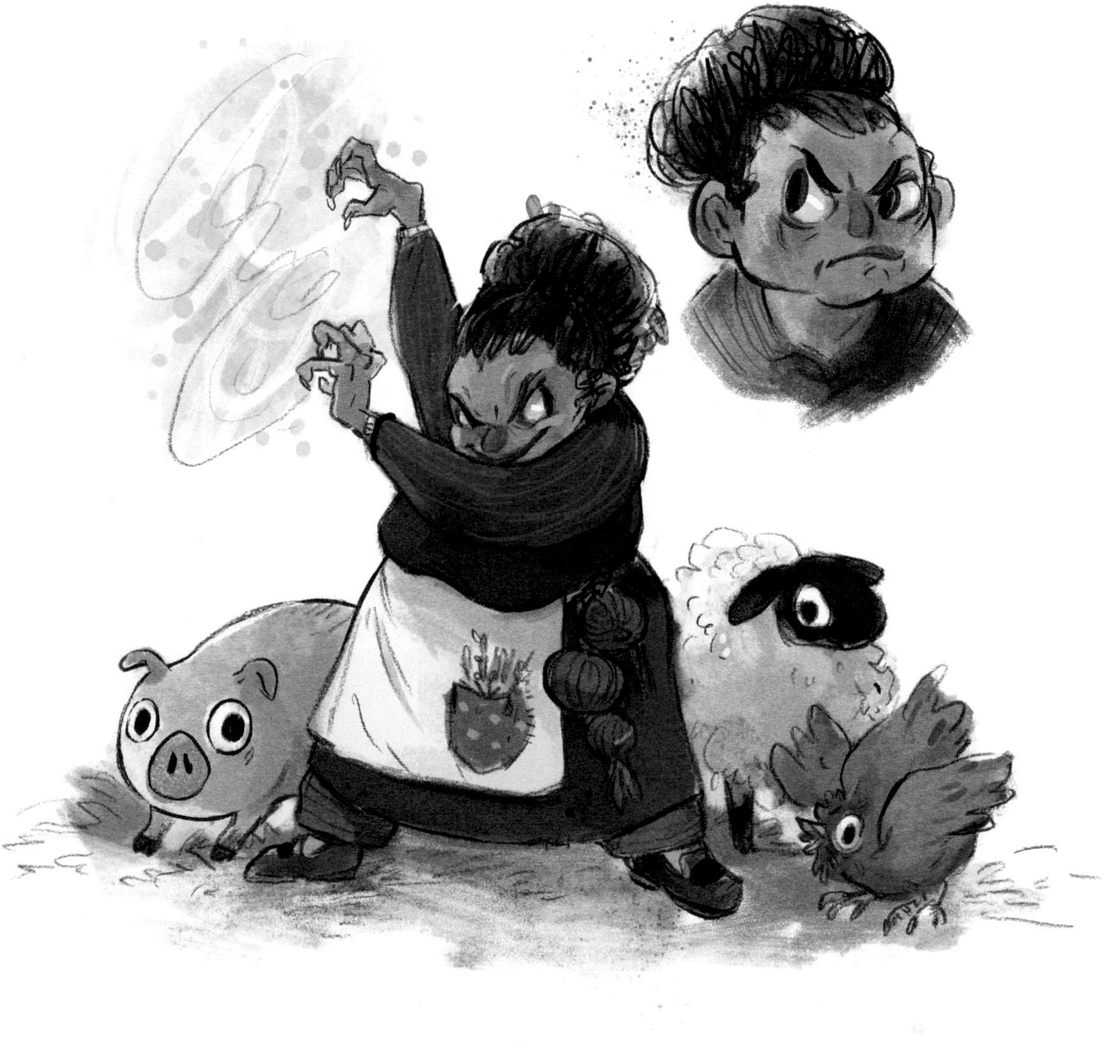

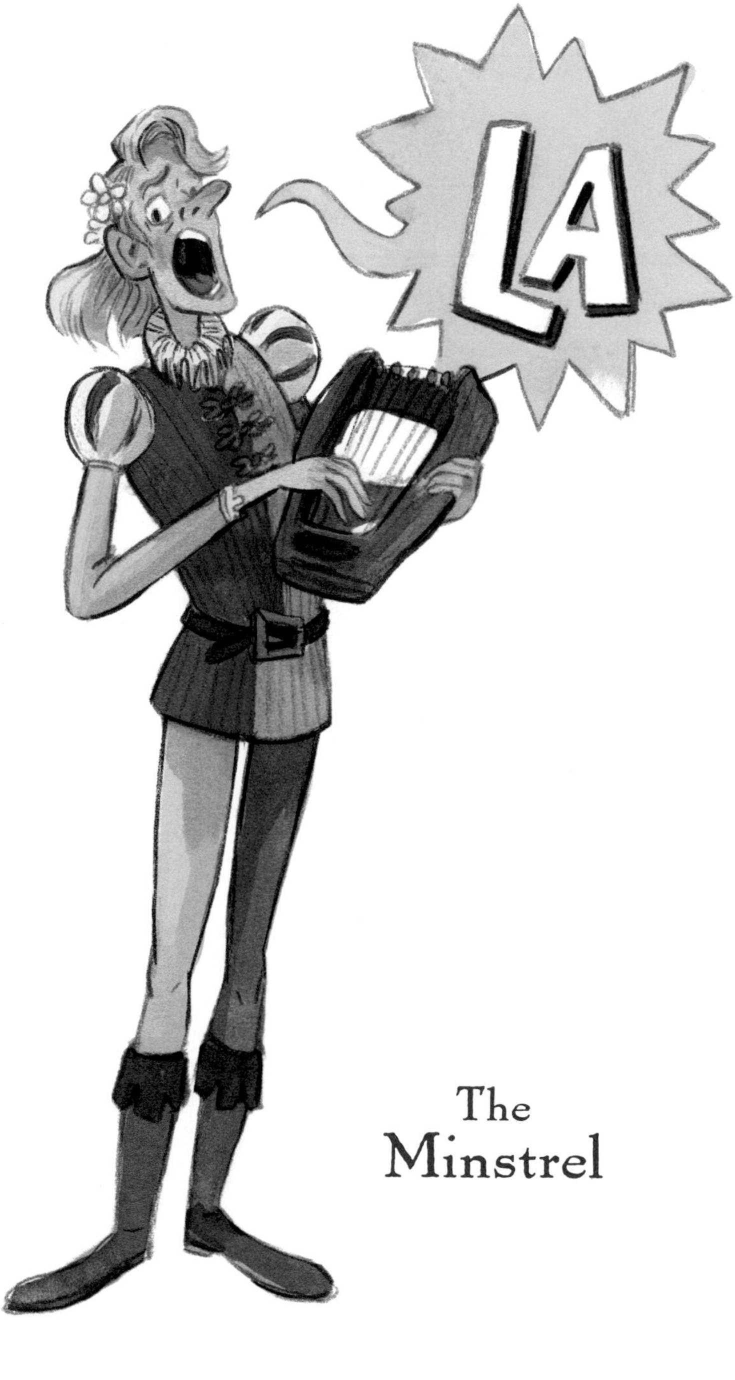
LA

The
Minstrel

Sebastian

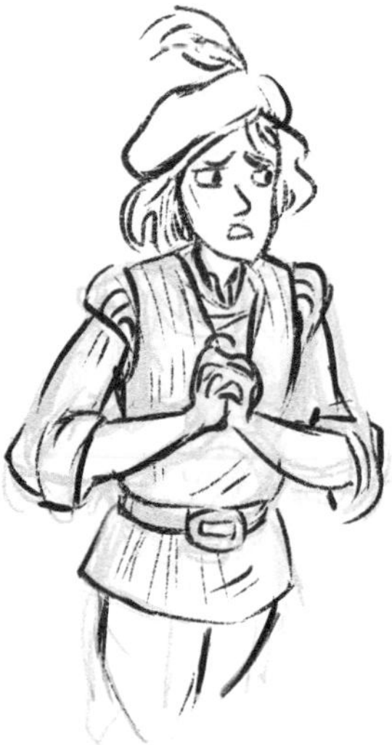

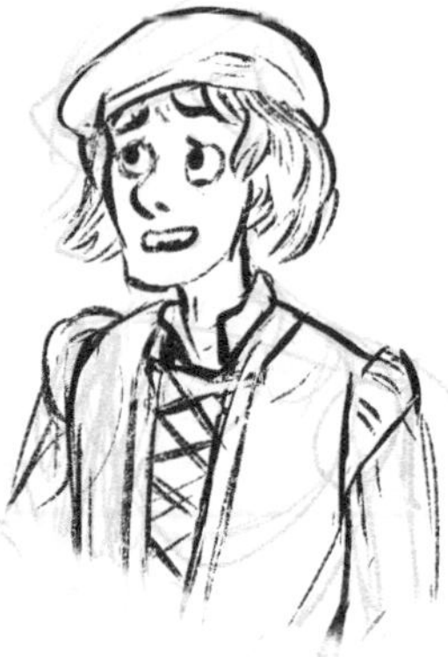

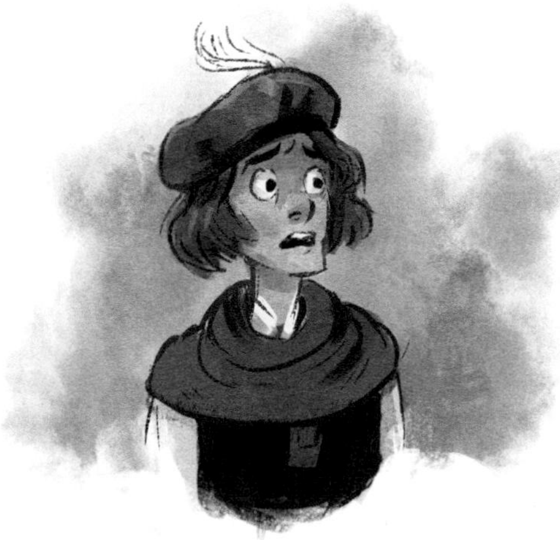

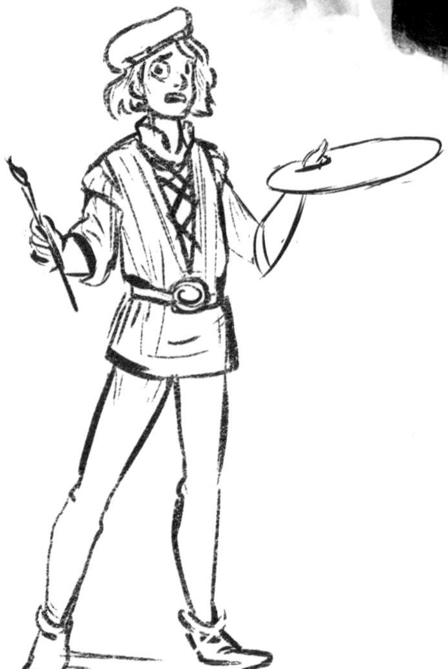

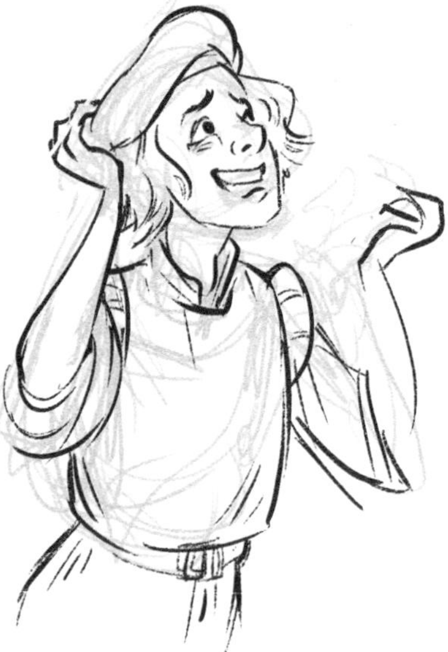

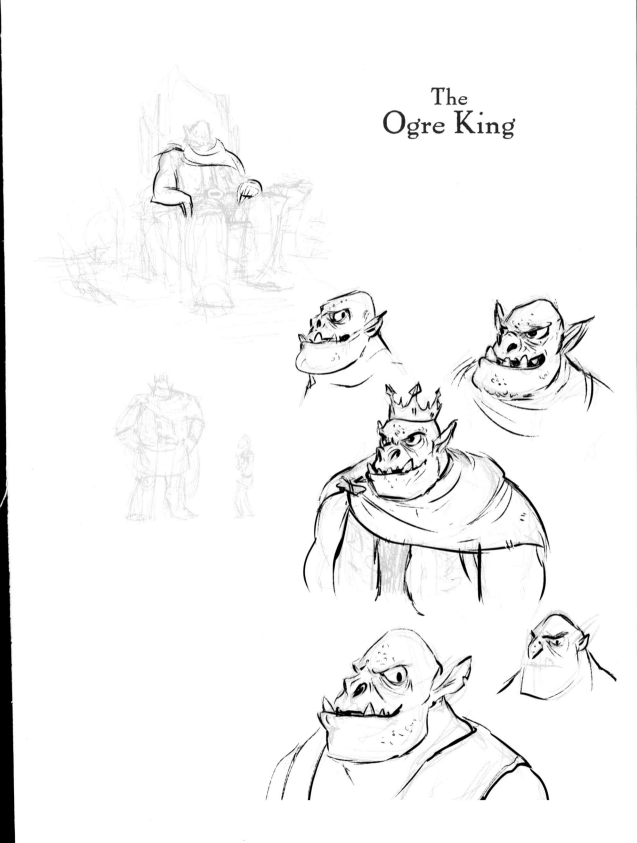

The
Ogre King

Text copyright © 2019 by Nathaniel Lachenmeyer
Illustrations copyright © 2019 by Simini Blocker

Published by First Second
First Second is an imprint of Roaring Brook Press,
a division of Holtzbrinck Publishing Holdings Limited Partnership
175 Fifth Avenue, New York, NY 10010
Library of Congress Control Number: 2018944914

ISBN: 978-1-59643-750-0

Our books may be purchased in bulk for promotional, educational, or business use.
Please contact your local bookseller or the Macmillan Corporate
and Premium Sales Department at (800) 221-7945 ext. 5442 or by
email at MacmillanSpecialMarkets@macmillan.com.

First edition, 2019

Edited by Calista Brill and Chris Duffy
Book design by Molly Johanson

Drawn and inked in Clip Studio Paint on a digital tablet and colored digitally in Photoshop.

Printed in China by Toppan Leefung Printing Ltd.,
Dongguan City, Guangdong Province

1 3 5 7 9 10 8 6 4 2